THE AMBASSADOR is Maxwell Gordon Amberley, a troubled man, left rootless with the death of his wife, trying to find renewed meaning in his life. Suddenly, in the midst of his personal turmoil, he is assigned to South Vietnam and brought swiftly into the deceptive calm of the eye of the hurricane ...

Here in this extraordinary novel are sharply-drawn portraits of men and women—Asians, Americans, Europeans—at the center and on the fringes of policy-making in a dangerous war—a vast panorama brought into focus through the vision of one passionate and dedicated man ... The Ambassador.

"WEST IS A MASTER NOVELIST."
—*San Francisco News Call-Bulletin*

"ILLUMINATING." —*Toledo Blade*

"ABSORBING." —*Wall Street Journal*

THE
AMBASSADOR
MORRIS L. WEST

A DELL BOOK

Published by DELL PUBLISHING CO., INC.
750 Third Avenue, New York, N.Y. 10017

Copyright © 1965 by Morris L. West

Dell ® TM 681510, Dell Publishing Co., Inc.

Reprinted by arrangement with
William Morrow and Company, New York, N.Y.

First Dell Printing—January, 1966

Printed in the U.S.A.

For **MICHAEL JOHN** *The innocent inheritor*

Heaven and earth and I are of the same root.
The ten thousand things and I are of one substance.

Attributed to Sojo the Scholar-Monk

'All things betray thee, who betrayest Me'

Francis Thompson, *"The Hound of Heaven"*

The shadow contains the undeveloped sides of our personality, the unconscious possibilities, abilities and intentions
of our soul. This shadow has often been known as the
dark brother.

Ernst Aeppli, *Psychologie des Bewusstens und Unbewusstens*

CHAPTER ONE

As a diplomat I have a good record. In his valedictory letter the President called it "a distinguished and meritorious career, the sum of whose service represents a great profit to the United States of America." I was able to accept the compliment with some irony, but with confidence at least that I had earned it.

I have served the Department for thirty-five years and have been an Ambassador for ten. I have taken my share of hardship posts, and been tossed my quota of hot potatoes. Even my enemies will admit that my failures have not been too blatant and that I have had one or two conspicuous successes.

Some of my friends tell me that this decision to quit the Service in mid-career is my shrewdest stroke yet. They point out that on the one hand, I am in high favor with the President, who can recall me to duty at will as a special negotiator, and that on the other, I am free to pursue my own political ambitions.

My friends, of course, assume that I have political ambitions, and I am hurt that they should credit me with so much calculation. And yet why should I be hurt? I have always been known as a cool-headed bargainer, and there is a certain diplomatic value in a reputation for ruthlessness. If I am changed, my friends have hardly had time or occasion to notice it. How can they possibly know the private conscience of Maxwell Gordon Amberley when he has come so late to knowing it himself?

To this point I have observed all the conventions of the Service, and I have arranged my exit with biblical decency. After the death of Phung Van Cung, I waited a full twelve months in office—more than enough to absolve the Administration from any guilt in his death or responsibility for its consequences. Then I made the statutory visit to Washington to kiss hands and discuss a new appointment. After that I went into a hospital in New York for a checkup. Three weeks later I was able to announce my retirement from the Service on the grounds of ill-health.

The real reason? That is what I am here to find out, here in the old Zen Shrine of Tenryu-ji, the Temple of the Heavenly Dragon, near Kyoto in Japan.

It is autumn, and the sacred maples at the gate are red as fire against the dark lift of the pines. The sky is like the skin of a pearl, and the fallen leaves lie quiet on the pools, on the pathways of raked sand, on the rocks and the vivid green of the moss patches.

Sometimes I walk in the garden and watch the monks tending the plants, steadily, particularly, "making of each grass blade a Golden Buddha." Sometimes I sit in the house of Musō Soseki, cross-legged on a straw mat, drinking tea which he has infused for me in ceremonial fashion and following him through that meditative method of dialogue which is called *mondō.* . . .

"Why do you come to this place?"

"To seek enlightenment."

"Why have you not found it?"

"Because I seek it."

"How will you find it?"

"By not seeking."

"Where will you find it?"

"In no place."

"When will you find it?"

"At no time."

The pattern of the dialogue is like the pattern of the temple and the house and the garden. Everything is spare, allusive, uncluttered, infinitely extended, just as the mat on which we sit seems to flow outward and merge with the sand of the pathways and the ripples made by the carp in the garden pools.

Musō Soseki is a monk of the Zen cult. He is also poet, gardener, master of calligraphy and the art of printing from wood blocks. The brushstrokes of his name signify Window-That-Opens-on-a-Dream. He is seventy-five years old, sturdy, brown and weathered like an aged stone. His face is calm with benignity and bright with humor. He has agreed to accept me as his pupil, and using the methods of Zen, to jolt, prod and jar me toward the moment of intuition and illumination which is called *satori*.

I have need of illumination—great need. I am only sorry I did not wait to find it three years ago, when, after the death of my wife, George Groton brought me down here for the first time.

I was Ambassador then—a gilded personage in the diplomatic drama of Tokyo. Look at a map, mark the vectors of political force in Asia and you will understand the nature and extent of my influence. I did well, I think. I have a flair for language, a taste for exotic custom, an ear for the minor key. These are valuable assets in an esoteric civilization. Whatever else I had was not mine by nature, but a gift from Gabrielle.

She had charm, tact, humor and a luminous harmony which spilled over from her life into mine. When she died, the harmony dissolved into a crashing discord. Every fissure and fault in myself seemed to open at once.

I had never had any firm beliefs of a spiritual kind—and being deeply blessed by a loving woman, I have never felt a pressing need of them. I had religious feelings. I was not averse to attending church services. I managed even to enjoy them when official duties demanded my presence. For the rest I was content with the comfort of my household gods—and of the priestess who ministered to them and to me.

Now that she was gone, it was as if all my shrines were tumbled down at once, and I must plow them underground, away from the light. I refused all sympathy. I became brusque, energetic, meticulous. My staff found me unbearable, my colleagues were alienated.

Only the Japanese, a schizophrenic people, seemed willing to accept my need of a period of curative madness.

Of my own people, only George Groton, the very junior Third Secretary, was shrewd enough to see what had happened to me. He was not abashed by my anger, nor put out by my arrogance. He was diligent, good-humored and quite unafraid. He was tall, gangling, bespectacled, with stooping shoulders and a shock of sandy hair. Yet in rare moments of softness I found myself wishing I had had a son like George Groton.

Then, one night when he was duty officer, he had to wake me with some late cables. I had drunk too much before going to bed, and I was in a foul temper. I was intolerably rude to him. He took a deep breath, planted himself squarely in front of me and said:

"Sir, you are destroying yourself and destroying the harmony of the Embassy. If you won't let any of us help you, then let us at least get the work done as best we can."

I gaped at him, speechless. Then he shrugged and gave me a disarming grin.

"You can send me home if you like, sir—but someone had to say it."

"Why you, Groton?"

"Mrs. Amberley was always very kind to me. Before she died she made me promise to look after you."

I was so ashamed of myself I could say nothing. I took the cables and locked myself in my room and wept like a child. The next morning I wrote Groton a stiff little note of apology and thanks. A week later he invited me to join a party of the staff who were going down to Kurama to see the annual fire festival. Since Kurama is only a short distance from Kyoto, it was the most natural thing in the world that we should visit the Temple of the Heavenly Dragon and that I should meet Musō Soseki.

If Groton had lived, he would have been a great diplomat. He was a simple man who cut swiftly to the core of a problem, yet he was delicate enough and good-humored enough to adapt to the devious processes of other minds. When I saw him die violently in Saigon, I wept again. And I have not shed a tear since for man or woman.

Musō Soseki received me with the easy courtesy of man in accord with himself, his history and his world. He walked me around the garden of the temple, interpreting it to me in the Zen fashion, not as a casual association of beauties, but as a place of subtle contrivance, of harmonious associations and revealing contrasts—an ambience designed for spiritual happenings, an instrument of enlightenment more potent than books or arguments.

He did not make a lecture out of those matters, but spoke of them as a man speaks of his intimate life, lovingly and with deep preoccupation. When he spoke of *satori*, he was at pains to make the notion clear to me. I remember two sentences very clearly:

"The root of human distress, Mr. Amberley, is a sense of alienation from the natural order of the universe. The effect of *satori* is an illumination of the mind, so that the nature of the self and the universe is finally clear and the sense of true relationship, or oneness, is restored."

My own distress was so recent and so vivid that I seized on the words and begged him to explain them further. He refused, smiling, and told me:

"Come back again, and we will drink tea and talk in silence."

I went back to Tokyo like a man walking in the afterglow of a calm but wonderful dream. I wrote to Musō Soseki, thanking him for his courtesies and asking to see him again. Ten days later his letter came back, a small masterpiece of beautiful calligraphy on handmade paper. The old man offered me his house, his friendship and what he called the "small and unworthy fruits of my winter harvest." I might visit him at any time and live with him as his guest.

As often as I could, I went down to stay with Musō, sometimes alone, sometimes with Groton, who had entered into a similar relationship with another monk.

Groton was more advanced than I, perhaps because he was younger, perhaps because he was by nature humbler, more flexible and apt to the disciplines of the Zen method.

The odd thing was that I had not then any notion of submitting myself to a religious exercise in the ordinary sense of the word. As Musō presented it to me, the practice of Zen belonged to the purely natural order and was in fact a preparation of the human organism for a higher state of awareness. On these terms I could accept it without self-consciousness. I might even hope from it a remedy for the weaknesses which pain and loss had revealed in my personality.

It was the measure of Groton's wisdom that, although he had led me to my teacher, he refused to enter into any discussion with me on our mutual commitment. He pointed out simply that in Tokyo we were separated by the formalities of the Service and that in Kyoto we were separated by the privacy of an incommunicable experience. When I expressed my gratitude for what he had done for me, he accepted it with a grin and a typical Zen comment:

"When we are silent we are one. When we speak we are two."

This, also, I was to remember much later, when we debated so bitterly the course to which I committed myself in Saigon.

For my part, I was content to be quiet and withdrawn—removed for a day or two from the press and complexity of my trade. I enjoyed the garden, the quicksilver flow of the old man's talk. I think, too, I did better work because of it. I understood better the elusive refinement of Japanese thought, the emotional shadow that haunts the most direct statement. I began to understand that this intuitive approach to enlightenment was not necessarily a rejection of reason, but an exploration of reason's most secret processes at the level of the subconscious mind.

For his part, Musō Soseki did not press me into any of the disciplines. Sometimes we would simply drink tea and talk discursively like friends anywhere. Sometimes he would take me through a *mondō* dialogue. Sometimes he would lay before me, as a subject of meditation, one of those apparently meaningless propositions which are *kōan*.

The one which he proposed to me, and to which he returned always with mild persistence was this:

"What will you do when they ask you to kill the cuckoo?"

My first reply was a challenge to Musō to define the terms of the proposition. Who, for example, were they? What was the cuckoo, and why should I be asked to kill it?

Musō smiled and refused the challenge. "You, Amberleysan, *you* must tell *me* what I mean."

In spite of myself, the question began to haunt me, irritate me and distract me from the formal and often formidable logic of practical diplomacy. It troubled me like a surrealist painting, each of whose symbols was plain to me, yet whose whole was a gibberish until I was given the key.

Yet, slowly, I began to see how and where I was being led: into a state of self-mistrust, into a dissatisfaction with the obvious, into a sphere of wordless communication. Even as I understood this, I understood how far I was from any term of arrival.

Then, without warning, the whole process of re-education was interrupted and I was thrust, without recourse, back into the realities—or were they the illusions?—of the Service. Festhammer flew in from Washington with a formal request from the Secretary of State, backed by a friendly note from the President. Would I give up the Tokyo post and take up special duty as Ambassador to South Vietnam?

No one is less like a Zen adept than Raoul Festhammer. He is the perfect pragmatist. A fact in his hands is as formidable as a rapier. There are some who call him the perfect opportunist, but I have too much respect for him to damn him so lightly. He is a cool appraiser. His situation summaries are a model exercise in tactical

logic. He drinks little, smokes not at all and has a fre-
netic appetite for beautiful women. He is an uncertain
friend and a dangerous enemy—but in his work as precise as a banker. In private life I have small taste for
him, but professionally I would stake my career on one
of his reports—which was exactly what he was asking
me to do now.

". . . It's a mess, Max. A bloody, thankless mess.
We call it a subversive war, but at bottom it's a civil war
as well. Son against father, family against family. We're
involved because we want to maintain a military foothold in Southeast Asia and deny China an access to the
southern rice bowls and the sea roads to Africa. If
South Vietnam goes, Thailand is outflanked and Singa-
pore is threatened. We've committed thirty thousand
men and God knows how many millions of dollars and
we're still 'advisers' with no final voice in the conduct of
operations.

"We backed Phung Van Cung and his family because they were the best and strongest administrators
available. I think they still are, but they're out of control. They won't listen to reason any more. They act
like men with a private line to the Holy Ghost. They're
minority Catholics in a country of Buddhists. Instead of
making friends with the Buddhists, they're putting pressure on them at every point. They're arresting students
—boys and girls—and putting them into forced labor
camps. They've alienated the capital and they're losing
control of the country areas. The military command is
divided, and in spite of ten thousand fortified villages
and a vast superiority in arms and equipment, the Viet
Cong are still winning every round on points. . . . Mc
Nally did a good job as Ambassador, but we gave him
the wrong instructions. We told him to make friends
with Phung Van Cung, to work by persuasion and
charm. Now the charms have worn out.

"We can't work like that any more. We have to play
rough and tough and bring the Administration to heel
with financial sanctions. There is a mass of papers I
want you to read, and then you'll see why we need a

strong man for this assignment, Max. There are no Os-
cars in it. Win, loose or draw, it's still a bloody mess
and all you get is a pain in the neck. . . . Everyone at
home hopes you'll take it."

I spent forty-eight hours reading the documents he
handed me, and then I accepted. Later, when I came to
tally the guilts I had to assume, I wondered how many
belonged to this precise moment.

Pride was involved—and who is not proud to say,
"I am here in the name of a great people. I am chosen
because I am shrewd and strong and it will be dangerous to provoke me." Under the pride was a fear—because Gabrielle's death had shown me how little strength
I had, and Musō Soseki had begun to challenge my wisdom, and George Groton had made me ashamed of my
angers. And under the pride and the fear was something
else—a compulsion to put off contemplation in favor of
action, to defer a decision about myself by assuming the
right to make decisions about millions of nameless
others.

And yet I was sworn to this kind of service. My
whole life was dedicated to it. I had been summoned by
a special call from the Chief Executive. I had no right
at all to interpose my private problems in the business
of the commonweal. I had to understand that I was two
selves in one body. The two were separate, disparate.
The self I knew in the garden of Tenryu-ji was a
different self from that which played so confidently the
gambits of power. So, it seemed, I must accept always
to live on two levels of existence, rejecting any impulse
to equate the one with the other.

And yet I was still conscious of uneasiness and foreboding. Who could say how long this precarious balance
of selves would survive the shocks of a hostile environment? Musō Soseki had helped me find respect for my
secret self, but there was no Gabrielle to love me and
hold me in harmony with the inward and outward
world.

So I turned to George Groton. I asked him if he
would be willing to go with me to Saigon as my special

assistant. He grinned in his boyish fashion, thanked me for my confidence in him and agreed. Then, innocently enough, he asked me whether I proposed to see Musō Soseki before I left Japan. In the flurry of discussions with Festhammer and the spate of talks to Washington, I had not given the matter a thought. Groton pointed out to me that a special kind of courtesy was involved —the courtesy of the pupil to the master, which is like the courtesy of a son to his father. Once again I was shamed by my own thoughtlessness, and I promised that, as soon as the round of diplomatic farewells was over, I would spend the last day with Musō Soseki in the Temple of the Heavenly Dragon.

The chill of winter was already in the air. The fire had gone out of the sacred maples at the gate. The leaves were scattered, the rocks were bleak and the water in the pools was gray and forbidding. Musō Soseki received me in his house and closed the screens so that we sat separate from the rest of the world in a tiny island of light and warmth. When I told him of my transfer, he nodded gravely and said:

"Every man wears a different pair shoes. He has to walk where the shoes take him. However, I think it is a great risk to take such an appointment at this time of your life."

I laughed and told him the risk was normal to a diplomatic career. He frowned and shook his head.

"I was not thinking of your career, but of your self. You have become conscious of imperfection in your own life. You may be tempted to try to impose an impossible perfection on the situation which confronts you. You are being sent to produce results. What kind of results are you expected to produce? An end to the civil war? An end to communism in South Vietnam? An end to the regime?" He held up a small, slim hand to stay my reply. "No! Don't answer! In the way of enlightenment you are my pupil. In the way of the world you are the American Ambassador. You must not discuss matters of state with me. . . . But the problem of politics is only a multiplication of the problem of the individual, and we try to solve it in the same way: by proposing to ourselves a limited end which, if attained, will signify 'success.' Thus a general says, 'If I win the war I shall have—and be!—a success.' He ignores the fact that war is a destructive violence that knows no bounds and that afterward a new act of creation is necessary to bring order out of chaos and laughter out of the mourning. You see, my friend, what I mean?"

"I see it. But it illuminates nothing. I know very well my situation as a professional diplomat. I am not free to propose the ends of my actions—but only to act so as best to accomplish the ends that are proposed to me."

Musō Soseki smiled and shook his head. "That is true only in part. You are called upon to counsel and advise, and so, in fact, you may help to propose the ends that are later proposed to you."

"That's true. But I counsel under pressure of daily events: plague, famine, war and fluctuations in the stock market. I have to remind myself and all those with whom I deal that a change is not necessarily an improvement. If I fail to convince them, I may be ordered to bring about a change in which I do not believe. On the other hand, the change in which I do believe may be only the begetter of other plagues and other wars."

"And you are content with this situation, which is in fact your whole professional life?"

"I accept it as a fact—a necessary fact of existence. In this sense I have to be content with it."

"Is it necessary because it is so—or because you will it so?"

"I wish I knew the answer to that."

"To wish is not enough. One must set oneself in the attitude of seeking for an answer."

I was reproved and I knew it. I had to accept the reproof because this man was the master and I the pupil. But it was hard to digest because, on the other plane, I was the great man called by the President of a great nation to change, if he could, the course of history. My pride shouted for release from this bondage to an aged mystic. Another voice cried, "Stay! Lest without him you destroy yourself utterly."

Musō Soseki was silent a long time. His eyes were fixed on the unseen garden. His lined face was set in the repose of contemplation. I found myself settling also into the physical and mental postures of meditation. My attention fixed itself on the small eddy of warm air above the charcoal brazier. My mind detached itself from the logic of the previous conversation and began to swing freely by associative impulse. Then, abruptly, the old monk spoke again:

"I regret very much that you have not yet answered the question of the cuckoo."

"I have thought about it a great deal, but I still do not understand it."

"Even now you do not understand it?"

"Even now."

"Then let us look for the answer again. Tell me. Why do you come to visit me?"

"To hear the silence."

"Have you heard the silence?"

"Sometimes."

"Have you heard the cuckoo?"

"How could I? The cuckoo is silent when winter comes."

"But you came to hear the silence. Why does not the silence of the cuckoo make itself heard?"

"I have never been able to ask him."

"But you wait all year for his song?"

"Yes."

"And when you hear it, you understand that spring is here?"

"Yes."

"So you do understand the cuckoo?"

"Yes."

"Are you afraid he will not understand you?"

"I know he will not understand me."

"Do you know, or are you reluctant to find out?"

"I am reluctant to find out."

"Why?"

"Because I have never trusted the cuckoo."

"Do you think the cuckoo will forgive you?"

"I hope he may."

"What will you do then when they ask you to kill the cuckoo?"

"Why should anyone ask me to kill the cuckoo?"

"Because he is reluctant to sing in winter."

And there I was, still a neophyte, back at the gate by which I had entered. The old man was aware of my discomfiture because he dropped the formal tone of the *mondō* and reminded me gently:

"Remember that what you seek is an 'inwardness.' It will give you no precise answer to the 'outwardness' in which you are involved. It will not show you how to succeed as an Ambassador or to 'solve' one problem by changing it into another. What it will show you is that the secret of life and survival and betterment is carried by the individual and not by the mass. So that whatever is done for the better in your work, or anyone's work, must be done by and through the inwardness of individual men . . ." He broke off abruptly and gave me one of his rare smiles. "I must not confuse you. Wisdom grows like a flower which opens when we do not look at it. Please write to me. I shall be concerned for you. And when you come back, you will come to visit me."

"I will come back—and thank you."

The question was still unanswered. There was no illumination, only a deepened sense of dissatisfaction and foreboding. One thing I did understand: that this relationship into which I had entered with Musō Soseki was very real; that he, the master, was as deeply involved in my life as I was in his. Thenceforth he would count himself responsible in part for my well-being and my rectitude. And I must honor him and concern myself with his health and comfort and with the dignities of his dying.

Much water—and much blood—have flowed under the bridge since that winter conversation with Musō Soseki. Now I am back in the garden of Tenryu-ji, trying to make some sense of my public triumphs and my pri-

vate betrayals. What is so strange to me now is that
I should have been so deeply stirred by a fanciful question about a cuckoo and so little disturbed by Festhammer's final word before I took off for Saigon.

"Any day now, Max, someone's going to knock off
Phung Van Cung and his family and set up a new government. Before they strike, they're going to ask you
how you feel about it and how far you're prepared to
back them in the name of the United States. . . . And
the rough edge is, Max, you'll have to give an answer—
and then justify it to the Department and the President.
. . . Good luck. Have a pleasant journey!"

A hundred miles from the Vietnamese coast we were
met by an escort of fighter bombers which flew in tight
formation with us for the rest of the journey. Our first
landfall was the giant delta of the Mekong River, which
fans out through a hundred miles of rice paddies and
tropical plantations and atap villages and dikes and
canals into the flat, shallow water of the Astrolabe
Banks.

They had brought me this way for my first look at
the military situation. The delta country was the stage
for some of the bitterest fighting of the whole war. The
Mekong River was the supply route by which arms and
military equipment were floated down to the guerrillas
by way of Laos and Cambodia. They came hidden under bags of rice and bunches of bananas. They were
paddled by women and children and tribal grandfathers
and Khmers from the border. The guerrillas came and
went the same way—by river, and creek, and backwa-
ter. They were as free as animals in a natural element—
for who could read the heart of a small brown man
planting rice or weaving palm fiber or selling sweet sug-
ar cane in a village market?

In the tight familial life of the thatched villages the
bitter tragedy of a civil war was seen in its simplest and
most brutal consequences. At night the villagers withdrew behind a bamboo stockade with their livestock.
Each family provided a lamp to light the walls and a

sentry to guard them against the Viet Cong, who came creeping through the rice paddies and the clumps of bamboos to make their raids. But the man on the wall and the man in the swamp below were brother and brother, or cousin and cousin. So, sometimes, a lamp was blown out and a hand stretched over the stockade to help the raiders to enter. Sometimes rice was passed, or medicine for the wounded. Sometimes there was the truce of simple inaction, so that the guerrillas could pause and rest themselves in a banana thicket while the villagers slept peaceably inside the stockade.

For the military command it was a nightmare. For the dwellers in the hamlets it was a natural accommodation to circumstance—for what was left to a delta peasant if the millennial structure of the family was destroyed?

At a safe fifteen thousand feet we circled above the vivid land. An Air Force major pointed out a small town which he called Travinh. He showed me the helicopters wheeling above it like ungainly birds. We caught the streak of rockets and the tiny flash of gunfire and saw smoke bursts rising from lilliputian tree clumps. But we saw no men, only small sorties of ants. We heard no sound except the high whine of our own jets. We were gods in the empyrean, looking down on the inconsequential flurry of human hostility, which tomorrow would be washed away by the sluggish river or sunk in the rice swamp or eaten by the jungle. We waited perhaps ten minutes, then turned north and began to slide downward into Saigon.

As we neared the airport, our escort peeled away from us and we dived, too steeply for comfort, toward the runway. The Air Force major made a wry explanation: the Viet Cong were active even on the outskirts of the city, and an occasional aircraft was hit by rifle fire as it came in to land.

When we rolled to rest and the doors were opened, we found ourselves in the middle of an armed camp. Helicopters and fighter bombers were parked around the perimeter of the airfield. There was a U.S. guard of honor, and a parade of Vietnamese paratroopers in camouflage suits and berets. The Foreign Minister was flanked by generals in full dress. Our Embassy officials were matched by a contingent of service personnel, headed by the Commander in Chief, General Tolliver.

George Groton made a whispered comment as we stepped onto the tarmac!

"They've brought you in like a military general and not like an Ambassador. I wonder who stage-managed that one."

My guess was Raoul Festhammer. He had always had a talent for diplomatic theater. But I had no time to dwell on the point. The Protocol Officer was at my elbow and steering me swiftly through the courtesies. The courtesies were cordial enough, but the whole ceremony was brief, almost brusque. I sensed a tension, an unspoken wish to have me off the airfield and safely installed in the Embassy as soon as possible. Wherever I moved, I was masked by an armed man. General Tolliver sat beside me in the car, and when we drove out of the airport and onto the wide boulevard that led to the city, my car was led, flanked and followed by armed vehicles.

After the subdued ceremoniousness of my life in Japan, it was a rude shock, and I found myself reacting to it in an unexpected fashion. Excitement took hold of me—an odd, almost sexual excitement, as though this parade of arms, this air of risk and physical threat, were a challenge to my virility. I was glad to be received like a military man, and not with the civilities of politics. I was here to act, to set forces in motion and then direct them to a favorable end. I must inspire confidence and courage and wear my office like a patent of power. It was a giddy, exalted moment. Tolliver's troops had me hedged in like a sacramental presence, but I wanted to stand up and show myself to the people as one sent to deliver them out of bondage.

Then I looked at the people and was shocked instantly into sobriety. They had no eyes for me, nor for my sinister cavalcade. They did not gather in groups to wave flags and shout hosannas for the new deliverer. They looked once and then averted their eyes. Their small, intelligent faces might have been carved out of teak.

The coolies trotted past with baskets balanced on bamboo poles across their skinny shoulders. A shave-pate monk in saffron robes held out a begging bowl to a housewife who offered him a rice cake and a piece of fruit. An aged Chinese amah scuffed along the sidewalk, clasping the hands of children scrubbed and beautiful as dolls. The police at the intersections were blank-faced and efficient. Girls, bright as birds in silk skirts and pantaloons, rode sidesaddle with students on motorcycles. Housewives sat like ancient and elegant princesses in the pedicabs, their faces calm, almost contemptuous, under their hats of plaited palm.

They were not hostile. They were cautious, disinvolved, indifferent to those who could make so little difference to the fundamental pattern of their lives. So many lordlings had come and gone in their historic memory—the Chinese, the Mongols, the Portuguese, the Dutch, the English, the French, the Japanese and finally the Americans. . . . And yet not finally because there was no finality in Asia. The vast and complex configuration of the continent forbade it. The tribal currents were kept constantly in movement by the pressure of mountain barriers, the fear of howling deserts, the lure of rice deltas, the traffic of mighty waterways, the seduction of islands full of spices and beaches sprinkled with jewels.

There would always be a tomorrow in Asia because man was proud to be potent and woman was honored to be prolific and, in spite of famine and cholera and dysentery and smallpox, the tribes multiplied and the Middle Kingdom was always bulging at its borders and stretching hungry tentacles toward the rice paddies and the roads that led to the sea of the Southern Islands. In the shadow of these tomorrows the city of Saigon with its shady boulevards, its comfortable villas, its air of musty Gallic elegance, seemed suddenly as impermanent and impertinent as I myself.

My eye was caught suddenly by a flash of color and movement. About fifty yards ahead I saw the brilliant blue tiles, the tip-tilted eaves and the golden woodwork of a pagoda. From its entrance there walked three monks, two young ones attending a very old man. They walked with him to the edge of the footpath, where they spread a small rug and helped him to seat himself on it. One of them laid a large earthenware vessel within hand's reach. They bowed respectfully and withdrew into the pagoda, so that the old man sat, a solitary and statuesque observer of our approach.

We were not yet abreast of him when I saw him lift the earthenware vessel and pour the contents over his head as if he were performing a ritual ablution. The liquid ran down over his face and shoulders, staining his yellow robe and the mat on which he sat. Then, quite deliberately, he laid down the vessel, fumbled in his robes and brought out a cigarette lighter. As he flicked it there was a muffled explosion and his whole body flowered into fire.

We were abreast of him now. I could feel the heat and smell the odor of roasting flesh. I saw people running and shouting and police beating them back with batons and rifle butts. I felt my car leap forward as the driver stood hard on the gas. But in that last suspended moment I saw the old man's face. It was covered and crowned with flames; but his eyes were closed, his lips were parted in a Buddha smile and he sat silent and quite motionless, waiting for the fire to consume him.

CHAPTER TWO

I was witness to a martyrdom—and I did not relish the experience. There was an impact of horror at the spectacle of a human body immolated by fire. There was a nightmare excitement in the flurry of violence around the sacrifice. There was a weird spirituality in the ecstasy of the monk and the mastery of his will over tormented nerves and muscles. There was a sudden nausea as I realized that this ritual suicide had been staged for me and that, through negligence or ignorance or political calculation, I had been made an accomplice in the act.

I was not yet an hour in the country. I had not even set foot in my own Embassy, yet I was involved, publicly and irrevocably, in the religious feuds of South Vietnam. Before I had even presented my papers at the Presidential Palace, I could be challenged by the press of the world to make a statement about a Buddhist martyr and a Catholic administration.

I was being challenged in another fashion as well. I was a student, if not an adept, in the eightfold path of the compassionate Buddha. I had accepted to walk in the way of Zen, and I was unprepared for the more primitive attitudes of the Vietnamese Mahayana. Musō Soseki had shown me that the way to enlightenment was by a series of small deaths inflicted on the self-centered spirit. But that a man should seek to attain it by a gross act of physical extinction was to me a brutal shock. The shock made me angry, and I said rough words to General Tolliver.

"For God's sake, General, who the devil let me in for this? Who's responsible for the security arrangements?"

Tolliver was blunt and equally bad-tempered.

"The Embassy, the CIA and the Palace. I was to provide the convoy and the convoy guards. I did that. Security was to be handled by the Viets in consultation with the CIA. The CIA approved their arrangements."

"But goddamnit, man! The Buddhists have been threatening this kind of demonstration for weeks. The press has been full of it. So have the Embassy dispatches. Surely someone must have tipped today as a good day to open the show."

"They were all warned," said Tolliver bitterly. "The

press knew. The Palace knew. The CIA knew. It was discussed openly at the final briefing. But Harry Yaffa said he would guarantee the arrangements. He's top brass in the CIA, so how can I argue with him? Besides, I've got my own war to fight—and I'm engaged on too many fronts already."

"And who, especially, wanted me involved in a Buddhist burning?"

"Everybody," said Tolliver bluntly. "The Buddhists because they want to stage a public drama of their wrongs. The Palace because they hope you'll be repelled by a display of primitive fanaticism. The press because they're accused of dramatizing the war from the Caravelle Bar and they can use a real-life story like this one. The CIA because they want to change the Administration and this kind of crisis is the best way to sell you the idea."

"And the Army, General? Your army, I mean. Where do you stand?"

"Knee deep in a delta swamp," said Tolliver with abrupt vehemence. "Fighting a war we can't win and daren't lose. We have no operational authority. We're here as advisers and storekeepers. In theory, we can't even fire a bullet until our personal safety is directly threatened. If we take over operational control, that makes us capitalist colonizers like the French. If we mount a full scale military drive into North Vietnam, we have escalation and a possible military confrontation with China. If we win on our own ground, we are victors in a political and social vacuum. If we pull out and let the Viets fight their own war, we lose face, foothold and all the southern peninsulas of Asia. . . . Your Buddhist is important to me, yes. He's a symbol of disunion and disaffection in our own camp. But I didn't stage his martyrdom. I've got enough martyrs of my own. . . ."

I apologized to him, and he accepted it with a shrug and a tired smile.

"Everybody here has his own version of the truth. But if you want the whole truth, you'll have to fish for it in the delta swamps. And they're pretty muddy just now."

"Bloody, too, they tell me."

"Bloody, too. I hope you'll take time off to see for yourself."

Then we turned into the gates of the Embassy, where I was to be installed like a satrap behind the bayonets of the guards.

George Groton summed up my welcome in one wry phrase:

". . . A crew of undertakers measuring a new client for his shroud."

I, too, felt a mortuary chill, but I was more prepared for it than Groton. Reformers and troubleshooters are suspect in the Service, the more so when they come from appointments of ease and distinction. Besides, McNally, my predecessor, had been a friendly man, beloved by his staff. I had always been known as a cool superior, and of late I had been reported as an exacting one. It was natural, therefore, that they should be chary of me.

But more, much more, was involved than the good or ill-humor of an Ambassador. This was a hardship post —a place of risk and daily danger to my people and their dependents. There were riots in the streets. Bombs exploded in bars and movie houses and public markets. A bicycle parked in a driveway might be packed with plastic explosive. Children were driven to school by predetermined routes, under armed guard. Gates were locked at night, and the father of a family slept with a loaded pistol under his pillow. A Sunday drive five miles out of the city might lead to an ambush by the Viet Cong. A peddler of rice cakes might be a gunrunner or an emissary of guerrillas. So beware of any newcomer who expected to change the face of Asia with a bold gesture and a bland new policy from Washington.

All the staff lay under the censure of a policy that had failed; but they would have to accept the consequences of the new one, as they had borne the perils of the old. They had a right, therefore, to put me on trial, and I had to justify myself to them before I could command their loyalty. I felt oddly naked as I took my place at the head of the conference table and waited for my colleagues to settle themselves. These were men who had been fighting an outpost war while I sat, contemplative, in the garden of Musō Soseki. I would speak to them with the voice of the Chief Executive, but they might well judge that it issued from the mouth of a biblical ass.

Over the last preparatory rustle George Groton passed me a note written in Kanji characters: "Harry Yaffa, CIA, is strong man. Friction between him and Mel Adams, First Secretary. Other opinion divided." I crumpled the note and thrust it into my pocket.

Melville Adams sat on my right, a lean, bleak, academic fellow in his late forties. He had been a long time in the Service and had earned respect for the studious impersonality of his attitudes and the stubborn courage of his convictions. There were those who thought him too dry a man for first-line appointments, but I had seen him work in Helsinki and the Argentine and I had always held him in sober respect.

Halfway down the table was Harry Yaffa, looking more like a fashionable surgeon than the Chief of the Central Intelligence Agency for South Vietnam, Laos and Cambodia. He was short, pudgy, dapper and benign. His hands were soft and beautifully manicured. His silk shirt was elegantly cut, with a monogram woven in blue thread under his left breast. His voice was soft. His manner was full of charm and deprecation. He was reputed to be devious, ruthless and without moral scruples of any kind. If I were to control him, I would need to know him much better than I did now, but I suspected that I would not much relish a closer acquaintance.

I looked down at the rest of my audience. They were all sedulously intent on the typewritten reports in front of them. It was time for me to make the opening gambit.

". . . I should like to dispense with formalities, gentlemen. . . . You've been running this store a long time. I shall lean heavily on your information, advice and help. I hope you will be frank with me, as I propose to be frank with you. . . ."

Their eyes were hooded, their faces blank. They were all case-hardened professionals. This was pure preamble, and they believed not a word of it. They were waiting to hear the true text of my instructions from Washington. I recited it briefly and baldly.

"I am here as the instrument of a revised policy with respect to the regime of South Vietnam. I am instructed by the State Department to make the following specific demands: the persecution of the Buddhists and the repressive measures against students must cease forthwith. Phung Van Cung must make whatever concessions are necessary to restore political and military unity within his own Administration. He, and members of his Administration, must refrain from any further public attacks on the policy of the United States. If he is not prepared to do this, I am authorized to threaten immediate sanctions: a closure on U.S. aid funds and a step-by-step withdrawal of our military personnel."

There was a sudden stir of interest around the table. General Tolliver demanded bluntly, "And if Cung doesn't do as he is told, will the sanctions be applied?"

"You may take my word that they will be, General. Within the next few days you will receive detailed instructions from the Pentagon on the method to be used in any withdrawal of military personnel."

Tolliver thanked me and then relapsed into silence. He was too canny a soldier to play politics with the professionals. He had said part of his concert piece already. The rest could wait until I understood my need of the men with the guns. The next question came from Mel Adams.

"Will these demands be made public, sir?"

"That will depend on the outcome of my first talk with Phung Van Cung, tomorrow morning."

"Meantime, what information do you propose to give the press?"

"None at all until after I have presented my papers at the Presidential Palace. I notice you have scheduled a press conference for five this afternoon. I would like it canceled."

"Do we make any explanation?"

"Yes. You make it clear that a diplomatic courtesy is involved. Tell them that I will be at their disposal for a full-dress conference at two o'clock tomorrow afternoon. . . . Speaking of the press, gentlemen, I expect their first request will be for a comment on the suicide of the Buddhist monk this morning. At this moment I would not know what public comment to make. However, I do have a private statement for you all. I think it points to a lamentable breakdown of our security arrangements. I would like to know who was responsible."

There was a short, uneasy silence. Then, bland as butter, Harry Yaffa answered me:

"I have already investigated the incident, sir. It is my opinion that responsibility lies squarely on the shoulders of the Viets. We knew something like this might happen. The city has been full of rumors for the last two weeks. We discussed security arrangements in detail with the Palace. We arranged that they would post a four-man guard detail at the gate of the pagoda. I had two of my agents located on the opposite side of the street. . . . Five minutes before your car arrived, the guard was moved. One of my agents left immediately to find the guard commander. He was still arguing with him when the monk was brought out. . . . After that there was nothing to be done. Everything happened too fast."

"And your second agent, Mr. Yaffa?"

"He is an undercover man with no police or military authority. If he had attempted to intervene, there might have been a worse disturbance. . . ."

"So the Ambassador has lost face on the very morning of his arrival and the Palace has affirmed its don't-give-a-damn attitude to the Buddhists. Is that the position?"

Yaffa seemed to smile faintly at my simplicity. "It's a little more complicated than that, sir. The Buddhists have scored a victory of their own." He fished among his papers and brought out a typewritten document which was passed to me from hand to hand along the table. "That's a translation of the last letter written by our martyr. It's already circulating around the pagodas and among the Buddhist laity."

I read the typescript in silence, while my audience waited. In any context it was a notable document: the last testament of a man on the eve of his voluntary exit from the world. It called up for me the vision of an aged ascetic, smiling and silent, immobile, even while the flames devoured him. In spite of myself, I was moved by the simple fervor of his final words . . . "Before closing my eyes to Buddha, I have the honor of presenting these my last words to President Cung, asking him to be kind and tolerant to his people and to grant them in truth a religious equality. . . ."

I laid the paper down and faced Yaffa again.

"That's an inflammatory document, Mr. Yaffa."

"I agree, sir." His tone was studiously formal, but I caught an undertone of irony. "It also raises a question that must be asked sooner or later at this conference. How far has Washington calculated the effects of your ultimatum to President Cung?"

It was out now. It lay naked as a knife blade on the table: a challenge that had to be answered. I wondered that this roly-poly little man was the only one who had the courage—or the calculation—to make it. Had any of my colleagues conspired to make him their spokesman? Or was he challenging them, too, from some standpoint of secret power? I felt like a man being coaxed off solid ground into a place of swamps and marsh lights. I decided to retreat a pace or two and fight this first skirmish in my own territory.

"Washington has made certain calculations, Mr. Yaffa. However, the Secretary of State has asked me to test them against the opinions of the men on the spot. So let me ask each of you in turn the same question.

What do you think will happen when I deliver our demands to the Palace?"

When the conference ended, I felt suddenly isolated and incapable. It was an eerie sensation, as though I had come, at one stride, to the limit of my mental and physical powers. I was tired and old; my judgment was clouded; my will was feeble. I resented Raoul Festhammer for having thrust me so easily into the seat of judgment. I resented the memory of Musō Soseki and his warning of my own inadequacy. I resented my colleagues, who caviled at the dissensions among the Viets and who were yet so little united among themselves. I wanted nothing better than to abandon all responsibility and retreat from this place of tension and intrigue.

After the swift, virile excitement of my entry it was like the sadness that comes after the act of love. It was like and yet unlike, because I felt, under the sadness, a terror and a danger—a desperation that might one day thrust me into action to end the sorry comedy and begin again. Even as I saw the shape of the danger, I put it away from me because I must smile and thank my colleagues and close the meeting with courtesy and a display of confidence.

It lacked only two hours to dinnertime, so I asked to be driven immediately to my house. Groton would wait at the Embassy until the transcript of the meeting was typed, and then he would bring it to me immediately. Mel Adams would dine with us and brief me on Embassy activities.

Then Yaffa came up and asked for two minutes in private. He had a gift for me: an automatic pistol in a shoulder harness of black leather. He asked me to wear it wherever I went, to keep it in my desk drawer by day and sleep with it under my pillow at night. He gave me advice as well: to stay away from open windows and to travel always with the bodyguard whom he would provide. I searched his smooth face for any sign of mockery, but I found none. His final words were sober and respectful:

"In this you must trust me, sir. Security is my business. Your safety is my personal responsibility. This is an assassin's town. I beg you to do as I ask."

I thanked him and promised to co-operate. Then he asked permission to ride with me to my house, to show me certain precautions that he had instituted for my safety. I could not refuse without seeming ungracious; and besides, I was intrigued by the swift change in his personality. In the conference he had been ironic, subtly assertive, a maker of controversy. Alone with me, he was urbane and deferent. His foppery fell away like a mask, and I saw what Groton had seen: the strong man who roused emotions of respect or mistrust. As we drove through the hot, sluggish evening to my house, Yaffa read me a short but pungent lecture on the city of Saigon.

". . . It has a kind of charm, hasn't it? A French provincial stage set, with Oriental actors. But the drama is all Asian. Nothing means what it seems to say. Look at this street. There are three policemen and four militiamen, but that's not all. The fellow pushing the hand cart is one of Cung's security boys. There's another one at the far corner. The woman at the window up there works for me. . . . This city is screwed down so tight you can't have a drink or a meal without tripping over a secret policeman. It looks calm, doesn't it? But underneath it's boiling. That man riding a bicycle may belong to the Viet Cong. That taxi driver may be carrying a grenade under the bucket seat. . . . In one way and another these people have been at war continuously for almost two thousand years. They're a very sophisticated race—very tough too. Chinese lacquer on Vietnamese bamboo . . . and the French added an extra veneer of their own. Over there is Cholon, the Chinese city. They trade and breed and lend money and breed some more and wait quietly for the time when they can be buried near the tombs of their ancestors. They have a man there you should meet someday—Number One Chinese. He's a big man, but he is rarely seen and his name is never spoken. He keeps his people quiet and

patient, and listens to the wind." Without a change in
tone he added, "That's what I'd like you to do, sir. Listen to the wind for a while. It speaks a different language from the one you heard at the conference table."
Before I had time to answer, he went on. "The Buddhist burning was only the beginning. Something big
is brewing, and I'm not quite sure what it is. It may
even happen tonight. If not tonight, then within a couple of days. I'll know half an hour in advance, then I'll
call you."

When I pressed him for details, he lapsed into vague-
ness. I was irritated and he knew it. He said firmly:

"Let's be frank with each other, sir. Let's understand
clearly what our functions are. You are the official representative of the United States. I have to serve in another way—as a political opportunist. There are things I
have to do that you can never approve, and therefore it
is better that you shouldn't know them. I have to kill
men and suborn women. I have to foment one plot to
ensure the success of another. I have to provide against
your success and your possible failure. If you want to
salve your conscience by having me lie to you, I can
do that, too. I'm very good at it, but I'd rather not lie
when it isn't necessary. I hope I make myself clear."

"Very clear, Mr. Yaffa, except in one particular.
What about your own conscience?"

"A luxury, sir. I found long ago I couldn't afford it."

And there, perforce, our private talk ended. We were
already at my house: a large stuccoed villa, surrounded
by a high wall topped with barbed wire and broken
glass. Two marines stood guard at the iron gate. Two
more patrolled the walls. Inside the gate was a small
guardhouse. When our driver sounded his horn, another marine swung the grille open and the guards stood at
the salute as we drove into the compound.

It was ablaze with tropical color and heavy with the
scent of frangipani; but after the sober, calculated order
of my Japanese garden, this place seemed lush and run
down, like a beautiful woman gone to seed. I found no
welcome in it, no rest for eye or spirit. I would always

be a transient here. There was nothing to coax me to spend that innermost secret self which was my last true possession.

Yaffa was already launched on a final brisk summation:

"Half your domestic staff is American. Anne Beldon is your private secretary; Humphrey is your major-domo—old Virginia, and very good at it. Mrs. Brendan is your housekeeper. The rest you'll meet in due course. The kitchen staff, the cleaners and the gardeners are all Vietnamese, members of three families who live in a compound at the rear of the residence. That way we can keep them under surveillance and away from threats or seduction. Your private rooms overlook the river. We've checked the field of fire from there, and the chances of your being sniped at are very small. But I ask you to remember that there is always that long chance. The whole building is wired with burglar alarms, and the guards have a security drill which I needn't bother you with now. Your personal bodyguard is Bill Slavich. He's a crack shot and a judo expert. He lives on the premises. If you'd like to go in now, sir . . . !"

He led me calmly through the ceremonies of greeting, and I noted with some satisfaction that Anne Beldon seemed good-looking and good-humored and that my bodyguard looked more like a graduate from West Point than the prize fighter I had feared. I am perhaps a snob in these matters, but I have a quick dislike of obtrusive people and it would have offended my pride to be guarded by a man who looked like a bully.

Then finally I was alone, in a large, airy bedroom that looked across the river to the flat green spread of the delta. In the last light of evening it looked strangely calm and beautiful—unreal, too, like the painted back-drop of a ballet.

It was hard to believe that only ten miles away, within the scope of my present vision, a pitched battle had been fought only a week before—a battle involving nearly a thousand men: Viet Cong, troops of President

Cung's army, and members of our own American forces. It was harder still to believe that this very night, when the swift tropic darkness came down upon the land, the Viet Cong would be on the move again, raiding this or that village along the canals, exacting tribute in rice or chickens or bullets, buying or frightening one family or another into allegiance.

Somewhere out there, I had been told, an American officer was being carried from village to village naked, blindfolded, caged like a beast, an object of mockery and derision. When morning came, a recalcitrant peasant might be found floating in a canal with his throat cut, another might be impaled, gagged and moaning, on the stakes of a bamboo fence. And before the sun was high, before the searching helicopters were out, the Viet Cong would be gone, hidden in the jungle fringes or mingling with the shoppers in a village market.

Even as I watched, the night came down and the first faint stars pricked out through breaks in the cloud banks. This was the sad hour for me, the hour of inaction, of doubt, mistrust and fear of the lonely night to come. I confess it frankly, I am a man who has always had great need of women, and if my life had seemed until now, regular and disciplined, it was because I was well matched in my marriage to Gabrielle. After her death I was saved for a while by a pride in her memory and by a certain fastidious vanity which prevented me from spending myself in sordid or temporary affairs. Now I saw clearly that these defenses had been slowly whittled away, and I wondered, with real anxiety, how I should support, alone, the strains and stresses of this new appointment.

I had found a temporary strength in the ascetic disciplines of Musō Soseki, but even this solace was denied me. No longer could I walk in the mystic garden of Tenryu-ji, but I must tread a perilous maze, as wary of my own passions as of the plotter's treachery or the bullet of the assassin.

As I stripped and bathed, I pondered the afternoon's conference, picking over the tangled threads of discussion to find the one that would lead me through the labyrinth to the monster—if monster there were—who dwelt at its center. But each thread I followed led me to a blind alley and then broke off, so that I had to retrace my steps and begin again.

General Tolliver, for instance, had a simple and precise view of the situation. This was a war which he must fight but could not win. He would come out of it with an extra star on his epaulets and he would hand back to our Government a corps of battle-proved veterans. American losses were small, and they might reasonably be balanced against a profit in campaign experience. For Tolliver the Viets were a military liability. Their High Command was divided by political intrigues. Their field officers were poorly trained. Their fighting troops were discouraged and demoralized. The whole campaign was an ulcerous wastage of material, manpower and fighting spirit.

Mel Adams was equally pessimistic. The political situation was an intolerable mess. The Cung Administration was a ramshackle dictatorship founded on mandarin ethics, warlord intrigues, the secret police and oldline Gallic Catholicism. Cung himself was an able politician, but he had lost the sympathy of the city dwellers and lacked the personality to rally the country folk. He had withdrawn into isolation and surrounded himself with sycophants who justified his most extreme follies. He was a Catholic in league with God. He had blundered with the Buddhists, but he could not admit it without losing face. So he had embarked on a breakneck course of repression and divisory tactics. My ultimatum would shock him. If he trusted me, I might perhaps help to change him. If he could not be changed, he would willy-nilly be deposed and removed.

And there, waiting in the wings, was Harry Yaffa, with the ready-made instrument of removal. The generals were ripe for revolt. They wanted only a firm sign of approval from the United States and they would topple Cung overnight. Working together, the generals could provide a stable government backed by military strength. They could reorganize the whole conduct of the war. . . . Therefore my ultimatum should be made public the minute it was delivered to the President. It should be couched in such terms that the generals would read it as an approbation of their plans. . . .

So there *was* a monster in the middle of the maze after all. His name was Cung, and all I had to do, to rally the country and win the war, was to have the generals chop off his head. It was all gloriously simple and seductive as a fairy tale. Like the fairy tale, it created its own air of reality. But the truth? Tolliver had told me to fish for it in the delta swamp. Musō Soseki had urged me to seek it in the inwardness of things.

"What will you do?" he had asked. "What will you do when they ask you to kill the cuckoo?"

The import of his question was clear to me now, but how I should answer it was not clear at all. I switched off the light, walked to the window and looked out once more across the dark delta lands. It was there, in atap huts and jungle bivouacs, that the verdict on my actions would be delivered.

There was both the simple outwardness and the complex inwardness of things. There the village headman was prince, primate and court of last appeal. There the *truong toc,* the clan chief, maintained the cult of the ancestors and the cleanliness of the altars. He kept the tombs and wrote the records of the clan and was the trustee of its inalienable property. There the family lived, three generations deep, under one roof, and all contributed to the purse and the rice bowl. They were grouped and held to the earth by a common root like the bamboo—and like the bamboo, they swayed and bent and survived under the wildest storms.

They were an accommodating people, slaves to an antique politeness. Come Christian priest or Buddhist monk or Confucian scholar or Tao magician, they would listen and learn a little and offer a share of the rice cake. And afterward they would retreat into the world of spirits, with its peopling of wandering souls and guardians of tree and rock and lily pool.

For them there was no monster in the middle of a maze—only a mandarin who lived in a distant palace in Saigon and published edicts that were politely received and politely forgotten before the sun went down. Or perhaps we were the monsters, the tall white barbarians —the long noses, the blue-eyed ones, who knew nothing of the spirits, but peddled powders and potions to purge out worms and guns to kill their cousins.

There was a knock at my door, and George Groton came in with the transcripts of the conference. He was flushed and excited as a schoolboy, and after my somber solitude, it was a relief to listen to his eager talk.

". . . It's like the thrillers they used to write, but don't any more because nobody believes them. While I was waiting for the transcripts, I walked up to the Caravelle for a drink. I almost expected to see Papa Hemingway perched on a stool in combat fatigues. The correspondents were whispering in corners and making cryptic telephone calls in bad French. Somebody dropped a soda bottle in the corridor and two Viets in the corner reached for their guns. Then everybody laughed and looked sheepish. . . . It seems there's something big brewing in the city but nobody is prepared to say what it is. Harry Yaffa's sidekick wandered into the bar after me and tried to pump me about you and your ideas. I told him I was just a messenger boy. I met your secretary downstairs, sir. She's quite a doll." He flushed and looked rather sheepish himself. "I'm sorry, sir. I was rattling away, wasn't I? But this is the way the place hits you—like a shot of benzedrine."

Then we both laughed, and I asked him, "Did Harry Yaffa's man give you a gun, too?"

"No, sir. But he told me the best bars to drink in. And he said if I wanted to sleep with the local B-girls I should wear a flak jacket."

"A knowledgeable man."

"He made that very clear. We're the new brooms. We're expected to clean out the old mess and leave a nice clean stable for everyone," said Groton dryly. "If the Ambassador plays ball with the CIA, all our trou-

bles will be over. . . . By the way, Mel Adams gave me
a message for you. He would like to bring a dinner
guest—the Apostolic Delegate. He's been recalled to
Rome, to report on the situation to the Vatican Secretariat of State. He leaves tomorrow morning. Adams
says a talk with him might be a good preparation for
your meeting with Cung. . . . I liked Adams. He came
out clean. He seemed like a man who wouldn't
panic. . . ."

We talked in this disjointed fashion while I finished
dressing, and I was impressed once again by the con-
trast between his boyish eagerness and his swift and
trenchant intuition. He had, too, a natural sense of the
fitness of things. He did not presume on the intimacy of
our private exchanges, but when we were in company
conducted himself always with modesty and deference.
More than I could express, I needed his loyalty. I
hoped that I might leave him, in return, a legacy of experience and training in the Service. When we walked
down for dinner, we found Mel Adams and a short,
shiny-faced Italian in clerical dress. Adams introduced
him as the Right Reverend Monsignor Angelo Visconti,
Apostolic Delegate to the Republic of South Vietnam.

He proved an ideal guest, witty and exotically elegant
in the English language. He was the perfect curial diplomat, secure in the knowledge that haste is no remedy
for urgent problems and that the wisest talk is made
between the pears and the cheese. He had a store of
anecdotes from half a dozen countries, and he made us
an urbane comedy that was a true relief from the tensions of the day. Then briskly he put himself at my
disposal for interrogation. My questions were blunt, but
he answered them with theological precision. I recorded
our dialogue in my diaries for this period:

"How far, Excellency, can the Catholic Church in
South Vietnam be held responsible for the acts of repression and cruelty which have been committed against
the Buddhists, who constitute eighty percent of the
country's population?"

"The Archbishop of Hué and the President, with

whom he is closely linked, can be held directly responsible. The Archbishop committed an incredible folly
when he forced the Government to forbid the flying of
flags on the birthday of Gautama Buddha. There were
riots. Nine people were killed by the police. Both the
Archbishop and the President took an intransigent
line. There were more disorders, more arrests. And now
we have Buddhist martyrs. . . . However, the Vatican
and the body of the Church in South Vietnam have
been clearly dissociated from the measures of repression. The dissociation was made publicly in a pastoral
letter from the Archbishop of Saigon, and also in a letter written directly from Pope Paul VI. Leaving out of
account certain regional and provincial attitudes among
certain of the lower clergy in the countryside, I
can state clearly that the great majority of Catholics are
shocked by and hostile to the repressive measures of the
regime. And yet," he added quickly, "neither are the
Buddhists all saints. There is an undercurrent of violence among them which may lead to more trouble
later."

"How would you describe the state of the Catholic
Church in South Vietnam?"

"Among the people there is a deep and lively faith.
However, clerical education is at a low ebb and in need
of reform. Pastoral authority has been shaken by the intransigent attitude of the Archbishop of Hué toward the
Apostolic authority of the Holy See.

"Yet Cung claims to be a good Catholic, and he
bases his policies on the so-called doctrine of personalism, which in practice strikes at the roots of personal
freedom, while claiming to develop it along Christian
lines."

He laughed wryly at this, and made a Roman gesture
of resignation.

"The best slogan the French ever made was 'Liberty,
equality, fraternity.' And that was a glorious lie! But to
try to unite a country around a philosophic proposition
—and a confused one at that—is sheer nonsense. I
made a pun in my last report: 'Maritain and Mandarin-

ism!' I am afraid the Secretariat of State didn't appreciate it. The truth is that Cung is a Catholic out of the Middle Ages. His attitude is that of an antique Mandarin. His practice is authoritarian and totalitarian. At bottom he is one hundred percent Marxist. The way this country is organized at the moment, it could be made Marxist overnight simply by changing the flags."

"How could the country be made Marxist overnight?"

"Because all the machinery of total political control is already in existence. The countryside, for example, is organized into strategic hamlets, which presently have a military function, but which also have a political one. Every resident in every household in every hamlet is registered by name, age, profession and description. The whole country, but especially the cities, are under constant surveillance by the secret police. The organization is similar to that of the Nazi Gau, or that of the Marxist 'cell' system. You can use it in whatever direction you choose."

His answer reminded me vividly of Harry Yaffa, the self-confessed opportunist. Whatever the system or the circumstance, he, too, could use it for a variety of contradictory purposes. I did not feel disposed to comment on the cellular organization of the hamlets since we Americans had our part in it, too, so I asked a less political question:

"What do you see as the greatest danger for Catholicism in this country?"

"I see a progressive danger for all the population— Catholics and Buddhists alike. First there is the apathy which afflicts those who live under repression and without a free voice for their grievances. Then there comes a passive resentment. Afterward they may find themselves forced into a desperate dilemma, thinking that there is little to choose between a regime of the extreme right and the extreme left."

"What does the Church propose to do about this situation?"

"We are setting about a campaign to deepen the spiritual life of our people, to reform clerical education and to dissociate the Church from bloc politics while leaving individual members free to make a legitimate political choice. We have to give our people the means of surviving as a spiritual entity, whatever happens politically or militarily."

I understood his point of view, though being a man without a settled faith, I was disposed to view it with a certain cynicism. I had no confidence that the Christian minorities would survive in Southeast Asia any longer than they had survived in China, under a hostile regime. Still, I was anxious to see how a Roman with the long view might judge the outcome of the argument.

"Will you have time to make the reforms in the Church and deepen the spiritual life of the people as you want to do it? Can you, in effect, maintain this last foothold of the Church in Southeast Asia?"

"From a human point of view, it is hard to say. This is Asia, not Europe. There are much ignorance, illiteracy and rank superstition. Education is the privilege of the few and they often misuse it. In the end we have to trust in Divine Providence and the working of the Holy Ghost."

His face clouded and he added the somber comment, "I have been in despair. I make no secret of it. But lately I have seen the small beginning of a miracle that seems to recur in the Church: the survival of a wise and lively faith in ordinary people which transcends the mistakes of those who rule them."

It was a temptation to comment that miracles like this were often illusions created for the comfort of the despairing. On the other hand, Angelo Visconti had what I longed for—a firm belief in the supernatural. And who was I to gainsay what I could not disprove? It might be more interesting to see how his faith was being translated into action. I asked him again:

"Is anything being done by the Church to restore and develop relations with the Buddhists in the spirit of Christian charity and the Ecumenical movement?"

"We have a few priests who are maintaining relations

with the Buddhists at this moment and trying to do what you suggest. . . . You must understand that though the actions of some of its members often appear to compromise the Church, the Church in essence and in itself is not compromised. Our ultimate affirmation is always an affirmation of fraternity and Christian charity."

My next question was perhaps an unfair one, but it was important for me to know how the affirmation of faith was heard by the Catholic President.

"The city is full of rumors that a certain number of students are held in prison, and that both males and females are being submitted to torture. Do you believe these rumors?"

"Unfortunately, I am forced to believe that some of the rumors are true. I believe also that there will be more arrests very soon."

"Have you made representations at the Palace about this matter?"

"I have made many representations, but it is impossible to change their thinking." He broke off at this point, I remember. He sipped his wine, and seemed to be weighing his next words with considerable care. Then he smiled and gestured in deprecation.

"What I have to say now may seem a contradiction of everything I have told you, but it is important that you know it. In justice to Cung, I have to say that if I were asked to judge him in the private forum of his own conscience, I should have to admit that he is probably in good faith. He is blind, yes! Stubborn and misguided, yes! But he did emerge as the savior of the country when it was sunk in disillusion and corruption. I think now that he is justifying his present mistakes by his past triumphs. But that is an error to which we are all tempted, and often in the best faith. This is a paradox, perhaps, but it is nevertheless the truth as I see it. I would add something else, too . . ."

I never did hear what he might have added. At that moment I was called to the telephone. Harry Yaffa had a message for me.

"It's happened. Cung's troops are moving out to raid the pagodas. I'd like you to come to the Embassy right away."

I looked at my watch. The time was fifteen minutes after midnight. As I put down the receiver I heard, distant but clear, the beating of a brazen gong.

CHAPTER THREE

The gong was still throbbing as we drove with pennon flying through the nighttime city. Then abruptly it stopped and we heard the crackle of distant gunfire. Mel Adams pointed to the military pickets along the street and the trucks parked at each intersection.

"Cung's a good tactician. The whole city must be staked out like this."

Harry Yaffa was waiting for us at the gates of the Embassy. He leaped into the car and slammed the door. He looked strained and disheveled.

"They're raiding the Xa Loi Pagoda and three or four others through the city. I've just had calls from Hué, Dalat and Danang. The same thing's going on up there. You should see this for yourself, sir."

"I agree."

"I don't agree sir!" For the first time since my arrival I saw Mel Adams come to life. He was harsh and abrupt. "I think it's bad diplomacy. It leaves you no room to move. If you're an eyewitness, you have to deliver a public verdict without any diplomatic reserves. The press will be there. Inevitably you'll be photographed, and you'll be photographed as a passive spectator of police violence. I think that's a bad thing."

"Is it any worse," asked Harry Yaffa coolly, "than

going to the Palace tomorrow with secondhand information? Cung arranged this little show just for the Ambassador's benefit. Come on, Mel! Brush the cobwebs away! This isn't kid-glove diplomacy. This is war."

"I've made my position clear," said Adams stiffly. "Even in war you need room to deploy your forces. This way you don't have it."

It was time for me to intervene. I needed to save face for both men.

"It's a risk, Mel, and you are right to point it out. The decision is up to me. Let's go."

Before the words were out of my mouth, Bill Slavich trod on the accelerator, wrenched us around a corner on two wheels and headed at full speed in the direction of the pagoda. There was more gunfire now and as we came closer we could hear shouts and screams and the angry murmur of a gathering crowd. The approaches to the temple were blocked by wooden barricades and guarded by riot police armed with automatic rifles and gas guns.

A crowd was gathering at the barriers, and the troops were beating them back with riflebutts. As we skidded to a stop, two policemen came toward us at a run. They saw the pennon and withdrew. Yaffa and I climbed on the hood of the car to look over the heads of the crowd.

The gates of the pagoda had been burst open and there were police wagons parked outside. As we watched we saw the police hustling a small group of monks toward the wagons. They were battered and bruised, and one was bleeding profusely from a skull wound. Behind them a nun was screaming and struggling in the arms of a junior officer. We heard a cry from one of the upper stories, and as we looked up we saw a man in a yellow robe topple from a window and fall into the courtyard below. From inside the pagoda there were more rifle shots and the duller explosions of tear-gas shells. The crowd shouted curses at the guards.

A pair of correspondents broke out of the mob and

came hurrying toward us. One of them raised a camera and took a flashlight shot of me perched on the hood of the car. His companion introduced himself.

"I'm Cavanna, Associated Press. You're Mr. Amberley, aren't you?"

"That's right."

"Have you any comment on tonight's proceedings?"

"Yes. I have seen violence and brutality. As a representative of the United States of America, I deplore it. I have no further comment until I have had time to discuss the matter with President Cung."

"This morning a Buddhist monk burned himself in your presence. Tonight this happens. This is your first day as Ambassador in South Vietnam. Any comment on the timing, sir?"

"My comment will be made at my press conference at two tomorrow afternoon. That's all for the present."

There was a new flurry of violence at the barricades. A bottle was thrown, and then a shower of sticks and stones. The police moved out from behind the barricades and drove the watchers back. They were brutally efficient. There were more broken heads, and a young girl was thrown down and trampled by the retreating mob. The police picked her up and carried her, too, back to the wagons. The crowd was being rolled steadily back toward our car.

Yaffa yelled, "Let's get the hell out of here. I know where to go."

He had us back in the car in five seconds, and we wheeled around the next corner into the grounds of the U.S. Aid Mission, which adjoined the property of the pagoda. The resident staff were all out in dressing gowns and pajamas. A young woman was taping the wounds of a monk whose face had been laid open by a bayonet. Another monk sat huddled against the garden wall, whimpering and nursing a broken jaw. One of the Aid staff came up to me. He was angry and shaken.

"Murder is being done in there, sir. Bloody murder! Can't we stop it?"

Harry Yaffa snapped at him, "No, we can't! So take

it easy! Get those two monks inside. Instruct the guards that if anyone tries to break in here they're to shoot first and ask questions afterward. Call General Tolliver. Tell him what's happened and have him send a doctor around and an extra guard detail." Then he turned to me. "If you've seen enough, sir, I think we should get you back to the Embassy."

I had seen enough. The senseless violence of the scene affronted me. I was boiling with anger. I turned to Mel Adams.

"You stay here, Mel. Collect all the information you can about this affair and report to me first thing in the morning. The two priests are under the protection of the United States Government. All inquiries are to be referred to the Embassy."

Adams nodded and added a reminder. "It might be well, sir, to inform all other Embassies about what's happened."

"I'll handle that, sir," said George Groton. "Do you want any more staff on duty?"

"Yes, please. Call Miss Beldon and the key personnel. We're going to be busy for the next few hours."

"What about you, Mr. Yaffa?"

"I have work of my own," said Yaffa grimly. "Bill Slavich will drive you back. I'll check in at the Embassy as soon as I can."

As we drove back through the picketed streets, I tried to suppress my anger and made a calm accounting of the events of the last twelve hours. I had no doubt at all that they had been timed to discredit me and weaken my hand in any negotiations with the President. I had lived long enough in the East to understand the importance of "face," which is another name for that display of public potency which makes for personal credit. My appointment was a blow at the personal credit of President Cung. Therefore, like a true Oriental, he must reduce me to demonstrate his own stature. But more, much more, was involved than my discomfiture, and I must not be betrayed into a hasty assessment.

President Cung was too shrewd a politician to make

a show of violence for its own sake. His actions would always be consistent with what he was—the man who had taken control of the country after the debacle of Dienbienphu, the man who had resettled nearly a million refugees from the North, who had revived the national economy and broken the power of the Binh Xuyen—the river pirates who had controlled five thousand troops and the whole Saigon police force. He had survived a dozen conspiracies and brought under control a collection of armed sectaries, feudal warlords and military plotters. It was he who had called in the United States to train and unify the Army and supply the military equipment necessary to fight a war against the guerrillas of Ho Chi Minh. He was a philosopher as well as a political strategist, and he would do nothing for a trivial reason.

No man in his right senses would try to win a war by launching a religious persecution against eighty percent of his own population. Therefore Cung must have at least a *prima facie* reason for his action against the monks, who were the elite of the Buddhist faith. I remembered a document which I had studied along with the other papers Festhammer had given me. It was a report from the Central Intelligence Agency on the infiltration of Communist agents into the *Sangha,* the Buddhist monastic system.

The report covered activities in Thailand, Laos, Cambodia and South Vietnam. It pointed out that in Thailand, where the Lesser Way was practiced and where the *Sangha* was centralized under the patronage of the Royal Family, Communist infiltration could be controlled. Under the more lax and diffused system of the Mahayana, control was very difficult. Young and aggressive monks were beginning to usurp authority from the older and more contemplative brethren. The yellow robe was a safe and simple cover for subversion inside the pagodas and among the people.

This was Cung's case, and he could plead it strongly in any forum. After the riots in Hué, where nine people had been killed by Government troops, Buddhist monks had organized open gatherings and made inflammatory speeches condemning the Government. In a country at war such public disorder was hardly to be tolerated. Here again the evidence would seem to justify strong security measures. But violence such as I had seen at the Xa Loi Pagoda was an intolerable political folly, and as the Ambassador of the United States, I had to dissociate myself and my country from it.

When we reached the Embassy, there was another surprise waiting for me—an elderly monk who had escaped from the Xa Loi Pagoda and sought sanctuary inside the Embassy. He had made it with a dozen yards to spare, and the Marine guards had held off the pursuing police at gunpoint. He spoke French but no English, and I talked with him for nearly an hour, while Anne Beldon recorded his narrative of the raid.

He was not, I found, an impressive figure. He was shallow, vulgar and ill informed. He gave me a blow-by-blow description of the raid on the pagoda, but when I came to question him about the nature of Vietnamese Buddhism, its history, its organization, its attitude and its problems, he gave me nothing but commonplaces mixed with rather scurrilous invective against the Cung family. I could not see him in the role of martyr, but I could cast him very well as an agitator. I could not help contrasting his bitter invective with the monumental self-discipline of Musō Soseki. However, he did give me two important facts. The police raiders had come prepared with a list of names. Any monk whose name was on the list was charged as a Communist conspirator. The police had also taken possession of the ashes of the monk who had burned himself that morning, but the charred heart, preserved in a vase, had disappeared. Cung, the knowing Christian, wanted no martyr on his doorstep.

Then the telephone calls began to come in from other areas. In Hué the soldiers had gutted one pagoda and robbed the temple treasury. There had been a pitched battle on a bridge leading to another temple. Thirty people were dead and several hundred wounded. It was estimated that nearly a thousand people had been arrested in various parts of the country.

I drafted a long message to Washington and others to U.S. representatives in Laos, Cambodia and Thailand. At six in the morning we were still working, and we heard President Cung himself come on the air from Radio Saigon. He proclaimed a state of siege and martial law throughout the country. He gave the Army full power to search and arrest suspected persons. A curfew was imposed, and a total censorship of internal and external communications.

Before he had finished speaking, Harry Yaffa came in and announced that Saigon was clamped down by first-line troops and that all exits from the city had been sealed off. Telephone communications had been cut throughout the country. Our own communication system was open, but officially South Vietnam was isolated from the rest of the world.

It was all so swift and thorough that it must have been planned long in advance of my coming. I must, therefore, regard it as a move to forestall a real threat to the Administration. What the consequences might be I could only guess. Now I had to act. Anne Beldon brought me a breakfast of black coffee and crackers. I shaved hurriedly with a borrowed razor and set off for the Palace with Mel Adams and my Protocol Officer. All the approaches were controlled by a network of guard posts and barricades. It was fifteen minutes before we were cleared past the first pickets.

Yet inside the Palace there was still an air of calm and formality. A Vietnamese secretary explained with pointed politeness that we were an hour in advance of our appointment and that the President, because of unusual pressure of work, was obliged to keep us waiting a little while. Frigidly Mel Adams explained that, as the United States was involved in this state of national emergency, the Ambassador's early arrival was a special courtesy to the President. The secretary assured us that the President understood this and would make himself available as quickly as possible.

We were given green tea and cigarettes, and we sat down to wait. Face was involved in the waiting time, too, and I set a mental limit of ten minutes, after which I was prepared to leave. Eight minutes and fifteen seconds later I was ushered into the presence of Phung Van Cung.

He was a small brown man, a head shorter than I, immaculately dressed in a tussore suit, with a gray silk tie and a diamond pin. His skin was sleek; his eyes were bright and smiling; he looked as though he had just stepped out of a bath—which he probably had. He greeted me formally in the heavily accented French of Vietnam. A servant appeared with the inevitable green tea. As we drank, he inquired after my health and expressed the hope that I had had a good journey. He smiled as he talked, and his shrewd bright eyes searched my face for any flicker of emotion. He spoke affectionately of my predecessor and asked me to convey his greetings and good wishes. He made compliments about my work in Japan and offered condolences on the recent death of my wife.

He was especially interested, he told me, in the fact that I was a student of the Zen way of Buddhism. He was sure it would help me to a better understanding of the difficult situation in South Vietnam. The shot went home. I had not expected to find him so well informed. He gave no sign of triumph, but went on smoothly to finish his prelude. He trusted that I would be happy in my new appointment, and if I had need of any personal service I should not hestitate to call upon him or any member of his staff. He regretted that I had not arrived on a more auspicious day, but he was sure that I understood the state of emergency in which the country found itself.

I told him that I was not at all sure that I understood it. On the contrary, I was counting on him to enlighten me. With that the courtesies were over and we were down to the business of our meeting. Cung leaned back in his chair, folded his hands on his silk front and launched into an eloquent exposition.

"You have come, Mr. Ambassador, from a country at peace to a nation at war. This is not a Japanese tea ceremony. Our very survival is at stake. We are being threatened from outside and undermined from within. We estimate that there are thirty thousand fully trained Viet Cong operating inside our borders. They are assisted by an estimated sixty thousand, irregular troops and subversive agents. These agents are trained to use any and every means to infiltrate our ranks and spread disloyalty and disorder. Certain Buddhist monasteries have become control points for espionage and subversion. In my position what would you do? Allow them to flourish unchecked? Let them do the work of Ho Chi Minh under cover of the yellow robe? Let them carry pistols and ammunition and intelligence messages in their begging bowls? Come, Mr. Ambassador, you're not so naïve as that. . . . I know that I am represented in the foreign press as a fomenter of persecution. This is not true. I should be a fool to encourage religious disputes in a country at war. I know, too, that certain of my officials and my colleagues have made mistakes. The first violence at Hué was one of these mistakes. I admit it frankly. I was prepared to repair it. I was prepared to enter into friendly negotiations with the General Assembly of Buddhists. I asked them to list for me their grievances and what they considered their legitimate claims. But consider what happened! First they demanded from me a humiliating avowal of personal responsibility whose sole purpose was to discredit me. I refused to make it, but I was still ready to discuss their problems. Even while the negotiations were going on, certain turbulent monks were addressing public gatherings and calling for the overthrow of the Government. . . . No country permits such open disorder even in peacetime. Do you permit it in Little Rock and Birmingham and Washington? Of course not! Do you expect me to allow it in a country bleeding from a subversive war? I should be false to my charge if I did so."

It was the case I knew he would make, and in the terms in which he expressed it, it was a very acceptable one. As calmly as I could, I tried to show him the other side of the argument.

"In general terms, Mr. President, I agree with your proposition. A country at war cannot tolerate civil disturbance. But last night I was present at the raid on the Xa Loi Pagoda."

"I know, Mr. Ambassador. I knew within half an hour. I have to tell you that your presence was a diplomatic indiscretion."

"On the contrary, Mr. President! I am here as the representative of my Government, which is your ally in this war. I have a duty to inform myself as fully as possible. Last night I saw brutality of the worst kind—calculated and unnecessary brutality! And that, if I may say so, Mr. President, was a political indiscretion! In the past ten hours it has been multiplied all over the country. God knows what the reactions will be in the rest of the world."

"The rest of the world! Mr. Ambassador, the rest of the world is as remote as the moon for us! We are a peninsula of Southeast Asia. We are a partitioned people. The shadow of China has hung over us for centuries. She has occupied us before, and she wants to do it again. Our world, Mr. Ambassador, is bounded by the sea and by China, and we can see, westward, perhaps as far as Burma. . . . Do they weep for us in Sydney or Paris or London?"

"Americans weep for you, Mr. President," I told him bitterly. "They sweat to pay your bills. They die for you here in your own land! You insult them and me when you talk like this!"

I had shaken him, and shamed him, too. He was too intelligent not to admit it. He said quietly:

"I apologize. I have said more than I meant. . . . I acknowledge our debt to the United States. But when you help us, you must not claim to own us, nor to judge us by your own standards."

"Because we are friends, Mr. President, the world judges us together. Even your own people will blame us for last night's bloody affair."

Suddenly he was angry. He picked up a folder full of photographs and thrust it at me across the desk.

"Are you afraid of blood, Mr. Ambassador? Does it turn your tender stomach? Look at those! They show you some other bloody affairs—what happens when a Communist bomb goes off in a public market! How the Viet Cong carved up a village family which opposed them! What a pregnant woman looks like when she has been disemboweled with a bayonet! Am I to be tender with those who plan such things and then take a hypocritical refuge in the Buddha, the Dhamma and the *Sangha* . . .? This is Asia, not Geneva or Manhattan! Here the man who holds power is the strong man armed—the man who exacts blood for blood. I am a Christian. I like it as little as you do. But I know my people better than you."

The photographs turned my stomach. I closed the folder and handed it back to him. It would have been all too easy to agree with him. But I dared not. I had, at all costs, to wrestle him off this breakneck path.

"Precisely because you are a Christian, Mr. President, you cannot afford the senseless brutality I saw last night. Don't you see? It's another weapon in the hands of the Viet Cong. You are the minority faith persecuting the majority. Do you want a holy war with every Buddhist in Asia? You will get it, I promise you! And the press of the world will damn you for an intransigent fanatic."

"The press are often liars, Mr. Ambassador! And even when they tell the truth, they are blind to its consequences!"

"They will not lie about last night's proceeding, Mr. President! And neither can I. When I am questioned by the press this afternoon, I shall have to tell the truth—

and the truth will condemn you and your Administration. It will do more. It will raise an outcry in America. Americans will ask why they should pay for your arms and send their sons to fight with you. What shall I answer them? What shall I say to my Department of State and my President?"

"Tell them the rest of the truth! Have them publish the photographs in that folder! Tell them that half of the names of the subversives in the monasteries were supplied by your own Intelligence Agency. Ride in one of your helicopters and see the war where it is truly being fought—in the villages and the fortified hamlets, among the Montagnards in the North and the delta people to the south. Ignore the cities, where people are spoiled, intoxicated by spurious ideas left over from the French or borrowed from the American press! Saigon and Hué and Dalat could be lost to us overnight, but we would still fight on. Do not be deceived! I am still in control of the situation, and I am not afraid. We shall survive our ills in spite of the press of the world. I rebuilt this country after Dienbienphu. I shall go on building it—with or without you!"

In spite of myself, I was impressed by the stubborn courage of the man. He was perched on a powder keg. There were bayonets at his back and breast, and he was still prepared to fight. But I had to deliver a warning. I laid it before him clearly and precisely.

"I beg you, Mr. President, do not invoke the omens. I am charged to deliver a message from the Government of my country. If you are not prepared to end the divisions between Christians and Buddhists, between your own generals and administrators, you may well have to fight alone—without money, arms or American troops!"

To my surprise, he took it very calmly. His lips twitched into a thin smile. He asked blandly:

"Are you really prepared to go so far, Mr. Ambassador? Are you really prepared to pull out of here and let Cambodia, Laos and Thailand fall like a house of cards? This is your last foothold in Asia. Will you abandon it because I cannot promise you an impossibility? You demand unity—an end to divisions! My God, Mr. Ambassador! How can you be so naïve? As a nation we are older by a millennium than the United States—and we are not yet united! The whole structure of our society tends to disunion, division and small enclaves of power. Like the Italians before Garibaldi, we have still only a half-developed sense of national identity! We are fourteen million people—Viets, Thai, Muong, Yao, Miao, Chinese, Khmers and Chams. Do you expect a miracle from me? Are you prepared to sell out my people because you don't get it?"

"I am instructed to inform you that we are so prepared, Mr. President."

He shrugged and smiled again. "Well, at least we know where we stand. You may inform your Government that I shall give the most serious consideration to the message you have delivered to me. You may inform them also that I object most strongly to what is, in effect, a political ultimatum. You will instruct them that I am aware that your Central Intelligence Agency is in daily contact with certain dissident elements who wish to overthrow the legitimate government of this country and set up a military junta. You may say that I request to be informed officially whether the Ambassador or the Central Intelligence Agency is the true and legal representative of the United States Government."

It was a shrewd blow, and it took me by surprise. I countered it sharply!

"I can give you the answer to that, here and now, Mr. President. I, and I alone, am the official representative of my Government."

"I am glad to hear it. Perhaps then you would like to study a report which I shall send you on the activities of the Central Intelligence Agency."

"I shall be happy to study it, Mr. President, and I shall guarantee to submit a copy immediately to my superiors in Washington."

"Good. I shall be interested to hear their comments and yours. . . . There is another point, Mr. Ambassador. I am informed that three monks from the Xa Loi Pagoda have sought sanctuary with the Americans. I should like to know what you propose to do with them."

"We propose to keep them under our protection until we have official assurance that they will not be harmed in any way after they leave our custody."

"I shall think about that, Mr. Ambassador. I may decide to leave them with you. In the end you may find them quite embarrassing. A final question. You have a press conference arranged for two o'clock this afternoon. Do you propose to reveal the terms of your ultimatum at this time?"

"At this time, no. We should prefer not to have to reveal them at all. You will no doubt wish to consider them at leisure. I shall be at your disposal whenever you choose to call me."

"Thank you, Mr. Ambassador." He stood up and held out his hand. "Let me add only that I am delighted to have met you and that I hope our meeting will be the beginning of a better understanding between your country and mine."

"I hope so, too, Mr. President. With all my heart I hope so."

I left the Palace in a state of deep perturbation. I needed time and wise counsel to make sense out of the confusions which the interview with Cung had raised in my mind. So I decided to bypass the Embassy and take Mel Adams to my house for a confidential talk. We were both full of the fatigue of the night's vigil, so we took a shower. I lent Mel Adams a clean shirt, and then we sat together in my study and rehearsed the main points of the conference with Cung.

Adams, I found, was a sage and sober counselor. He did not attempt to conceal his own uncertainties, and he weighed each issue with admirable detachment.

". . . On one point I have to agree with Cung, sir. We are asking for a miracle if we expect him to unify the country overnight. You'll see for yourself when you get out among the villages just how tight and exclusive is the family and tribal structure. There's an ingrained historic mistrust of outsiders, whether they be generals, administrators or foreigners like ourselves. Buddhism itself can be a divisive influence because it accommodates but does not unify all shades of opinion and practice. In the West we regard it as a religion of contemplation and quietism, but there are violent strains in it, too. It has always had militant sects, and the militancy flowers from time to time into strange manifestations. You've seen what is happening with the Soka Gakkai in Japan. . . . I have to agree on the evidence that there is a certain amount of subversion originating from the pagodas. But subversion is a colored word. To a great many Viets, Ho Chi Minh is Uncle Ho—a noble patriot and a successful revolutionary, while Phung Van Cung is a reactionary backed by capitalist America. . . .

"We, too, contribute to the problem of disunity. We are too pragmatic. We demand the short-term result and are often too impatient to explore its later consequences. We like to define things in precise terms, and the definition betrays us into fixed positions from which we cannot withdraw. It's like Quemoy and Matsu and the legend of the two Chinas. It's only a legend, but we created it and we're stuck with it. That's why I don't like Harry Yaffa. He's a first-rate intelligence man. But he's always too ready to act; he has no sense of history, continuity or consequence. Give him any situation and he'll undertake to change it for you. He's organized to do it, too. When one action doesn't succeed, he'll mount another overnight.

"Action! Action! We're a people educated to action. 'Get up and go! Go west, young man! There's gold in them thar hills!' You know the East, sir. You know how treacherous this temptation can be. And what does action mean to the peasant in the rice paddy? Communism comes with a philosophy as well—but what do we promise after the guns are silent? Democracy? Self-determination? It's the ancestors who rule the tribes, and how do we give them a vote? . . .

"I've tried to ask myself many times what would I do if I were sitting in Cung's place. I confess I'm not sure. How do you break down this warlord mentality among the generals? If you give them an extra slice of cake, they think they're entitled to a bigger one. Face is not saved by egalitarian distribution of power and influence. You still have to prove that you are more important than the man next door. In political terms, Cung's method makes the best sense: divide and rule. In military terms, of course, it leads to the mess we have now.

"Take the Buddhist question. I believe Cung does want to negotiate with them. But he's afraid that when he stretches out a hand they'll want to bite off his arm as well. The monks in the pagodas are not fighting the war; their profession absolves them from it. So, according to Cung, they have no right to foment public disturbance to the detriment of the fighting man, who's getting his ass shot off in the delta. . . . Again, it's a reasonable point of view." He grinned unhappily and poured himself another cup of coffee. "I'm not being very constructive, sir, but I think we have to explore the situation very carefully before we commit ourselves to a change. You've delivered the ultimatum. What happens now?"

"Cung will think it over; then he'll get in touch with me."

"What do you expect him to do about it?"

"If you put it that way, Mel, I'd say that he has now to make a clear and public gesture to invite the Buddhists into friendly negotiations, and to redress whatever real grievances they have. I think he has to release the students and monks who are held in prison. After that he's in a position to enforce law and order."

"I don't think he can do that, sir. Not all of it, anyway."

"Why not?"

"Because the violence isn't over yet. They told me at the Palace that they expect more riots."

"From whom? The Buddhists?"

"No. The students. Before the day is out they will begin their own demonstrations, and that will be another bloody affair: more batons, more bullets, more arrests. So then what?"

"The United States makes another public protest."

"And then Tolliver's officers have to lead Vietnamese troops into action—Buddhists and Catholics alike —while their sons and daughters are in jail! Pretty, isn't it?"

"Then let's look at Yaffa's project, Mel. We back a coup. Cung goes. Who runs the country?"

"A junta of generals."

"The warlords again?"

"Put it that way, yes."

"Juntas are notoriously unstable."

"I agree. Yaffa thinks the generals would be more united without Cung in the saddle."

"And you, Mel?"

"I doubt it."

"Could they pull the Army together?"

"I doubt that, too."

"Improve the morale?"

"Hard to say."

"Could they run the country?"

"With the Army, they can perhaps regulate it better. But whether they could govern it, inspire it, wrench it out of disillusion and cynicism, I don't know. I doubt that any one of them, or all of them together, could have done what Cung did after Dienbienphu. I doubt that any one of them is as singleminded as Cung or, strangely enough, has the moral sense that Cung has. This is where Uncle Ho is so strong in the North. He's a revolutionary leader with a fully developed Marxist philosophy. Cung is a philosopher, too; but this doctrine of personalism which he has borrowed from the French has no popular appeal. It's a Gallic subtlety. I don't think it makes any sense at all to the mass of the population. If Cung were a grass-roots politician who had a talent and a personal magnetism to sway the people, he could sell them Kant, Hegel, Aquinas and the Grand

Panjandrum because the people know his record and respect it. But he doesn't have that sort of charm. He's a recluse, a celibate, an autocrat—and a Christian, which doesn't help either."

"So I ask you to vote, Mel: Cung or a junta of generals? How would you mark your ballot?"

"I don't know sir," said Mel Adams quietly. "I wish I did. Maybe I've been here too long. Maybe I've succumbed, like the Viets themselves, to a kind of creeping despair. Maybe Yaffa is right when he accuses me of vacillation and inaction. It's not that I'm afraid, you understand. It's just that all our actions force us down a road that leads nowhere . . ." He broke off and sat a while in silence, looking down at the backs of his long nervous hands. I felt a pang of pity for him because his dilemma was so like my own. I felt respect, too, because he was prepared to accept responsibility for his own uncertainty. Finally he raised his head and looked at me with somber eyes. "I want to tell you something, sir. After I've said it, you may want my head. I'll give it to you willingly on a silver dish. Tolliver is the only American in this country who has an honest set of orders. He is ordered to fight a war that can't be won, but nobody expects him to win it. For him and for the Pentagon it's a holding action. If the Viets are divided, he fights with a divided army; if they're united, he fights with a united one; and the final responsibility falls not on his shoulders, but on the Vietnamese High Command. With us it's different. We are being asked by Washington to intervene directly in the Government of this country. You have come here with an ultimatum which says, in effect. 'Do this and this or we will make you bankrupt and remove our military support.' On another level the CIA intervenes, too. We are doing all this in the name of democracy and self-determination. But at bottom it is a political and military move to contain China and limit the spread of indigenous revolutions—revolutions that have their roots in colonial exploitation, warlord tyranny and corrupt administration.

"I tell you bluntly, sir, the only people in this country who truly know what they are fighting for are the Catholics. If this country goes Communist, they know their Church will be wiped out in half a generation, while Buddhism will accommodate itself as it has already done in China. That's why I understand Cung and sympathize with him—even while I know the mistakes he's making. That's why I think we're making a mistake, too. We're looking for a new man and a new policy—but we don't know what we want. We're backing the jockey instead of the horse. And because we're in a hurry we get the wrong jockey. That's where I find myself in disagreement with our policy in Southeast Asia. I am a servant of that policy and I try to be a good and honest servant, but I don't believe in it any more."

It was a harsh confession from a man who had spent so long in the Service. I took it as a compliment that he had elected to make the confession to me. As gently as I could, I put another question to him:

"If you were asked to frame the policy, Mel, how would you do it?"

"I'd neutralize. I'd neutralize while we still had strength to bargain. Then I'd pull out and let the country determine its own future."

"And let Uncle Ho take over within a year or two?"

"He's taking over now," said Mel Adams flatly. "He's taking over because the man who truly wants to rally the country lacks the talent to do it; because we are bankrupt of everything but arms, men and money; because when the sun goes down, the peasant in the rice paddy sees no torch, but only the darkness of his own disillusion. . . . So now, sir, if you'd like me to resign, I'll do it."

"Do you want to resign, Mel?"

"No, I don't."

"What do you want to do?"

"I think I can still be useful here, if only as an opposition voice. I think you have a chance—a slim chance, perhaps—to change Cung and preserve the gains he has already made. But it won't be easy because the hounds will be baying at your heels to stage a coup and start a new dynasty. I'd like to play conscience for a while. I'd like to check out the stories they'll give you and show you where the truth is buried."

"It's a thankless role, Mel. Even I can't guarantee to be grateful."

"It's not a question of gratitude, sir. It's a question of my own self-respect. If Cung goes they'll kill him, and I'd rather play conscience than a political assassin."

CHAPTER FOUR

Assassination is an ugly word, but in the climate of Saigon that morning it sounded like a commonplace. The city looked like an armed camp. There were pickets at every corner and a constant passage of armed patrols in jeeps and trucks. There were few citizens on the streets, and their movements were furtive and fearful. The shops were empty. The bars were deserted, and the girls sat, peering out through the iron grilles, like captive birds. I had the momentary illusion that this old-fashioned provincial city had turned suddenly into a jungle where all the beasts had gone to earth, while the hunters stalked them nervously, afraid of the silence and the solitude. There was a smell of thunder in the air, and when a car back-fired it sounded like a gunshot.

At the Embassy they gave me the first reports of student disturbances. The University was in revolt. Students had walked out of classes and held protest meetings. One professor had been stoned by his pupils. Government posters proclaiming martial law had been torn down and defaced. Groups of youths, perched on walls, jeered at passing troops, challenging them to fight the Viet Cong, and not their own people. Many of the demonstrators had been arrested and carried off to detention camps near the outskirts of the city. On the stroke of midday a new edict had been broadcast closing all schools until further notice. American students had been escorted back to their homes by our own military personnel. Extra guards had been posted around the Presidential Palace and anti-aircraft batteries were being set up in the Palace grounds.

On my desk was a curt cable from Festhammer in Washington:

ALL HERE DEEPLY CONCERNED NEWS OF FRESH VIOLENCE AGAINST BUDDHISTS. YOU ARE DIRECTED TO PROTEST IN STRONGEST TERMS AGAINST BREACH OF FAITH BY GOVERNMENT AFTER REPEATED PROMISES OF RECONCILIATION. OUR PROTEST TO BE ANNOUNCED UNEQUIVOCALLY TO PRESS. PLEASE REPORT FULLY AND URGENTLY ALL DEVELOPMENTS.

I had already made my protest at the Palace. Within an hour I would publish it to the assembled press. There was nothing I could usefully report on the situation until I had made some sense of it myself, so I laid the cable aside and called General Tolliver for his summary of the military situation. He gave it to me crisply:

"So far the city is quiet. Cung has moved in three battalions under the command of a Catholic general who is known to be loyal to the Administration. As an additional precaution, the troop dispositions are being changed every four hours. Hué is also clamped down tight. The rest of the country is fairly quiet. Last night we had a report of brawling between Catholic and Buddhist troops in Travinh, but the local commander stopped it quickly. Apart from that, there are no signs of open revolt in the Army, or of any troop movements ordered by dissident generals. Field operations against the Viet Cong are proceeding normally but morale is low among the fighting units. I've posted extra guards at all United States offices and military installations. I have small mobile patrols checking on the safety of American families. That's about all for the moment, sir. If there's any change, I'll let you know."

So far, it seemed, I could trust Cung's reading of his own position. He was in control of the situation. How long he could stay in control was another matter. Those aircraft batteries in the Palace grounds indicated a healthy doubt of the loyalty of his troops. I called for Harry Yaffa and asked him to give me his reading of the signs. Somewhat to my surprise, he agreed with General Tolliver.

". . . At this moment there is no doubt that Cung is master of the country and there is no one well enough organized to unseat him. The city is boiling and discontent, but Cung has jammed the lid on the pot so you can't see all the bubbles. I've been out and around, and I'm getting hourly reports from various agents. There's no doubt at all that Cung has executed his move beautifully."

"Let me put it to you plainly, Mr. Yaffa. If I gave my consent to a coup at this moment, could your generals bring it off?

"No, sir." He was very emphatic. "If they tried it at this moment, they'd be crushed in half a day."

"So maybe Cung is the man we need after all—the strong man armed, who can maintain the kingdom."

"I don't think so. You've seen the city this morning. It's in a condition of shock and stasis. Everybody's run for cover. The first one who pops his head up will get a bullet in it. But you can't blockade any city indefinitely. People have to eat, drink and relax a little; the troops have to relax, too. So give it a week or ten days, and Cung will feel safe enough to take the lid off. Then you'll really see the pot boil."

"Let's go along with your thought then, Mr. Yaffa.

Martial law is revoked. The troops move out of Saigon. Will your generals be ready to take over at that point?"

"If this garrison is dispersed, yes. But let me be clear with you, Mr. Ambassador, because the generals have been very clear with me. None of them is prepared to move without at least the tacit support of the United States. They're too vulnerable, you see. They have to have our protection."

"And if we don't give it?"

"Then you're stuck with Cung, a dictator ruling in a vacuum. If the Viet Cong made any big move, morale and discipline might collapse altogether."

There was a short uneasy silence. Then Yaffa put a question of his own:

"Where do you stand, sir? You've met with Cung. You've heard the opinions of your staff. I've been as frank with you as I can. What solution do you see?"

"I don't see any at the moment. I'm being honest with you, too, Mr. Yaffa. I've been in the country a little more than twenty-four hours. I'm under orders from the Chief Executive to treat with President Cung and to see if I can beat some sense into him. If I can't, then I will have to make recommendations for an alternative solution. But I'm not prepared to do that yet. I don't have enough facts or enough firsthand knowledge. In a sense, Cung's present action works to my advantage. It gives me a little more time to inform myself."

"I see that," said Yaffa quietly. "Now I'd like you to take a look at my position. I must go on preparing for that moment of crisis when Cung may have to be removed. I must be able to offer alternative courses of action. That's the whole meaning of my job. Let me ask you then: How far are you prepared to trust me?"

"I am prepared to trust you, Mr. Yaffa, so far and so long as you are prepared to be honest with me. When we first met, you told me you were a good liar. But I cannot make any recommendations to our Government on the basis of a lie—even a professional one. I am sure you see that."

To my surprise, he leaned back in his chair and laughed. His small soft hands made circular motions in the air.

"Round and round the mulberry bush! Fine, sir. You make your point. I accept it. Now let's be specific. What's the first thing you want?"

"First, I want to meet those generals who are, or might be, involved in a move to overthrow the Cung Administration."

He frowned at that and tugged at his pink jowls. "That's an awkward one. Put them all together in a room and the dumbest agent would see the shape of the plot. There is one way we can arrange it . . . The Australians, the Italians and a couple of other Embassies are helpful to me from time to time. They'll arrange a dinner or a cocktail party and add any name that I ask for to their guest list."

"Let's do that then. How long will it take?"

"Three, four days for the first meeting."

"Fine! . . . Now there's another matter. Cung claimed this morning that he knew all about your operations. He's promised to send me over a full report on them. I've promised to study it and send a copy on to Washington."

Yaffa laughed again. "I'd like to see the report, too, sir."

"Can it possibly compromise you, Mr. Yaffa?"

"I'm sure it can. But there's an odd thing about this country, Ambassador. Security doesn't mean a tinker's damn. It's the cards you hold, and how you play them. It's the way the family alliances work, the way the financial strings are pulled. Sure, Cung knows the people who are working against him. But, like an old-time mandarin, he accepts conspiracy as part of the normal climate. So long as he doesn't see the shape of the final plot, he believes that he can buy this one and frighten another and exile someone else to be Ambassador in Cairo. So I don't really care about this report. I'm more interested to persuade you and provide you with the means to do the expedient thing at the right time."

"The expedient thing, Mr. Yaffa?"

I could not resist the jibe, but Yaffa was unmoved. His answer was swift and definite:

"Yes, sir. There is no right or wrong in politics. Only the expedient and the possible."

"There is a phrase in the Scriptures, Mr. Yaffa: 'It was expedient that one man should die for the people.' Have you thought about that with respect to Cung? If the generals depose him, will they also kill him?"

The question caught him unawares, and he looked up at me with an air of fastidious surprise.

"Kill him, sir? The question has never been discussed."

"Then I want you to discuss it, Mr. Yaffa! I want to be assured that the Government of the United States cannot be made the scapegoat for an expedient execution!"

It was then that I saw, under the bland, effeminate mask, the true shape of the man. He did not flinch from the proposition, nor from me. He faced me squarely and laid the answer before me like a dollar on the gaming table.

"Assurances you can have, Ambassador! They come cheap! I get them and give them every day. But not promise! Who can guarantee anything when the guns go bang-bang? Not I! I'm an intelligence man—a professional conspirator. You want a new government? I'll give you one, like an omelet for breakfast. You want a napkin to wipe the egg off our faces? I'll provide that, too. But don't ask me to make the omelet without breaking eggs. I can't do that. Nobody can!"

When he had gone, I felt suddenly cold, as if a goose had walked over my grave.

Anne Beldon brought me coffee and a plate of sandwiches, and fussed over me until I consented to eat them. It was the first time since my arrival that I had paid any attention to her, and I felt obliged to make an apology for my preoccupation. She accepted it simply, and we fell into one of those desultory conversations which are a relief from the tension of high affairs. She was a widow, she told me. Her husband, a Navy pilot, had been killed in Korea. She had joined the Service in Japan and had served for a while in Tokyo, Taiwan and Bangkok. She spoke good French and was learning Vietnamese from a retired professor of the University of Saigon. She talked easily and moved well, and when she smiled her eyes were lit with humor and a hint of mischief. I guessed her age at about thirty-five.

The Service, I find, does odd things to women of a certain age and status. It is demanded that they be efficient; some end by becoming dry and possessive. They live in a community of males of whom half are married and the rest accustomed to temporary and sometimes exotic love affairs. However, the conventions of diplomatic life place them at a disadvantage. In hardship posts like this one they are often condemned to a kind of purdah, so that some lapse into hysteria and a few into inversion. It is rare enough in my experience to find a senior secretary who maintains an emotional balance and a flexible womanhood. Anne Beldon was such a one, and I was grateful for her company before the inevitable harassment of the press conference.

She was too wise to be drawn into discussion of Embassy personalities, but she did give me a shrewd comment on the tenor of life among the Vietnamese:

". . . You can't imagine how tired and disillusioned these people really are. I visit them, dine with them, talk with the women. Before things got too bad, I used to spend an occasional weekend in Dalat with the daughter of my professor. Nobody seems to remember that this country has been at war continuously for twenty-two years—ever since the Japanese came and Ho Chi Minh raised his first guerrilla bands. I think you have to be a woman to understand what that means. You see the pundits come and go. You listen to all the promises—and suddenly your child is a man carrying a gun like his father."

"How do they regard us, Anne?"

"Their feelings are very mixed. They see us as symbols of a liberty and a prosperity they do not have. They like us. They are grateful for what we try to do. But they think we're very simple—too simple for the old, old complexity of Asia. They don't like the French, but in a queer way they respect them more than they respect us. They make the point that the French are still running the country—the banks, the movie theaters, the rubber trade and the airlines; while Americans do the fighting to keep them in business. It happens to be true, too!"

"And what do they really want, Anne? Do they tell you that?"

"Just peace. Peace at any price, I'm afraid. And I can't say I blame them."

I had heard it first from the Roman monsignor, again from Mel Adams; now it was said for the third time, by a woman. The people were tired. They had lost faith. They wanted only to sleep quietly at night. What did I bring that could restore the vanished aegis? The coffee was lukewarm, and sour on my tongue. I pushed it away and asked Anne Beldon to bring me my notes for the press conference. When she laid them before me she asked:

"May I say something, Mr. Ambassador?"

"Of course, Anne. What is it?"

"Be careful of the press here. Most of them are very young. They are deeply involved; they take a lot of risks, and they've seen some horrible things. They've been accused of reporting the war from the Caravelle Bar, and they're very angry because it just isn't true. They've been fed a lot of sweet talk from our people, too, so they'll be after your head."

"Thanks, Anne. My grandfather was an Indian fighter. I'll do my best to keep a whole scalp."

As I stood up my hand brushed hers, and I was surprised to feel how cool and soft it was. I remembered that it was a long time since I had touched a woman's skin.

Mel Adams and my Press Officer had marshaled the correspondents in the Conference Room of the Embassy. I had asked for a full-dress meeting, and they had given it to me with bell, book and candle! There were newsreel cameras, tape recorders and a full platoon of reporters from a dozen countries. Most of them, as Anne Beldon had warned me, were young and they all had the strained, intent air of those who live at risk in a hostile environment. Some were in shirt sleeves; two or three were dressed in stained fatigue uniforms, as though they had come straight from a military operation. One or two were unshaven. Others had the yellow, pinched look that goes with malaria or a long hangover. Their dean was a lean, gangling young man from Brooklyn who represented an international wire service. The Press Officer presented him to me, and he made the swift round of introductions without a falter. I sat down. The cameras began to turn. The recorders rolled. The conference—or was it a trial?—was in session. They had planned the interview well. The questions came from everywhere in the room, but they followed a careful pattern of inquisition.

"Mr. Ambassador—does your appointment signify a change of United States policy toward the Cung regime or the conduct of the war?"

"A change of policy? No. We are here to help the Republic of South Vietnam to prosecute the war against the Viet Cong and prevent the spread of Communism in Southeast Asia. We have never wavered from that purpose."

"A change of attitude then?"

"No. We came as allies, military advisers and suppliers of strategic equipment. We still have that attitude."

"Has your advice always been accepted?"

"Unfortunately, in certain vital matters, it has been rejected. The United States Government has urged strongly that the Government of South Vietnam take steps to redress the grievances of the Buddhist community and apply to them the full religious equality which is guaranteed by the Constitution. This has not been done. Instead there have been new acts of repression and violence. My Government deplores them and dissociates itself from them in the clearest terms."

"You yourself were an eyewitness of certain acts of violence at the Xa Loi Pagoda?"

"I was. Immediately afterward I lodged a strong official protest with President Cung."

"Can you tell us the terms of the protest?"

"They were the strongest possible terms, I assure you."

"Was there any mention of sanctions for noncompliance? The cessation of aid payments, for instance? Or the withdrawal of military aid?"

"No comment at this time."

"But President Cung has already made a comment. At eleven this morning he stated that the United States was intervening in the internal affairs of South Vietnam with a brutal threat of economic sanctions."

"That's the President's comment. Not mine."

"He claims also that American agents are stirring up trouble and inciting a revolt among disaffected elements in the Army and the Administration."

"I suggest, as I have already suggested to President Cung, that repression and brutality will stir up revolt much quicker than we Americans could ever do it."

"Do you deny, Mr. Ambassador, that the CIA or any other American agency is plotting against the Government?"

"I've been here just about twenty-four hours. I've heard of plots among the Buddhists, and plots among the Catholics, and plots by the Viet Cong. But so far I haven't stumbled across any conspiracy in my Embassy!"

They laughed at that; but it was a hollow sound, like the laughter in a bull ring after a comic pass by the matador. The dance of death was still going on, and we were still a long way from the moment of truth. A rawboned fellow with shrewd eyes and an Australian drawl thrust a microphone under my nose and started a new line of questioning:

"Are we winning the war, Mr. Ambassador?"

"My information is that we are."

"A month ago General Tolliver stated that the war could be won by 1965. Do you agree?"

"I am a diplomat, not a military man. I cannot answer that question."

"Could it be won, Mr. Ambassador, if the United States took control of the military situation and launched an all-out offensive?"

"It might be won in a military sense, but it would be a victory in a vacuum, leaving us in the same position as the French—colonial troops in a politically disaffected area. It would also lead almost inevitably to 'escalation' —a head-on confrontation of America and China. No one is prepared for this at the moment."

"What, if anything, troubles you about the military situation?"

"Division in the Vietnamese High Command and lack of a fully trained and cohesive corps of field officers and noncoms."

"Has the Buddhist repression introduced a major discord into the South Vietnamese Army?"

"As yet, no. But it has contributed to a general undermining of morale, whose real cause is the divisive tactics of the regime. This is something that cannot be changed except at a political level. From a military point of view, we have to do the best we can in the situation that exists."

"And what is being done at the political level, Mr. Ambassador?"

"As I have told you, we have already made very strong representations to President Cung. We shall continue to make them, and we shall take such other steps as the circumstances may dictate."

"Can you be more specific about those steps?"

"Later, perhaps, but not now."

"Suppose the Cung regime proves unacceptable to

the majority of the people. What will the United States do then?"

"That's a hypothetical question. It has no present relevance."

They hammered at me for nearly an hour, until Mel Adams stepped in and closed the conference. My mouth was dry. My clothes were damp with perspiration, and my head was drumming. As we walked upstairs to my office, Mel Adams handed me his verdict:

"They gave you a rough time of it, sir. They were well briefed and in deadly earnest."

"How did we make out, Mel?"

"On a trial balance, I'd say we're a little in front. Your protest was well received. They got the message about sanctions. You registered a discreet dissatisfaction with the military situation. Now we'll just wait and see how it comes out in print. But I'd be prepared for some body blows. They know—forgive me, sir—they know we're selling smoke instead of a real solution. . . . Just for safety, I had the whole conference recorded on tape. We'll type it up and send it to Washington. It might be an idea to send one to the Palace as well—just for the record."

"Sound idea. . . . Sometimes, Mel, I'd like to go back to the old days of secret diplomacy. All gentlemen together—and let the peasants mop up the blood!"

"I, too!" said Mel Adams fervently. "How the hell can you negotiate under the TV cameras? How can you deal with Cung when you're both on record in a public argument? You're always stuck with the statements you made last week. When you get them back, they're graven on rock like the Decalogue."

"That's where the Marxists win every time, Mel. They can always rewrite the records. I wish we could rewrite some of ours. . . . Would you like a drink?"

Two drinks with Mel Adams, two hours at my desk with reports, dispatches and cables, then, suddenly, I was in the grip of a deathly tiredness. My eyes burned, my body ached as if I had been beaten with rods, the typescript blurred and swam in front of me. I remem-

bered with vague surprise that I had been working continuously for nearly thirty-six hours. It was enough, and
more than enough. Come all of Asia in arms with banners, elephants and tuckets of trumpets, I was going
home to sleep.

For a long time sleep would not come. My body was
slack and poisoned with fatigue, but my mind spun
around and around in a fury of speculation, like a motor thrown suddenly out of gear. The axis on which it
spun was always the same question: why this country,
harassed by war, yet propped up by enormous aid, had
not yet found the strength, the inspiration or the men to
gather its forces and complete the revolution that had
been begun twenty-two years before.

A dozen people had given me as many answers—but
none was adequate to explain the massive disintegration
that was taking place under my own eyes. A recluse
dictator? Not enough: other dictators harsher than this
one had produced, for a time at least, a sense of purpose and an impulse to unity. Divisions among generals
and administrators? Still not enough: there was nothing
to gain for anyone in a national collapse. Weariness and
disillusion among the people? These were the symp-
toms and not the disease itself. Religious feuds? They
were sporadic in the best-ordered societies. Police brutality? Asia was a brutal continent. Nature herself
inflicted far greater cruelty than man; and the people
were millennially passive under plague, famine,
smallpox, hookworm and the lash of the prince's
minions.

So what was missing? What, in fact, was the basis of
all unity? To what straw did a man cling finally to
maintain his precarious hold on existence? I was a man
like any other. I was naked now and sweating through
the tropic evening on a solitary bed. I, too, was threatened from within and beleaguered without. By what did
I, or could I, maintain my wholeness? My leaping
thoughts carried me at one stride back to the garden of
Tenryu-ji, where Musō Soseki had given me my first
lesson in the way of enlightenment.

"The root of human distress, Mr. Amberley, is a sense of alienation from the natural order of the universe. The effect of *satori* is an illumination of the mind, so that the nature of the self and the universe is finally clear, and the sense of true relationship, or oneness, is restored."

Identity! That was the word! That was the key to the whole human problem. Unless a man understood, however dimly, what he was and how he was linked with his fellows and with the cosmos, he could not survive. Put him in a padded cell, separate him from the sight, sound and touch of the world, and you would in a short time reduce him to madness and physical disorder. This was the true meaning of the ancient animism of Asia: unless the spirits of rock, river and trees were placated, the necessary relationship between them and man would be broken and the universe would dissolve into chaos.

Without knowing it, Mel Adams had expressed the same thought in different words.

"The only people in this country who truly know what they are fighting for are the Catholics."

Catholicism was a religion founded and rooted in a definition of human identity. Man was a person created by a personal God. He stood, therefore, in a familial relationship to every other man. The physical universe was an ambience provided for his growth, survival and continuity. His status was affirmed by the doctrine of the Incarnation, according to which the Creator himself took on human flesh and gave it an irrevocable dignity.

Communism, in its own gospel, was equally specific. The identity of man was affirmed and maintained only by his collective activity. He was a dependent creature, spawned out of chaos and proceeding to extinction. Alone, he was damned for his life span to a howling wasteland, prey to injustice and exploitation. His identity was therefore contingent upon his serviceable membership in the mass. But an identity he did have, and subject to his conformity, the mass would guarantee it and protect it.

By a strange paradox, Buddhism affirmed identity by preaching that perfection lay in its ultimate extinction in the All-self of pure enlightenment. . . . But this was an esoteric doctrine, accessible only to the adept; so the common folk had corrupted it and adulterated it to make it more comfortable to their needs.

Beside these deep, if divergent affirmations the American gospel of which I was the new prophet in South Vietnam sounded strangely hollow and unsatisfying. Democracy! Self-determination! Liberty, equality, fraternity! What did they mean to the man who sat under a boab tree and heard, through the trembling leaves, the whisper of an outraged spirit? How could he identify himself with us—the blue-eyed barbarians who possessed so much and understood so little?

Cung was a philosopher. He must have thought of these things, too. He was a man of Asia. He must have heard in his own heart the ancestral voices making the age-old cry for identity, continuity and community. Perhaps if I could make him listen to them again, I could rouse him to proclaim them in the common tongue, so that his people might hear them above the clatter of politicians and propagandists. Perhaps it was not too late for one last ride along the frontiers, one last echoing call on the trumpets. . . .

But it was already too late for me. Darkness and silence overwhelmed me, and I slept for a straight twelve hours.

I came down to breakfast, to find George Groton already on his last cup of coffee. He was red-eyed and tired, and when I questioned him he told me he had sat up late studying the Embassy documents on the Buddhist situation. In his view, they were dangerously incomplete. I asked him why.

"Because, sir, they deal with the current situation only from the point of view of political observers and intelligence agents. They are vague about a number of essential matters. For example, the majority of Vietnamese follow the Mahayana—the Greater Way; but there are a number of pagodas where the Lesser Way is practiced and these have definite links with the Hinayana of Laos and Cambodia. They have also a historic connection with the Cao Dai and the Hoa Hao; and these are politico-religious sects whose private armies were disarmed by President Cung. What are these connections? Are they being used for political or military purposes? The reports don't say. Therefore we have no way of knowing what may be the effect of Cung's repression on Buddhist activity over the border. Another thing. The Mahayana pagodas are autonomous institutions. The abbot is the titular head of his own community. But there are all kinds of loose affiliations and associations between temples. The documents are vague about these, too. The Chinese have their own pagodas and their own Buddhist monks. About these we have no precise information at all. And yet the whole present crisis began with the Buddhists. Was it wholly manufactured by Cung? Or is it part of something bigger—a left-wing Pan-Buddhist movement coming out of Ceylon and Burma, bypassing the monarchists in Thailand and showing its real face here? It's not so crazy as it sounds, you know. There's been polite regret but no big protest from Thailand over the pagoda troubles. But the Ceylonese have fired off rocket after rocket. It's at least significant. I think something should be done about it, sir."

"What, for instance, George?"

"I have a suggestion; I worked it out in detail last night. I'd like you to consider it, sir."

"Go ahead."

"Yesterday I spent most of my time with the monk at the Embassy and the other two at the Aid Mission. I told them that although I followed the Zen path I was still a Buddhist and, therefore, in sympathy with their aims and problems. I told them that you, too, were studying the Zen way, although you are not yet a full believer. That impressed them. The monk at the Embassy was shrewd enough to propose the next step. Why didn't I make a private investigation and report to you personally? He promised to give me letters to his friends, and with these I could move freely around the pagodas. . . . I thought it was a good idea, too, sir. It's obvious they'd try to use me because I look—and sometimes am—a simple guy. But at least I'd be getting firsthand information which we don't have now. If necessary, I could shave my head and put on a yellow robe." He gave me that boyish grin of his and added, "I've worn it before, sir. It's not too uncomfortable. I don't speak the language, of course; but French is common currency among the educated monks."

"Have you thought of the risks, George? What would happen if you got caught in a raid like the one last night?"

"I'd be an embarrassment to Cung and to you."

"You might also get your head broken by a rifle butt. There's another thing, too, that you may not have thought about."

"What's that, sir?"

"The Army is running one intelligence service, the Embassy has another and Harry Yaffa has a watertight operation of his own. That would make you the lone ranger, with no status and no protection. It could be awkward—for you and me."

He grinned again and said blandly, "On the other hand, sir, the Constitution of the United States guarantees religious liberty for all. I am a Buddhist and I do wish to keep up my religious practice. . . . Besides, you brought me here as a special assistant. This is one service I can give you that no one else can offer."

It was a tempting service, too—a private and practiced eye on the newest phenomenon in Asia, a Buddhism of public martyrs, secret printing presses and global propaganda. We talked over the project for another half hour, and I agreed to it, subject to certain conditions.

" . . . You try it for ten days, George, and see where it leads you. You report to me every three days. No risks, no heroics. If there's the slightest hint of trouble, I want to hear about it. After ten days we'll discuss it again. Is that clear?"

"Very clear, sir, and thank you. When can I start?"

"Now if you like."

He went off happy as a sandpiper, leaving me to finish my breakfast and make sense out of the clamorous reporting of the Saigon newspapers. I did not know—how could I?—that I had just signed a death warrant.

I remember the day which followed with peculiar bitterness, because it seems to me now to be the beginning of all the betrayals in which I was involved. Diplomacy is a dichotomous business at best, since it demands a total cleavage between the accidental and the absolute, between the just and the expedient, between the difficult truth and the desirable casuistry. No one can avoid the dichotomy; everyone is changed by it; some are destroyed by it. All too often one ends by accepting the opinion one has come to change or by committing the act one is charged to condemn.

Once in the Argentine an agreeable, if inept, colleague gave me a very Latin definition of a diplomat:

"He is, in effect, an antique augur who foretells the future by studying the entrails of a bird. The folly is that he must kill the bird before he can look at its guts."

I repeated the story of an Englishman who, with the admirable deprecation of the Foreign Office, gave me another version:

"It's not really like that at all, my dear chap. It's more like shooting grouse. You have to flush your bird before you can take a potshot at him. If you're unlucky you miss the bird and kill a beater instead."

That morning it seemed I was the beater with the bird shot in his breeches. I arrived at the Embassy clearheaded and relaxed. The reflections of the night before were still vivid in my mind, and I saw—or thought I saw—the beginnings of a constructive dialogue with President Cung. There would be a preliminary skirmish, of course. Rough words had been said on both sides, and they were already being shouted across the rooftops of the world; but at least I was prepared to offer the first olive twig, even if it made me look a little lopsided, like Picasso's pigeon. I was already drafting a note to the Palace when Anne Beldon came in and laid before me a cable from Festhammer:

WORLD REACTION TO LATEST SAIGON REPORTS STRONG AND HOSTILE. BUDDHIST ISSUE TO BE DEBATED IN UNITED NATIONS GENERAL ASSEMBLY. ALGERIA, CEYLON, INDONESIA AND OUTER MONGOLIA ARE SPONSORING A MOTION FOR THE APPOINTMENT OF A U.N. COMMISSION OF INQUIRY INTO THE VIOLATION OF HUMAN RIGHTS IN SOUTH VIETNAM. OUR OPPOSITION TO REPRESSIVE MEASURES HAS ALREADY BEEN EXPRESSED IN WASHINGTON AND MADE DOUBLY CLEAR BY YOUR PRESS STATEMENT IN SAIGON. WE SHALL THEREFORE BE OBLIGED TO VOTE IN SUPPORT OF THE MOTION. . . .

So, at one stroke, my plan for reconciliation was demolished. How could I possibly talk philosophy with Cung once my Government was aligned against him on the floor of the United Nations? I was angry, bitterly angry. This was power play and not diplomacy. I might just as well have plastered our threatened sanctions on every wall in Saigon. . . . The beaters had flushed the birds, but there was no place for them to fly. Both Cung and I were backed up into the corner of the aviary, snapping at each other and flapping our wings against the wire.

I paced my office for ten furious minutes, trying to make some sense out of the situation. Then the telephone rang and Arnold Manson, the Australian Ambassador, came on the line. He gave me a few brisk words of welcome and then asked for an immediate interview. I pleaded pressure of work, but he was not to be put off. The matter was urgent, he said, and if I could not see him he would be forced to take independent action. So, grudgingly, I agreed.

He was at my office in ten minutes, a surprisingly young man, with a shock of curly hair, a good-humored smile and a well-prepared brief. The United Nations debate on South Vietnam was a matter of grave concern to his Government. Australia, like the United States, disapproved of the repressive measures against the Buddhists, but she disapproved equally of the notion of a Commission of Inquiry. The only U.N. commission which could claim a legal right of entry into a sovereign state was a Commission on International Security. Whether or not Cung accepted a Commission on Human Rights, it would still be a breach of the U.N. Charter and a dangerous precedent for Australia as the Administrator of Trustee Territories. Clearly she did not want a mixed bunch of Algerians, Pakistanis and Outer Mongolians passing judgment on the lives of Stone Age primitives in New Guinea.

I agreed with him. I showed him the effect of a U.N. debate on my own relations with the Palace. I told him that I proposed to send an immediate cable to Washington, setting forth my personal objection to the move. I told him, too, that I saw little hope of changing the course of events in Washington and New York. For them, Cung was totally intransigent and must be subdued—with a bludgeon if necessary. For all his apparent youth, Manson was a good diplomat who did his homework. He showed me a feasible solution.

"There is one way to get everyone off the hook."

"What's that, Mr. Manson?"

"If President Cung were to invite the General Assembly to send a team of observers to study the Buddhist issue. He could forestall the sponsors of the motion. He would also avoid a long and bitter debate, and there would be no question of a formal commission with all its awkward consequences."

"Do you think Cung would accept such a proposal?"

"I think he might."

"Who puts the idea to him?"

"I'm prepared to do it, if you agree. Though it might be a useful gesture if it came from you."

It was an attractive notion, and I thought about it for a few moments; then I was forced to reject it.

"It raises too many problems. First, it makes me

speak with a different voice from Washington, and I can't do that; second, it gives Cung a strong argument that we say one thing in public and another in private. On the other hand, Australia is a small nation, and in this matter her interests and those of South Vietnam are identical. You're giving Cung an idea to use for your mutual benefit. . . . You know, Mr. Manson, you just might bring it off."

"And how would Washington react?"

"After they get my cable, I think they might like to get off the hook, too. But I can't promise anything."

"I understand that. I'm glad you and I are agreed at least."

"I'm glad, too, Mr. Manson. It's a small ray of sunshine in a damned gray day. Will you let me know how Cung takes your suggestion?"

"I'll call you as soon as I've talked with him." He hestitated a moment, and then asked deliberately, "Can we talk off the record for ten minutes?"

I was pressed enough and frayed enough to be irritated by the phrase he used. I reminded him rather too tartly that in diplomacy everything, sooner or later, went on the record. I was even more irritated when he refused to be put out of countenance. He simply smiled and answered calmly:

"I'm sorry. It's just a difference of idiom. Frankly I don't really care whether it goes on the record or not, provided it is stated as my private opinion and not necessarily as the opinion of my Government."

Everyone in Saigon wanted to ram a private opinion down my throat—and I was still too new to have formed one of my own. So I questioned him brusquely:

"Your opinion on what, Mr. Manson?"

"The question of sanctions."

"So far as I am aware, Mr. Manson, no sanctions have yet been applied."

"They have been threatened."

"Allow me to correct you, Mr. Manson. The question of sanctions was raised by the press, not by me."

"I know that, Mr. Amberley, but it is very clear that a notice, or a threat, has been delivered to the Palace."

"How is it clear?"

"I received a telephone call this morning—from the Minister of Commerce—asking me to use my best efforts to procure from Australia immediate shipments of wheat, rice and other foodstuffs and, if possible, to arrange suitable credit terms with my Government. It was a formal request, and it puts us in an awkward position since we are already supplying wheat on credit to Communist China. If we refuse the request, they can accuse us of starving our allies to feed our enemies." That shook me and he knew it, but he went on in the same calm fashion. "I took the trouble to find out the present financial position of the Cung Administration. They are in fact holding dollar credits to the amount of about thirty-five millions, and the French banking system is prepared to carry them for about the same amount. At his present rate of expenditure, therefore, Cung could keep his Government operating for about six months even if sanctions were applied. If you impose military sanctions as well, you will begin by a token withdrawal of administrative personnel. That will not affect the conduct of military operations. In my view, it will serve only to depress the national morale, which is low enough already, God knows."

This was too close to the bone for comfort. I saw very clearly why he had chosen to express a personal view and not an official one. He did have to use the guarded language of the trade, but could be as blunt as he chose.

"May I ask where you got your information, Mr. Manson?"

"American diplomacy is very public, Mr. Ambassador. Too public, I'm afraid, for everybody's comfort. Some of my information came from sources in Saigon, the rest from Washington by way of Canberra. We Australians are in a curious position. We're a small and ill-defended nation. Our future is bound up intimately with events in Southeast Asia. We've just been jockeyed

neatly into supporting the British over Malaysia—
which, in my very private view, will prove a historic
mistake. We are also committed to the United States by
treaty obligations which we intend to honor in public
and private. Because of these obligations I am bound to
be frank with you, and to urge you very strongly to re-
consider the whole question of sanctions, and of your
personal relations with President Cung."

From a junior member of the Southeast Asia Treaty
Organization this was strong talk indeed. There was
sound sense in it, too, but he had left me no time to
compose myself, so I took refuge in formality.

"Thank you for what you've told me, Mr. Manson.
Rest assured that I will give it the most serious
consideration."

"There is one other point before I go, Mr.
Ambassador."

"And what is that?"

"The Buddhist monk who has taken refuge in your
Embassy. He may prove an embarrassment to you and
to your friends. He is, as you know, the titular head of
a newly formed body called the National Union for the
Preservation of Buddhism. I am given to understand by
certain people that this was the man who incited the
Buddhist burnings. The word is out in the city that he is
the custodian of the heart of the martyr, which disappeared from the Xa Loi Pagoda during the police raid.
It may be true, it may not; but to the ignorant that
means that the relic is under the protection of the
United States. . . . More important, I think, is the fact
that this man is known to have connections with militant Buddhist organizations in Burma and Ceylon, and
with certain agitators recently expelled from the *Sangha*
and imprisoned by the Thais in Bangkok. I've written
to our people in Thailand, asking for more information
on that point. When I get it, I'll be happy to pass it on
to you."

"I'll be glad to have it. I appreciate your frankness,
Mr. Manson. I hope we may be able to find a solution
to our mutual problems."

"I am sure we shall." Good-humored as ever, he stood up and offered me his hand. "Thank you for your time, Mr. Ambassador—and good luck!"

On which inconclusive note our talk ended. I had the uncomfortable feeling that my junior colleague had behaved much better than I, who had twice his experience and ten times his authority. It is a cardinal rule in diplomacy that one should cultivate friendly and accurate informants. Instead I had been abominably rude to a man who had done me a professional service. If I could not count on my self-control in a discussion with a well-disposed ally, how could I guarantee it in the critical negotiations to come?

Once again the grave voice of Musō Soseki admonished me: "I think it is a grave risk to take such an appointment at this time of your life!" The odd thing was that I knew myself to be living at risk. I was lonely and therefore vulnerable to expressions of friendship. I was in a position of power and therefore swift to mistrust those who challenged my opinions or authority. I was charged to make a change, but in the full glare of public opinion I could be tempted to make it like a magician pulling a rabbit out of a silk hat. But there were darker deeps yet, cracks and fissures in what passed for the soul of Maxwell Gordon Amberley. These I was still unready to explore, lest, under the panoply of the tetrarch, I might discover a hollow man—no oracle either, but a gourd full of clattering pebbles. Besides, it was easy to absolve myself from self-examination when every moment challenged me to action and every action committed me to a new chain of consequences.

I was still working through the morning's dispatches when Mel Adams came in with troubling news. President Cung had decided to make an appearance in the National Assembly that same afternoon. He would deliver a public statement on the war situation and the Buddhist crisis. The Palace had been at pains to inform all members of the diplomatic corps and the international press that a French translation of the address would be distributed just before the President began to speak.

The meaning of the move was plain enough. Challenged in the United Nations, publicly threatened by the United States, Cung was making a bid to be heard in open forum. As head of a sovereign state it was no more than his right to speak to his own legislators. As leader of a nation at war it was no less than his duty to make to the people a clear proclamation of his position. Since I was a friendly diplomat, I had no grounds to blame him, and as a defender of democratic procedures I ought to commend him. In fact, however, I held a sword over his head, and if he said a word to displease me I could cut him down with it.

Mel Adams read my thoughts and asked me soberly, "Will you be in the Assembly, sir?"

"I must be there, Mel."

"It could be an explosive speech."

"I can always walk out."

"With all respect, sir, I think you should make that danger clear to President Cung. The way things are, you're both being pushed toward a head-on collision. I think you should avoid that at all costs."

"I'll try to talk to him, Mel."

It is a matter of record that I did try. I called the Palace while Mel Adams was still in my office. I asked, as a matter of extreme urgency, to talk with the President. With the unfailing politeness of the Vietnamese, I was informed that the President was in conference and that he had left strict orders not to be disturbed for any reason. He would no doubt telephone me as soon as the conference was over. I called in Anne Beldon and dictated a clear and friendly note. An Embassy official delivered it personally to the Palace, and the signature in his receipt book showed the time of delivery as twenty minutes before midday.

Midday came, one o'clock, then two, and I still had no word from the Palace. At three o'clock I sat with Mel Adams in the diplomatic gallery of the National As-

sembly and waited for the testament of President Phung
Van Cung.

He looked very small and insignificant as he stepped
forward to speak. The applause they gave him was duti-
ful, but scarcely affectionate. There are some men
whose very presence wakens deep emotions, as if they
were vessels of power. Often, of course, they are simply
mountebanks, natural actors endowed with a trick of
presence or some excess of virility which creates an illusion of spiritual potency. Phung Van Cung was not one
of these. His manner was detached and academic. He
read his speech, and his delivery was quite passionless.
There was even a touch of contempt in the performance, as if he had said, "I know you all very well, and
there are very few of you whom I respect. Some of you
I have bought, some I have made and some of you are
already in league to betray me. I will not truckle to you,
nor make a drama for your diversion. This is what I
have to say. Take it or leave it . . .!"

His address was delivered in Vietnamese, and the
high accented tones of the language made it harsh and
monotonous. But as I followed the French translation,
page by page, I had to admit that it was a beautiful
piece of political dialectic. He began with a swift but
precise review of the military situation:

". . . We are a nation under siege. To the north are
China and the armies of Ho Chi Minh, who holds our
brothers in bondage. To the west are Cambodia and
Laos, who, under the shelter of a spurious neutrality,
offer aid and cover to our enemies. To the east and the
south is the sea, where under cover of darkness junks and
fishing boats ferry arms to the traitors in our midst. . . .

"Even as I speak to you a full-scale battle is being
fought at Tânan, thirty kilometers south of this place.
There is heavy fighting also at Bentre, in the delta, and
at Danang, near the border of Laos. Our enemies, im-
placable and ruthless, are operating in battle strength
inside our borders within half an hour's drive of our

capital. We are fighting them, yes! But not all of us are fighting. There are those who make factions and diversions and civil disorders which work to the advantage of the enemy.

". . . We cannot tolerate such things! In the face of a ruthless foe, any factional activity which damages national unity is an act of treason!

"We are fighting for freedom, yes! For religious and political and economic freedom, yes! These freedoms are guaranteed by the Constitution of the Republic of which I am the guardian. But freedom is not an unlimited state. It is not a license for treachery and betrayal and violence in our own cities. We have built eight thousand six hundred fortified hamlets and grouped inside them nearly ten million persons to keep them safe against the Viet Cong. Shall we place these ten million persons again in jeopardy because a handful of turbulent fantatics—who do not and will not carry arms—demand a liberty to incite good and religious people to riot . . . ?"

To this point I had no quarrel with him. I mistrusted myself enough to be aware of the dangers of misused freedom and of the necessary limitation of personal liberty in times of social crisis. I was skeptic enough to split the blame fairly between political Buddhists and political Catholics and political cynics who saw a profit in disorder. Then his brusque monotonous delivery changed and a note of bitter irony made itself heard.

". . . Here in this land of ours blood is shed every day to check the aggressive and expansionist moves of Communist China. Yet in New York, a city at peace, in the Assembly of the United Nations, our friends—or those who call themselves our friends!—commit another kind of treachery against us. They are prepared to vote for a breach of our national rights and of the United Nations Charter by the appointment of a Commission of Inquiry on a question of Human Rights. We are not afraid of this Commission, but unhappily, we are forced to be afraid of our friends. So our observer at the United Nations has been instructed to issue a public invitation to the General Assembly to name a team of observers to study and report on the Buddhist question in South Vietnam. We have invited them, remember, we are not afraid of free inquiry. We have nothing to hide. But it seems that our friends have things to hide because they work in secret and not in the honesty of public debate. . . ."

This was rough talk, and a glance at the following pages of the text proved that it would get rougher yet. The other diplomats were watching me and not the speaker. Mel Adams scribbled a note? "Do you want to leave?" I scrawled a reply: "No, let's sit it out!" Phung Van Cung talked on in the same ironic tone.

". . . It is strange and sad to me that what our enemies have failed to do our friends are doing for them. We, the last bastion against Communist expansion in Southeast Asia, are being threatened with a withdrawal of military and economic help. . . . What kind of madness is this? What must Americans themselves think of it—the men who are fighting with our troops in the delta; the men who work with our people in the hamlets to teach them better farming and how to wipe out diseases that have plagued us for centuries? These we do not blame—they are true friends. But the others, the ones who speak with two voices, the ones who proclaim a public friendship and yet make themselves party to secret conspiracies against a legitimate government . . . ? If they are tired of the battle, let them go! Let them leave us the money and the arms and we will fight alone! We began our revolution without them and we are prepared to complete it without them, secure in the rightness of our aims and in the hope of a final victory!"

As he stepped down from the rostrum, the applause was thunderous; but whether his friends were acclaiming his boldness or his enemies cheering his folly I could not say. Mel Adams said unhappily:

"Jesus! He really tossed the fat in the fire! Let's go, Ambassador."

We went. The air outside was hot and heavy, and thunderclouds were piling up over the uneasy city.

CHAPTER FIVE

On the military front it had been a day of disasters.

The battle at Tânan had gone badly. Some three hundred Viet Cong had engaged a mixed formation of four hundred South Vietnamese troops: infantry, mortarmen and machine gunners. It had been a bloody fight, ranging over half a dozen square miles of rice paddies and fruit plantations. The Viet Cong had left thirty-five dead and a dozen too badly wounded to escape. The Republican troops had lost forty-eight killed and sixty-odd seriously wounded. They had also lost three machine guns, a mortar and eighty-odd small arms of American manufacture. The number of captured Viet Cong weapons was considerably smaller, and the arms themselves were mostly low-grade items from China and Czechoslovakia. The tally of the action added up to a notable victory for the guerrillas who were already reported to be regrouping much nearer to Saigon.

Up near the Laotian border there had been a more spectacular tragedy. A T-28 fighter-bomber with an American pilot and a Vietnamese crewman had crashed in guerrilla country. A search and rescue party of twelve men in two Marine helicopters had set off immediately from Danang. Flying at low level down a river valley, both aircraft had been caught by ground fire from the ridges. One had crashed into the river bed, the other had limped across a hill and tumbled into the jungle.

A second rescue party of six helicopters, manned by U.S. marines and Vietnamese gunners, had reached the scene. They, too, came under heavy fire, and lost two wounded and one killed; but they dispersed the guerrillas with rockets, napalm and machine guns. When they landed beside the wrecked choppers, they found all twelve men dead. They had flown the bodies back to Danang, and they would be brought to Saigon on the morrow for burial.

General Tolliver brought me the news himself. His lean aging face was tight with anger, and he cursed at the bloody futility of the whole situation.

". . . So while that half-assed virgin of a President is standing up in the Assembly, shouting betrayal, while Washington is bleating about sanctions and withdrawals, my boys are getting shot out of the air, and those poor dumb bastards of Viets are bleeding like pigs in the paddy patches. It isn't good enough, Mr. Ambassador! It isn't half good enough! I'm going to tell Washington! I'm going to tell the brass in the Pentagon—and I'm going to tell President Cung and the whole goddamn world! When they bring my boys' bodies down tomorrow, I'm going to give them a military funeral that will knock your eye out! Every correspondent in Saigon is going to be there and every cameraman, if I have to take 'em at gunpoint. Somehow—anyhow—I'm going to tell what this son-of-a-bitching war means to the men who have to fight it! . . . I want you there, too, Mr. Ambassador. You're the representative of our President. I need you."

"I'll be there, General."

"And what about Phung Van Cung? They're his dead, too!"

"I can't speak for him. I'm not even sure I can speak *to* him at this moment. . . ."

And then, suddenly I saw it—coolly and cynically—a way to make a profit from the dead and resolve the diplomatic dilemma which Cung's speech in the Assembly had created. I did not want to discuss it with anyone, lest I be confused again by conflicting opinions. I was thinking very clearly now, and I saw a swift and very possible end to political brawling. I went straight to my office and put through a personal call to President Cung.

There was no delay this time. He was prompt, polite and friendly, like a man who had wiped out an affront to his dignity and who could now afford to be magnanimous. I made no mention of his speech in the Assembly, but simply summarized the reports I had received from General Tolliver. He told me that he had just heard the same news from his own military staff. He expressed official sympathy and asked me to convey his personal condolences to the relatives of the dead men. It was clear that he was deeply shocked. I asked him whether, in spite of the lateness of the hour, he would grant me an immediate interview. To my surprise, he agreed without demur and suggested that I join him for dinner at the Palace. We would be alone, he said, and he would welcome the chance of a more intimate acquaintance with me.

It was more than I had hoped. I had to admit, too, that he had made the gesture with considerable grace, and skeptic though I was, I could not believe it was all calculation. In spite of the tragedies of the day I began to feel cheerful again. I had been a diplomat long enough to know that often the best way to solve a problem is to create a crisis which then precipitates its own solution as the thunderstorm sends down rain to clear the turgid air. All the public talking had been done: vile humors had been purged on both sides. Blood had been spilled in the mountains and in the lowland swamps. Remembering the dead, perhaps we might both discover a calm and a sobriety to serve the living.

Anne Beldon came in to tell me that the press were waiting for a comment on Cung's address to the National Assembly. I dictated a handout saying that I was now studying the text of the speech and that I wished to reserve any statement until the study had been completed.

There was a note on my desk from Harry Yaffa. He would be out until six in the evening, but he wanted to talk with me urgently. I left word that I would see him at my house between eleven and midnight. I was glad I did not have to talk with him at that moment. I had had enough reminders of death, and Yaffa was beginning to look more and more like an elegant undertaker.

Finally Mel Adams came with a summary of Cung's speech for inclusion in my cipher to Washington. I told him to send it as a bald document, adding only the report that I had arranged an immediate conference with President Cung. If there was anything urgent to report, I would have it ciphered and sent by the night staff; otherwise it could well wait for twelve hours.

"A good idea, sir," said Adams dryly. "I think we've all had a bellyful of 'swift reactions' and 'sharp protests.' We need time to sit down and smooth our feathers. We've been running this business like a cockfight for too long already!"

I had nothing to cap that piece of salty wisdom, so I closed up shop for the day and went back to my house, to bathe and shave and dress for dinner.

It was still an hour to curfew time as we drove across the city to the Palace. The streets were still picketed, but there were more people on the sidewalks. The bars and restaurants were open, and the little whores were on patrol again in pedicabs and taxis. Virtue in Saigon was a matter of Government regulation. One might drink with a bar girl but not hold her hand. Public dancing was an indictable offense. Love songs were banned as an incitement to crimes against morals. Houses of prostitution were closed; the ancient trade was now carried on by private treaty, and the bordello barons had turned to other businesses.

The approaches to the Palace were still closely guarded, and the snouts of the anti-aircraft batteries sniffed cautiously at the night sky. This time, however, we were not kept waiting; the guards waved us through without question, and on the steps of the Palace the President's aide was waiting to greet me with effusive courtesy.

Cung received me in his private drawing room, a sparse but elegant chamber paneled in teak and fur-

nished in the cool style of the Swedes, with pieces made
by Vietnamese craftsmen. The pictures were good, too
—an excellent Rousseau, a Gauguin from the islands, a
Rouault Christus and a large and magnificent triptych
of the Nativity carved by a local sculptor. I paid him a
compliment on his taste and he accepted it with a smile
and a dry joke.

"The French are fine artists, Mr. Ambassador. They
are less successful as colonial rulers."

A servant brought us drinks—whiskey for me and
Cung a glass of fruit juice. We talked in desultory fashion for a few moments, and it was clear that, while he
was at pains to be pleasant, he was by nature shy and
reluctant in social intercourse. If our dinner was to be
halfway successful, I had to take the initiative. I told
him I had a personal favor to ask.

"What is it, Mr. Ambassador?"

"It's quite simple. We've both had a hard day. I'd
like to enjoy my dinner with you and talk no business
until after the coffee."

He brightened immediately, and for the first time a
real warmth crept into his tone.

"I should like that, too. In this trade of ours it is hard
and sometimes dangerous to relax. Besides, it is my nature to be solitary, and I have never learned the trick of
easy talk."

"Come, Mr. President! I would never have said you
lacked eloquence."

He laughed at that, and the ice was broken. He began to talk, haltingly at first, then freely and vividly, of
his student days in Paris, of his exile in the United
States and of his life as a child in an old mandarin family. He did not lack humor, but it was quirky and sometimes barbed—the humor of a man who found more
malice than folly in the human comedy and less dignity
than degradation in the tragedy of man's condition. He
lacked the warmth to be a visionary, but he was a shrewd
observer of men and a well-informed student of affairs.
Of women he professed himself woefully ignorant, and
I gathered that he was afraid of them. He had the cel-

ibate's bleak disapproval of sexual excess, and it was easy to see that this attitude would not endear him to an Asian people, perennially permissive in sexual relations, for whom the potency of the prince was a matter of civic pride.

The meal he gave me was good; the wines were excellent; but I noticed that he ate sparingly and drank not at all. What struck me most, however, was the fact that he crossed himself quite casually and said grace before the meal. The religious bent of his character was of great interest to me, and I tried to set him talking by a reference to my own experiences in the Zen path. He questioned me closely, and revealed a wide and accurate knowledge of illuminative phenomena in both Eastern and Western religions. He added, a little ruefully, I thought, that he had never felt drawn to seek such experiences. Then he said something that interested me very much.

". . . Temperament is involved here, Mr. Ambassador, and the degree of dissatisfaction which the individual feels with himself, or with the social framework to which he belongs. The Hindu, for example, has a more febrile temperament than the Chinese. He is subject to the rigid and arbitrary caste system, while Chinese society depends upon the natural continuity of the family. So in India you see the development of mystical and metaphysical religion, culminating in the extreme refinement of original Buddhism. The high point in China was the pragmatic purity of the Confucian ethic. In Japan the social system is more rigid and complex, the pressures on the individual more intense. So there again you find an extreme refinement of sentiment, both artistic and religious. We Vietnamese are much more like the Chinese; so with us pure Buddhism has degenerated into a mixture of folk religion and Mahayana ritual, while our Catholicism tends to a too Latin formality. I myself have less sympathy than I should have for the intuitive simplicities of the Gospel. I am a Pharisee and a Jansenist by nature, and even the discipline of reason and experience has not changed me enough.

. . . I am called a Grand Inquisitor, you know—but for that one needs a streak of cruelty and I am not cruel."

"Do you find it hard to be tolerant, Mr. President?"

"No . . . not exactly. As a private Catholic, I am very much prepared to let every man damn himself in the fashion he chooses. But in public life—in Asian public life especially—there is no respect for any but the strong."

"Then surely the strong should try to make himself loved as well?"

He brooded over the question for a moment, and then answered it haltingly. "This is a personal problem for me. . . . I have always been aware of it. . . . I myself do not like to be touched and the notion of patting village children and embracing village maidens and grandmothers is alien to me. . . . I ought to do it, I know. But having no talent, I know I should do it badly."

Whatever he was then, he was not a fanatic, and I had nothing but respect for the honesty with which he had revealed himself. Neither was he a fool, though his Gallic regard for reason might well betray him, as it had betrayed the Gauls themselves, into some monumental stupidities.

When the meal was over, he led me out to a terrace which overlooked a garden enclosed by high walls. The walls were topped with barbed wire, and at each angle was a sentry box where an armed guard stood, dark and sinister against the sky. The air was warm and still and full of the scent of jasmine. Coffee was brought, and a brandy for me. Cung lit a cigar, the first luxury I had seen him use. Then he leaned back in his chair and watched me through the spiraling smoke drifts. His eyes were veiled now, his face composed into the mask of the scholar-prince; his voice took on the formal, ironic tones of the mandarin.

"So our small vacation is over, Mr. Ambassador. We are back to business. Where do we stand now?"

"In jeopardy—both of us!"

"And so?"

"So, Mr. President, I will tell you the truth as I see it. As Ambassador of the United States, I shall deliver to you tomorrow a formal note of protest against the unjust and unfounded accusations you made against my country in the National Assembly. Tonight, privately, I tell you that I am not in favor of sanctions—though I shall impose them if I am either directed or obliged to do so. I tell you also that I am not in favor of this move in the United Nations and that I think you have done well to counter it by inviting an open inquiry. . . . This being said, I must also tell you that you went much too far this afternoon. You said things which you will find it very hard to retract. It is possible that you have so much damaged your relations with us that we can never repair them. I want them repaired, believe me! I am prepared to co-operate with you to that end. But you must help me."

"And how do you propose that I help you, Mr. Ambassador?"

"I think you will agree it requires a gesture—a joint and public gesture that will save face for your Government and mine."

"Gestures are dangerous things, Mr. Ambassador. A gesture is a symbol, and symbols mean different things to different people. In America a kiss is a normal salutation. In Japan—a country which you know well—it is a public obscenity."

"There are certain gestures common to us all. Respect for the dead, for instance."

"Agreed. And what gesture do you propose?"

"Tomorrow the bodies of our marines and their Vietnamese comrades will be flown from Danang to Saigon. They will be received with full military honors at the airport, and then the burial services will take place according to the rites of each man's religion. I should like you to be with me at the airport and at the services. That way we, too, might make a public burial of our differences."

He gave me a thin smile and a nod of approval. "You are a good diplomat, Mr. Ambassador. I have much respect for you."

"Then you agree?"

"I have not said that. I think we need to examine very closely the meaning of such a public act and also its possible consequences. First, this ceremony will be arranged and conducted by the American military command, yes?"

"That's true."

"But this is our war, is it not? American troops are here as advisers and not as combatants."

"They get killed, whatever you call them."

"But should not we offer the military courtesies instead of the Americans?"

"If you are prepared to offer them, Mr. President, I think I could say we would accept them."

"But suppose I did offer them, what then?"

"It would be interpreted as a magnanimous gesture and an affirmation of our continuing friendship."

"In America, perhaps, where people are sentimental and dramatic. But here, do you know what would happen?"

"What, Mr. President?"

"In the villages, in the city markets, they would bring out the abacus. They would make a count, clicking the wood balls—and clicking their tongues, too! They would say, 'In Danang ten Americans and two Viets died. So the President makes a big ceremony and cries at the funeral. In Tânan forty-eight Viets were killed and he does not burn even a stick of incense for them. . . . See! The President is a Christian—a crab's claw that holds us in subjection to the foreigner.' "

"Do you really believe that would happen?"

"I know it. Some of my generals would make it happen. The yellow robes would whisper it as they went from house to house, begging the daily offering of rice. The Viet Cong would print it in the pamphlets they scatter through the hamlets at night."

"But you could answer them!"

"How?"

"Make the gesture complete. Come with me around the country. Fly from hamlet to hamlet in a helicopter. Show yourself to the people. Let them hear your voice and feel your presence. You could drown out the whispers and shame the plotters!"

For a few moments I thought I had convinced him. He sat, eyes hooded, head sunk on his chest, staring at the glowing tip of his cigar. Then, slowly, he raised his head and looked at me. His voice was gentle and touched with a kind of pity.

"Still you do not understand! The crab's claw! Do you know what that signifies in this country, Mr. Ambassador? It is the symbol of the foreign exploiter and the puppet who serves his interests. The memory of colonial rule is sunk deep like a thorn in the flesh of my people. I cannot parade myself with you in an American helicopter. Now if the helicopter were mine and you were my guest—you see the difference? No matter what help I accept, I must show myself always independent even if to you I seem stubborn and heedless of foreign opinion. There is no other way for the hope of liberty, peace and independence to be preserved in this nation!"

"Then for pity's sake, Mr. President, go out yourself with your own staff! Show yourself in the hamlets! Proclaim yourself as the leader! But at least announce us as your friends and not your enemies! You cannot go on locked up like a crusty hermit who abuses those who bring him bread while his adversaries make mocking legends about him!"

"I cannot leave this place, Mr. Ambassador—and you know it!"

"In God's name, why not?"

"Because this is the seat of government, and if I leave it, it may fall overnight into the hands of traitors and conspirators." He pointed a small hand at the watchtowers and the dark shapes of the sentries. "They are not there for ornament, you know. There have been several attempts on my life and many efforts to compass my downfall. Even as we sit here, men in high positions who have sworn to me their loyalty are engaged in conspiracy. You should know that because the plots are being made in your own Embassy."

"You have no right to say that, Mr. President."

"Why not? I have already made it a matter of public record." He sat bolt upright and stabbed his cigar at my chest. "Very well then! I will strike a bargain with you! I will attend the funeral with you tomorrow. I will tour the country with you and announce that we have settled our differences. I will release the Buddhist agitators and the students—on one condition!"

"And that is?"

"That Mr. Harry Yaffa leaves the country within forty-eight hours."

"That's an impossible condition."

"Why?"

"Because it would constitute a public acknowledgment that the United States is plotting against the Administration. Had you not made that charge in the National Assembly today, I might have been able to arrange Yaffa's transfer. But now you have made it impossible! I am very, very sorry."

"I am sorry for you, too, Mr. Ambassador."

"Why for me?"

"Because, much as I like you, much as I respect your experience, I find you an unresolved man. I think also that you are a very unhappy one. You know the truth, but you will not admit its consequences. No matter that you do not admit it to me—that is a question of diplomatic tact. Tonight I have tried to show myself to you as honestly as I could, I have shown you my defects and my strength. I think you understand them, too. But you are not prepared to accept them—let alone gamble on them. I read you very well, Mr. Amberley. You are an intelligent, cultivated man. You are drawn to me because you see in me a person who is concerned with spiritual values, who makes mistakes yet is honest enough to know them. . . . Yet in spite of this you are not willing to give me any mark of confidence or personal trust. You have a suspicion that I may be right, but you want to absolve yourself in case I am wrong. You are like the roulette player who wants to straddle all the squares at once. You demand an impossible perfection. You want a simple solution to an ancient and complex problem. You cannot have these things this side of eternity. You want a puppet who will dance to your music? In time you may carve yourself one. But you will find that, like the little Pinocchio, he will lie and cheat and his nose for profit will grow longer every day. You call me a monk and a hermit. Perhaps that is what I am. But I do have a conscience, even if it is not yours, even if it is not as flexible as that of Mr. Harry Yaffa. . . ."

"May I say something now, Mr. President?"

"You are my guest. It is your privilege to speak freely."

"Then I want to tell you something about Harry Yaffa. I don't like him either. I don't like his trade, but it is a trade we all use because we need it. In personal terms I find Yaffa unsympathetic. But whatever you or I may think of him, he has done a good job for this country. You would not have the hamlet program so far advanced without him. You would not have the Special Operations Groups among the Nungs, nor the junk patrols on the East Coast. Without his agents in Cambodia and Laos you would have no control whatever over the smuggling of arms down the Mekong River. . . . One more thing, Mr. President. If there are plots against you—and I have no doubt there are—it is your own people who make them. If ever you are deposed, who will rule from the Gia Long Palace? Not Harry Yaffa, surely! You say I demand an impossible perfection in our relations. Are you not demanding an equally impossible one? You are being armed and fed and equipped by the United States, a country whose politics are the most sensitive in the world to public opinion. And yet you provoke us and insult us and accuse us publicly of treachery. Then in the next breath you ask our taxpayers for more money and more arms! You are the man of reason, Mr. President! But this is a madness! Not even Congress can control one hundred and eighty million people. And yet you—you who need them so much—provoke them as you did today!"

"Should I make kowtows to them, Mr. Ambassador? Should I come like a beggar, cap in hand, because I am holding America's front line in Asia? I have seven hundred million Chinese at my back door! I provoke them, too, but I am still on my feet and fighting! Do not forget the history of this affair, Mr. Ambassador. It was you Americans who uttered the first public reproof about a situation on which you were only half informed. It was you who made the first threat of sanctions. And that was your big mistake. How can you threaten anyone who has come to terms with death?"

"Am I to understand then, Mr. President, that you will not be present at the airport tomorrow?"

"I will not. I cannot. But I shall be represented by my Foreign Minister and members of the General Staff."

"Neither will you make a tour of the military areas with me?"

"While Yaffa is in the country—no!"

"Will you undertake to release those Buddhist monks and students who are presently in prison?"

"When our investigations are complete, each case will be reviewed on its merits."

"With the assurance of my personal goodwill and my willingness to interpret in your favor with Washington and with the world press—will you consider or offer any gesture at all to repair this damage?"

"Do you have any suggestion?"

"I think it must come from you, Mr. President."

"At this moment I can offer nothing."

"So we are back to stalemate?"

"It is you who say it, not I."

"Then permit me, Mr. President, to take my leave. Thank you for a pleasant dinner."

"Good night, Mr. Ambassador."

"Good night, Mr. President."

As I walked out of the Palace, into the close and cloudy night, the monstrous irony of the situation overwhelmed me: that two men sobered by disaster could sit down at a dinner table prepared to mend their differences and that an hour and a half later they could end in a futile dialectic that might cost a million lives and change the history of the Asian peninsulas.

I was filled with a bleak and bitter anger. The more I thought of it, the more Cung's judgment on me sounded like a calculated insult. I could accept it from Musō Soseki because he was my master in the way of enlightenment, but from this man it was an intolerable presumption, and I would not endure it. It was in this black mood that I arrived at the Embassy and dictated the crucial cable to Festhammer:

TONIGHT I DINED WITH PRESIDENT CUNG AND DELIVERED STRONG VERBAL PROTEST ON ASSEMBLY SPEECH. SUGGESTED AS FIRST GESTURE OF RECONCILIATION THAT HE BE PRESENT TOMORROW AT FUNERAL OF U.S. HELICOPTER CREWMAN AND THEN JOIN ME ON TOUR OF BATTLE AREAS. I OFFERED MY FULLEST CO-OPERATION TO RE-ESTABLISH GOOD RELATIONS AND STILL SAVE FACE FOR HIM WITH PRESS. HE REFUSED YIELD GROUND ON THIS OR ANY OTHER POINT. THEREFORE PROPOSE USE MY DISCRETIONARY POWERS AND CUT OFF ALL FURTHER AID PAYMENTS FROM 1200 HOURS WEDNESDAY 9TH. AM INSTRUCTING TOLLIVER PREPARE FIRST WITHDRAWAL MILITARY PERSONNEL. FULL REPORT FOLLOWS—AMBERLEY.

I called General Tolliver and told him the news. He grunted unhappily and gave me another piece of information to round out my day: members of the small Australian Military Mission in the northern mountains had identified two new battalions of Viet Cong, and another had been positively identified by the interrogation of prisoners after Tânan. Uncle Ho and his military mastermind, General Giap, were taking full advantage of disorders in the South and large-scale Viet Cong action could be expected soon in all sectors. I told Tolliver I wanted to make an immediate tour of the battle areas. That made him unhappier still, and he spent ten minutes painting the risks for me. I heard him out and then told him that I needed to go, if only to let Cung digest his medicine and meditate a change of heart.

After that I went back to my own house, where I found Anne Beldon entertaining Harry Yaffa at a late supper of coffee and doughnuts. I felt an odd pang of jealousy at this scene of domesticity, and I was weak enough to ask Anne to wait up with us and take some notes of our discussion.

Yaffa had his own crop of troubles. The conspirators were terrified by the defiant tone of Cung's speech in the National Assembly. They took it as a sign that he had won his diplomatic battle with the United States and felt himself strong enough to stand alone. There had been leakages, too, and treachery in their own ranks. Several highly placed officials were now under open surveillance by the security police. Two generals had been transferred from field commands to administrative posts in Saigon, where they could be kept immobile and out of contact with their own units. If the opposition movement were not to collapse altogether, the plotters would need a clear and definite sign of our support.

Oddly enough, Yaffa's own confidence seemed to have evaporated. He was edgy and uncomfortable, as if all his careful arithmetic had turned to double-Dutch. He brightened somewhat when I told him that sanctions would be enforced within twenty-four hours. When I told him also that Cung had requested his own transfer out of the country and that I had refused it, he became almost good-humored and told me that my personal approval was of great importance to him. It was my private opinion that it wasn't worth a hill of beans, but I was prepared to accept the fiction so long as it suited my purposes.

Then, because I was still angry with myself and with Cung, I took a second impulsive decision.

"I am going to tell you something now, Mr. Yaffa, and Miss Beldon is going to take it down. Each of us will have a copy, and I shall send one to Washington. If I fail to make myself clear, I would like you to tell me and I will revise the text for you, but once we are on the record I want you to work strictly within the limits of the assignment. If you go outside them, I will hold you personally responsible. Is that clear?"

"Very clear, Mr. Ambassador."

"Good! Anne, we begin from here. 'At this moment it is very clear that President Cung has no intention of changing his attitude toward the Buddhists. It is clear also that he will not recant any of the tendentious and damaging statements he has made to the National Assembly. It remains to be seen whether he will change these attitudes after sanctions have been imposed. If he does not change, it may be necessary to consider the possibility of transferring our support to another government more able to unify the country and prosecute the war. . . .' Check, Mr. Yaffa?"

"Check," said Harry Yaffa.

" 'As Ambassador of the United States, I am therefore prepared to authorize contact and consultation with such persons as may show themselves willing and able to set up an alternative government as and when it may seem necessary. I am not, however, prepared to give either formal or tacit approval to any move to overthrow the present regime until I have fullest information about the personages involved and the methods they propose to use, and until I have received approval from Washington. . . .' "

"Check again," said Harry Yaffa.

" 'I am charging Mr. Harry Yaffa to make it clear to his contacts that we cannot, under any circumstances, give our approval to a political assassination. I am also charging him to exact guarantees that in the event of a coup to which we give even tacit approval the persons

of President Cung and his Cabinet will be protected.
. . . Mr. Yaffa has already told me that even if such
guarantees were given he could not personally ensure
that they would be honored. This is a reasonable disclaimer, but it does not absolve him from using his best
efforts to carry out our policy in the matter . . .' Is that
fair enough, Mr. Yaffa?"

"I wouldn't call it fair, Mr. Ambassador. But I'll accept it."

" 'Finally, our approval of any move to depose the
Cung government will be given by a code word, arranged beforehand between Mr. Yaffa and myself. Until this code word is given, the United States cannot be
regarded as committed in any way to the support of a
new regime. . . .' That's a classified document, Anne,
and its distribution is limited to me, Mr. Yaffa and
Washington."

"Thank you, Mr. Ambassador," said Harry Yaffa
with bland approval. "It's a move in the right direction
—and at least I am no longer working alone. When
you're ready to talk with the generals, let me know and
I'll set up the meetings."

"I am proposing to leave Saigon for a few days, to
take a look at the military situation. If there are any
people you want me to see on my travels, please let me
know."

"You can see one man tomorrow, if you wish, sir.
His name is General Tran Hung Dao. He'll be repre-
senting the Army at the funeral tomorrow morning.
General Tolliver will probably invite him to headquarters for a drink after the ceremony. At present he is
Assistant Chief of Staff, which, the way Cung runs
things, means precisely nothing."

"Can he be trusted, Mr. Yaffa?"

"Let's put it this way, sir. His position in the Government is very insecure. He's looking for a change. He
thinks we're the people who can give him the best deal.
After that you play it by ear, like a tin whistle."

When he had gone, dapper and confident once more,
Anne Beldon offered to make me fresh coffee, but I

poured myself a whiskey and then began to dictate a summary of my dialogue with Cung. Long practice in the Service has given me a good verbal memory and a sensitive ear for the rhythms and nuances of the spoken word. So, as I reconstructed the conversation for the shorthand record, I found myself forced to a far different conclusion from that which had prompted my cable to Festhammer and my perilous commitment to Harry Yaffa.

I could justify them both, of course, and no one would dare to question my judgment. I was Johnny-on-the-spot—the man of experience and integrity, the urbane negotiator who never let his temper get the better of his judgment. But in this last hour of a disastrous day I knew that I had deceived myself. I had made an interpretation that salvaged my vanity and damned me for a cheat. Cung had not insulted me; I was truly the unresolved man, the man who would not gamble on the truth he saw, but tried to hedge it with opportune casuistry.

Phung Van Cung had been very frank with me. He had shown me his personal defects and his public dilemmas. He had asked me to trust him, but I had insisted on an immediate and public recantation—an auto-da-fé which would have destroyed altogether his prestige as a head of state. He had not asked me to justify his imperfections but only to suffer them for fear of greater ones. And I? I had refused to be patient, I had cried for action and swift change. I had tried to bring off a coup of my own. Hey, presto! I am a stranger in town, and yet look what I produce out of the air! A white rabbit, two live pigeons, a purple scarf, a bunch of grapes, a maidenhead and a miracle—a reformed dictator wiser than the Holy Ghost!

Before I had finished the dictation the words were like alum on my tongue, and I drank two more whiskeys to wash away the taste. But my head was full of cotton wool and my hands were unsteady. I was dizzy from the liquor and the impact of another thought. I had demanded that Cung retract his statements in the

Assembly. But how could I retract the subtle falsehoods which I had sent to Washington?

Finally Anne Beldon closed her notebook and said quietly, "You should go to bed, Mr. Ambassador. You've had a big day, and there's another one coming up tomorrow."

"Why go to bed and court the nightmares?"

"If you like, I'll get you a sleeping pill."

"I never use them. I did once and found them a lethal temptation. I'd like to go for a walk."

She smiled indulgently and shook her head. "There's no place to go. The city's under curfew. You'd be shot before you went a hundred yards."

"There's the garden."

"You'd set off the alarm system."

"That's an interesting thought. 'A Garden is a lovesome thing, God wot!' Especially when you plant it with trip wires and electric eyes. . . . Do you think there's a cuckoo in the garden?"

"A cuckoo?"

"It's a riddle, Anne. Tonight I found the answer to it. . . . I'm sorry to keep you so late. Let's call it a day."

At the foot of the stairs I stumbled, and she reached out a hand to steady me. I was very careful not to touch her because tomorrow I must be Ambassador again.

The funeral of the helicopter crewmen was, on all counts, an interesting piece of theater. I was an actor in it, and I have nothing but praise for the stage management of General Tolliver. At ten thirty precisely I was to leave the Embassy with my aides and my military attaché. I would arrive at the airport at ten fifty and inspect the guard on the tarmac. At eleven the transport would touch down and the bodies would be unloaded. A military chaplain would read a Valediction. I would make a short obituary speech on behalf of the President of the United States and then ride with General Tolliver in the cortege to the cemetery.

However, as happens all too often in the theater, the backstage drama was more significant than the one delivered across the footlights. At nine thirty Mel Adams brought me the news that the Vietnamese Foreign Minister would not be present at the airport ceremony. He had been taken ill overnight, and his doctor had confined him to bed. He sent his deep regrets and heartfelt sympathies. Since no mention was made of a substitute, it was clear that the whole of the Ministry of Foreign Affairs must be suffering from the same diplomatic dyspepsia. At nine forty-five Tolliver called me to report that the local commander in Danang had taken possession of the bodies of the Viet crewmen and that he was under orders to have them buried in Danang with the minimum of ceremony. There was more yet. The Vietnamese guard of honor for the airport reception had been withdrawn, and the only official representatives of the Republic would be the Assistant Chief of Staff and his personal aide.

It was all very Oriental and very, very effective. At one stroke we were isolated: from the people, from the war, from our comrades in arms. Our status was defined more precisely than by any treaty. We were bankers, purveyors of equipment, military advisers. Our losses were a regrettable but minor incident in the life-and-death struggle of a nation. If we wished to make a drama out of our dead, that was our own affair. Tolliver was furious, as he had a right to be. For myself, I nursed a secret satisfaction. There was justification now for my political action, if no true absolution for my uneasy conscience. Yet when I stood on the tarmac and watched the bulky, battered transport roll to a stop, I found myself touched to tears by the brutal simplicity of the moment.

There were ten coffins in all: long caskets of jungle timber, made by village carpenters. They were raw, unvarnished, bare of ornament, and on the lid of each was a name and a number, scored into the wood with a hot iron. They were carried out of the plane on the shoulders of young men, grim and stubbled-faced, like heroes out of some old, violent legend.

The troops who waited to receive them were spruce

and clean, and their weapons shone in the morning sun. But the young men wore combat fatigues and were harnessed with leather and canvas, with pistols at their hips and killing knives worn high up on their breasts. Their cheeks were lean and stained with sun and jungle fever; their eyes were sleepless and somber. They walked slowly and defiantly, contemptuous of those who had come to pay this belated homage to their comrades.

Between the serried guards there were ten gun carriages, with a color sergeant standing beside each one. The young men laid the coffins down upon the limbers, and the color sergeants spread upon each one the flag of the United States. The young men ranged themselves four and four around each coffin, as if to affirm their right of possession over their own dead. There was a whirring of movie cameras, and an indecent scurry of news photographers as the chaplain stepped forward to read the Valediction. I did not hear the words he read because I was trying to frame my own, and struggling at the same time with a poignant guilt for my own hypocrisy.

Young men had died violently and would be buried in alien earth to a sound of gunfire and bugles. Young men! Not I, nor Tolliver, nor Cung, nor Harry Yaffa, but young men, inheritors of the past, fabricators of the future, who might have bred children, planted gardens, opened new doors to knowledge, seen visions on mountains to which we were blind. Now they were the blind ones and their mouths would be stopped with mud. Only the worms would breed out of their loins, and rank tropic flowers would feed on their hearts. . . . We were holding a wake for them, but political opportunists like myself had turned it into a mockery.

I am very practiced in ceremony, and I had prepared a safe and simple homily on the merit of those who died for a noble cause. Suddenly I knew that I could not speak it. The words would choke me if I tried. The chaplain finished the prayer and called me forward to the microphone. I heard a voice that was not my own pronounce a different obit, while the flashbulbs popped and the reporters scribbled furiously.

". . . I am ashamed today. I am ashamed that we must bury our dead alone, like enemies, in a land to which we were invited as friends and allies. I am ashamed that the money we spend, the aircraft and the arms we bring, should seem more prized than the men who fight and die so far from home. . . . It is a sad and terrible thing to me that in the midst of this war for survival there should be civil disturbances and religious feuds and brutality in police cells and detention camps. These things are an insult to our dead and to our dead comrades of the Army of South Vietnam, whom we are not permitted to honor here today. . . . They are voiceless now; they count on us to speak for them. Yet we spend ourselves in public debates and private squabbles and accusations calculated to make headlines in the daily press. I am ashamed that I, who was sent by our President to bring agreement and concord, should find myself involved in these fruitless wrangles. I pledge myself now, in the presence of the dead, to try as best I can to wipe out this shame. I adjure those who govern this country to join themselves with me to this end. . . . May God help us all!"

As I stepped back from the microphone, General Tolliver whispered, "That was great, Mr. Ambassador. Thank Christ someone had the guts to tell the bastards the truth!"

He had missed the whole point; or more truly, by an instinctive trick of self-deception, I had refused to make it. Cung was still the villain. I was still the white knight, beyond fear or reproach. It was too late now to say what I knew in my secret heart: that for all my noble words, for all my outraged virtue, I was one of the bastards, too.

CHAPTER SIX

After the funeral General Tolliver took me back to his headquarters for luncheon with his staff.

I was glad of the diversion, grateful, too, for this brief sojourn in the simpler world of the professional soldier. As a young man I had nursed, for a long time, a secret contempt for those who were content to live a whole lifetime under the benevolent patriarchy of the military system. They absolved themselves too easily, it seemed to me, from the search for a philosophy and the necessity for an enlarged moral judgment. They were mercenaries dedicated to a brutal art which must in the end be stamped out if the human race was to survive at all. Like the policeman, they were a constant reminder of man's frailty, ineptitude and tyranny. They were passive instruments of policies, good or bad, which they had no voice in making. They created a caste for themselves with its own cosmogony and its own illusions of utility, sanctity or heroism. They were dedicated to the national and not to the universal. They were like sorcerers, puttering in secret with a dangerous alchemy against the day when they might be required to launch death and destruction on an ignorant world. . . .

Alas, for my youthful cynicism! Today, in my secret dishonor, I envied them. I envied the innocence of their lethal purpose. I envied the morality of their obedience and the absolution which was implicit even in the misguided command of a superior. Their dignity was more deeply founded than mine because it was rooted in a notion of service, and their lives were always in pawn to affirm it.

Tolliver was a good host, and it was clear that his staff respected him. There was good talk around his table, free critical talk, laced with memories of home and seasoned with stories of campaigns and cantonments. There was a note of kinship, a pride of family which even the Vietnamese general seemed to share. They shared it with me, too, because I was the representative of their Commander in Chief, and they did not spare me their courteous contempt for the sterile and intricate trade in which I was involved. For a while I felt cleansed even while I knew I was not forgiven, but when the lunch was over I was back again to the intrigues of my business. General Tolliver beckoned me aside with Tran Hung Dao and led us to a private room. He gave us coffee, cigars and a good brandy, and then left us. He was a soldier and not a diplomat. He wanted no part in our devious enterprises.

Tran Hung Dao was a surprise in more ways than one. For a Vietnamese he was almost a giant. He was nearly six feet tall, brawny and broad of shoulder; his eyes were bright, his smile was engaging and his English almost faultless. He looked more like a Shanghainese than a Viet, and his opening gambit was equally unexpected.

"As you know by now, Mr. Ambassador, I am, in the view of my President, a conspirator. That is to say, I am a general who believes we are losing the war and a citizen who is dissatisfied with his Government. I am looking for a way to change both situations. I understand from Mr. Harry Yaffa that you yourself have certain opinions on this matter."

"I have, General. But this is not to say that I am ready to disclose them."

I am always annoyed by Asians who adopt the brisk and hearty approaches of the West. It seems to me they abandon a precious refinement for something vulgar and insincere. So I was curt with this muscular general. He knew it and he knew why, and his next words were much more temperate.

"Forgive me, Mr. Ambassador, but you have already

made certain drastic disclosures. But perhaps it would be more discreet to say that you would like to see a change in the political climate."

"In the climate, yes. Not necessarily a change of government."

"Do you think you can have the one without the other?"

"At this moment I am not sure."

"But if events should prove that a change of government is necessary—if, for example, your protests go unheeded, if the sanctions which you propose to apply fail of their effect, what then?"

"Then we must look to the Vietnamese people themselves to bring about a change."

He lifted his brandy glass, sniffed it approvingly, sipped the liquor and set down the glass. His tone was light and ironic.

"I see, Mr. Ambassador, that you are a very precise man, so I must be precise with you. The Vietnamese people . . . who are they? The Montagnards who live like primitives in the hills? The delta fishermen who cannot read or write? The Thais? The Chams? The peasant in the rice paddy who has no vote and could not use it if he had, because we do not have elections like the Americans? If a change is to be made, it must be brought about by those who have the education, the organization and the physical means to do it. When the change is made, the country must still be governed, the war must still be fought, if we are not to fall into total confusion and end in the sorry neutralism of our neighbors. You see that, of course?"

"I see it, yes. But to this point, General, you show me what *must* be done. I am more interested to know what *could* be done and how."

I was so accustomed to Oriental dialogues that I expected him to balk at the question, or at least to hedge his answer. He did neither. He gave me a wide smile, leaned back comfortably in his chair and told me:

"First, what could be done? A coup could be staged. If I define it correctly, a coup is a change of government brought about at a single stroke. It is not a revolution, which, for us, would be a bloody and tragic affair. A coup means the application of pressure at a single point, at a chosen moment in time so that the Government is overbalanced and a new one takes over. . . . Now who can apply such a pressure? Only the Army, which has organization, manpower, and the threat of arms."

"So willy-nilly we should be committed to a military junta?"

"Would it be so much different, Mr. Ambassador, from the military dictatorship which we have now?"

"It might be less stable."

"It would also be more moderate because the internal checks and balances would operate against the extremists."

"There is still a big *if*."

"There is always an *if*, Mr. Ambassador. You remember the little Christian prayer, 'If I should die before I wake . . .' Death is the only certainty we have."

"So a coup is to be staged by the Army. How can it be organized?"

"A very practical question, Mr. Ambassador. . . ."

On the wall facing him was a large campaign map of South Vietnam. He pushed himself out of his chair, walked across the room and stood beside the map, for all the world like a tutor instructing a dullard pupil. He continued to irritate me with his brawny confidence. "The Republican Army is divided into four corps. Number One Corps controls the northeastern sector of the country, from the border of North Vietnam through Tourane and over to the western frontier. The Second Corps, based on Pleiku, controls the provinces of the central highlands. The Third Corps controls the delta, and the Fourth Corps controls the Saigon special sector. Apart from these formations we have a small naval force, which is of no importance to our considerations, and a small Air Force—which is very, very important. Now . . . !" He thrust a long, emphatic finger at the map. "The Saigon special sector constitutes a protective ring thrown around the capital and the seat of government. It is held at the moment under martial law, and the corps commander is a Catholic, rigidly loyal to the regime. The troops themselves—except for the Palace Guard—can be swung this way or that. So the strategy of a take-over requires four steps. First, we move down two hand-picked battalions from the northern and central areas. We move up another from the South. We then have three spearheads pointing at the heart of the city. Step number two. We take control of the staff headquarters of Number Three Corps so that this formation is left without leadership. Once this is done the unit commanders can easily be persuaded to join forces with our three battalions. Step number three. Units of the Air Force hold the Palace and the city under threat of bombing. Step number four. We are in control of the capital and of the armed forces. We set up a government controlled by a committee of three or four generals. We administer it with civilian personnel who are already running its various departments and who can carry on their jobs in a normal fashion."

He broke off at that point and faced me, confident and smiling, as if he had just written Q.E.D. at the end of the theorem of Pythagoras. But I was not prepared to accept his demonstration as confidently as he had made it.

"As I see it, General, you could make this move at any time on your own initiative. Why do you wait? Why do you come to me?"

"Because we need—what do you call it?—a catalyst to start the chemical reaction. Look! I will show you! The commander of Number One Corps is a strong man, tough, a good soldier. And he hates our President's guts, so he is with us all the way. But in order to move his troops down to the capital he must pass them through the area of Number Two Corps, whose commander is a waverer. He doesn't like the Government any more than I do, but he is based in a province whose Governor is hostile to him, so he wants to take out in-

surance. The man in the delta is in the same position.
. . . This is where our President has been so very
shrewd. He has always matched his staff one against the
other. He never puts two friends together in the same
area."

"Where do you fit into the pattern, General?"

"I am here in Saigon. I am responsible for plans to
take over Number Three Corps headquarters and swing
the unit officers to our side."

"And the Air Force?"

"The Air Force is with us to a man. But the Air
Force depends on the United States for fuel and ser-
vicing, so they need to be assured that they will not be
kept out of the air by their own allies."

"In effect, General, you wish to make us partners in
the rebellion."

"No, Mr. Ambassador. All we ask is that you write
our insurance for us."

"And what are the precise terms of the policies you
would like us to write?"

"They are three, Mr. Ambassador: no betrayal, no
interference and your continued support with arms and
money when we have established a workable government. . . . Oh! There is one other, which is very important. We need a clear sign that you will honor the
policy in the terms I have indicated."

"It's a very clear document, General, even if it is still
only a hypothetical one. However, from our point of
view, it is still incomplete. We would need to see another clause added to it."

"And what is that, Mr. Ambassador?"

"That in the event of a change of government no violence would be offered to the persons of President Cung
or any of his Cabinet; that they would be taken into
custody and then given safe conduct out of the
country."

He thought about that one for a long moment. He
sucked in his cheeks and puffed them out again. He
came back to the table and swallowed his brandy at a
gulp. Then he sat down and puffed meditatively on his

cigar. He said evenly, "If we could give you that guarantee, Mr. Ambassador, would you then support us, on the limited terms which I have outlined?"

"Provided always that it seemed the present Government could no longer function effectively."

"That would be in your view, of course, Mr. Ambassador?"

"In my view and that of my Government in Washington. . . . Of course, you are always free to act independently and at your own risk."

"You drive a hard bargain."

"I am not bargaining at all, General. I am discussing a hypothetical circumstance which we would prefer did not arise."

His smooth face darkened; his eyes were shrewd and wary. Yet he held himself well in control and talked on in the same even fashion.

"You are a very good poker player, Mr. Ambassador. But you can't wait all your life for four aces. You can win with worse hands."

"Let me explain something, General. We can't win anything because we're playing against the house with a stacked deck. Yesterday, for instance, how did the game finish? We lost ten men and we spent one and a half million dollars of our taxpayers' money. Today, at a guess, we have already spent eight hundred thousand dollars! So far what have we got? A request for an all-risk policy on a military coup to be organized by three waverers and an overwilling general who can't guarantee his lines of communication. . . . You see the way it reads?"

"So what do you want, Mr. Ambassador—an auction between the devil you know and the devil you don't?"

"No. We want a friendly government which can maintain order with justice and bring this war to a conclusion that will guarantee the security and peace of South Vietnam."

"If I promised you that, you would know me for a liar."

"What can you promise then, General?"

"Friendship, yes. A united army, yes. Peace with the Buddhists, yes. An end to civil disorder, yes. The rest is a question mark, but I am sure we can do better than the present regime."

"But you are not ready yet."

"No."

"When could you be ready?"

"Six weeks—provided we had a reasonable hope of that insurance policy."

"If you can organize yourselves for armed rebellion, why can you not organize yourselves for a reasonable settlement with the present Government? With three army corps and the Air Force surely you can bargain with President Cung."

"But he will not bargain! He will divide and sub-divide and buy and threaten until our bargaining power is dissipated. This is his method. He is a master of it. No one can reason with him. You know that. You've tried. He won't talk to anyone but God—and even then I think God comes off second-best!" He slammed his fist on the desk, and his voice was high and harsh with anger. "Give me something clear, Mr. Ambassador! We're not children! The Viet Cong are three battalions stronger than they were last week. We're weakening every day because there is no confidence in our leadership. What do you say? Yes, no or perhaps?"

"Perhaps."

"Very well. One more question: How do we know when the perhaps becomes yes?"

"You will know. That's all I can tell you."

"And how do we keep in touch with you?"

"You don't, General. From this moment I can have no further contact with you or your friends on this matter. As Ambassador, I am accredited to the legitimate government of this country—whatever it may be."

"And how do you define a legitimate government, Mr. Ambassador?"

"In a system where no free elections are possible, we have to define it simply as that government which does and can govern."

"So while we are not yet a government, but only an opposition, to whom do we talk if not to you?"

"To Mr. Harry Yaffa."

"And what is his status?"

"Mr. Yaffa is an intelligence agent whose activities may be disowned and discredited at any time by his Government. That's the way the game is played. You know that."

He stared at me for a while, grim and thoughtful. Then his face broke into a grin of reluctant approval.

"Talking of poker, Mr. Ambassador . . . I wonder who really stacked the deck?"

After Dao had left, I spent more than an hour with General Tolliver, planning my tour of the combat areas. The project had, for a number of reasons, a singular importance for me. First, it was vitally important that I have a firsthand knowledge of the country, the conditions of life and very special problems of a subversive war in a partitioned and multiracial country. I still had hopes that with more knowledge and experience I could set up a working relationship with Cung, who—for all his knack of making me angry— was a man much more worthy of respect than Dao. Second, I wanted to be out of Saigon when the sanctions came into operation. I did not want to be available to the press, whose daily comment might aggravate the situation. And Cung himself might prove more amenable to my absence than to my accusing presence. Finally, I myself needed the harsh and curative contact with reality. After these few days of diplomatic dialogue I felt like a man walking in cloud-cuckoo land and talking in jabber-wocky. Tolliver repeated his warnings about the risks of the tour, but it was clear that he was glad to have me make it. He, too, was impatient with talk and intrigue, and deeply concerned for the morale of his troops. When I told him of my conversation with General Dao, he snorted impatiently and damned the man for a liar.

"All that talk about moving a battalion from each

corps area is poppycock! . . ." He pointed to his own operations map. "Take Number One Corps, up here near the northern border. The man who runs it is a General Tho. He's a fine soldier, and he knows damned well that if he pulled out a whole battalion the Viet Cong would pour in like water through a bottleneck! Besides, that's mountain country. All Tho's units are split into small formations because you simply can't move large concentrations of troops. . . . And that nonsense about the Air Force being afraid of us! They've got their own supplies of gas, ammunition and spare parts. If they want to fly straight from here to Hanoi, we can't stop them!"

"Then why did Dao tell me such stupid lies? He must have known I'd check his information with you!"

Tolliver grinned and shrugged in comic despair. "That's the way it goes out here. Dao was simply telling you that he knew you didn't trust him and he wasn't going to trust you. Oh, he's got plans, all right! Probably very workable ones, too. But so long as you're sitting on the fence you'll never hear them."

"I'm damned if I'll give him or anyone else a blank check."

"I wouldn't give him a wooden nickel!" said Tolliver emphatically. "If there's going to be a coup, the man who'll head it will be Khiet, down in the delta. He's the best strategist they have, and a tough fighter as well. Dao will be part of the junta, of course; but from our point of view he's the part we need least. He's playing both ends and the middle. Don't forget he's still Assistant Chief of Staff to Cung."

"So we're at one end and Cung's in the middle. Who's playing off Dao at the other end?"

"If you want my guess, Ambassador, it's the French. This whole country's crawling with Gaullist agents, and they've got money running our of their ears. They're subsidizing the rubber planters and the factory owners to pay off the Viet Cong so that they can stay in business. They're buying up neutralist opinion wherever they can because ultimately that's what they want—

another neutral state like Laos and Cambodia, with free access for France to Hanoi and the North as well."

"And General Dao is a neutralist?"

"An opportunist!" said Tolliver. "Like so many of them. I don't like Cung any more than you do, Mr. Ambassador; but he's twice the size of any man I've met here so far. He may be sold out, but he can never be bought out!"

"Do you think we should back him unconditionally?"

"We can't," said Tolliver unhappily. "And that's the devil of our situation from Taiwan to Bangkok. We're like the fellow with a blackmailing mistress. He won't marry her, he can't leave her and he sure as hell can't love her!"

The rest of the afternoon I spent back at the Embassy, composing a long and a detailed report to Raoul Festhammer, in Washington. The text of my final summation is still very clear in my mind because it represents my nearest approach to total honesty. When I am tempted, as I have been tempted many times, to assume all the guilt for what later happened, I remember it and I am held one step short of utter self-contempt.

". . . So in spite of his many dangerous shortcomings, I find myself leaning to President Cung as the one man strong enough and incorruptible enough to hold the balance of power in this country. However, I cannot and I dare not offer him absolute trust. So I am forced, through the medium of the CIA and Mr. Harry Yaffa, to maintain contact with dissident elements who are presently plotting the overthrow of the regime and who may one day bring it about. In doing this it is clear that I am making it more difficult for President Cung to maintain stability, order and loyalty. Yet I cannot leave us unprepared for a change of government or without friends in a new regime. All I can do is make the risk clear to you and make clear also the reasons why I have accepted it. . . . There is another risk, too, which I must put before you clearly and frankly. The risk is that I myself, through defect of knowledge, experience or character, may be forced into a wrong decision, which may cost us all very dearly. I think, for example, that I have done less well with Cung than I should have because he finds me too precise and not subtle enough to be sympathetic to his own very complex situation. Against this I believe that he is a man who would take quick advantage of any show of weakness. . . . It would be easy for me to abdicate this personal risk simply by handing you the information and asking you to issue the directives from Washington; but this is not what you asked of me, and having made the risk clear to you, I can only do my best. . . . I wish it were always possible either to be sure of one's own morality or to be totally without it. . . ."

I finished the report, and I passed it to Mel Adams for his opinion. When he had finished the reading, he handed it back and gave me an odd searching look. "It's a very honest document. I respect you for it."

"But you don't agree with it?"

"I think it's inconclusive, sir."

"That's just the point, Mel. It has to be. I'm not ready to come to a conclusion yet!"

"In one sense, that's true, sir. In another, it's quite untrue. You *have* come to a conclusion. You have decided on a continuance of divisions in the hope that one side or the other will present, on its own initiative, an acceptable solution. That's fine if you go all out for neutralism. But if you want to stay in the power play you have to make a clear choice. In that document you don't make it."

"I'm not ready or informed enough to make it. Don't push me, Mel."

"I'm not pushing, sir. I just want to be on the record."

"You're on it, Mel."

He thanked me stiffly and withdrew. I drafted a formal note to the Ministry of Foreign Affairs, announcing the imposition of sanctions. Tomorrow I would deliver it in person and open battle would be joined.

Then there was another fencing session with the press, and a chatty little telephone interlude with the

British Ambassador. He presumed—a little pointedly for my taste—that I was much too preoccupied to make the customary round of calls on my colleagues. However, they were all very anxious to meet me and perhaps, even at short notice, I would come to a cocktail party? Some of the Asians were a trifle sensitive, and they might think it remiss if I made no effort to meet them. The British and the Americans had to stick together, no? Especially with our French friends playing hell with a big stick. Tomorrow evening then? He was delighted. . . .

All of which meant that the French were treading on his toes and he wanted to wave the Atlantic Alliance at them. However, he did have a point about the Asians, and I could not afford the time to go trotting from Embassy to Embassy all over Saigon. So it was a reasonable bargain. I thought a little guiltily that, with so many people to see, I should send out some invitations of my own; but above all, I needed a reserve of time to bring my own study up to date. Also I needed at least a minimal diversion, but where did I get it in a city screwed down by a curfew and where I, of all people, was a man marked for assassination? . . . I gathered up the rest of my papers and took them home to work on after dinner.

Cocktails, conferences and reams and reams of paper! It is one of the ironies of diplomacy that the rise and fall of nations and the life and death of nameless thousands depend on such trivial things.

I walked in the garden before dinner because if I walked in it afterward I would break the beam of an electric eye, alarms would ring and guards would come running to protect my sacred person. I breathed the heavy perfumed air and fingered the thick velvet fabric of tropical flowers. I tried to talk to the Vietnamese gardener, but his French was as little as my Vietnamese and we ended in an exchange of bows and gestures. I chatted a few moments with the sentries, but they were constrained and formal, not having learned as yet that an Ambassador is always mortal, often lonely and sometimes puzzled by the intricate jigsaw of politics, from which key pieces are always missing. Bill Slavich passed through the garden, on his evening rounds, checking the guard posts and the alarm systems and the families in the compound. We paced a few moments on the damp moss of the lawn. He, too, had his problem with me. He was Harry Yaffa's man, a member of that curious demimonde of public servants whose trade is secret, violent and thankless. Our talk was banal, and I ended by asking him to find me a masseur who would attend me for an hour a day and work the tensions out of me. He promised to do it and then left me. I found myself wondering with prurient interest what were the diversions of a young man like this whose purlieus were the alleys of the world's underground.

Which brought me by a round turn to Harry Yaffa, the professional conspirator, whom I myself had named as my confidant and courier in all negotiations with the rebellious generals. I had read all his reports and made notes of all our talks, and on review I found them skilfully incomplete. The French agents? Their activities were noted, their influence assessed. The Army plotters? There was a biography of each, and even a running total of their bank accounts and holdings in real estate. The agents among the Buddhists, the reactionaries among the Catholic clergy? There was a dossier on each and an up-to-date record of his activities. Our agents in Vientaine and Pnompenh, our contacts among the pilots who flew the opium routes out of Burma and the skippers who plied the coastal trade from Bangkok around the Gulf of Tonkin? They were all listed. What more did I want? And if I did want more, I had only to ask for it.

Why then did I distrust this man? He had refused to lie to me. He had admitted that there were secrets to which I should not be party, but my experience told me that this was the normal and prudent custom of the trade. What was it about the man that irked me so that I must always be formal with him and never use his given name? Was I afraid of him or he of me? Did a man like him become a miser of secrets, hoarding them for his private enjoyment or for the exercise of an ignoble tyranny? Was there a special vice to which men who worked in this half-world fell victims—an ambition to rule from behind the king's arras, or a perverse impulse to destroy because they themselves walked in daily danger of destruction?

It was a dark thought, and it troubled me as I paced up and down in the clinging fragrance of jasmine and frangipani. But there was a darker one yet which troubled me even more. Every one of the men with whom I had dealt in the last few days had shown a patent distrust of me. To Cung, I was the unresolved man who wanted to straddle all the squares on the board; to Yaffa, I was the potential failure against whose default he had to prepare; to General Dao, I was a dubious ally; to Mel Adams, an honest reporter whose honesty was not enough. I had experience enough to know that a man in high authority is always suspect, even to his staff. In the past Gabrielle had been both my conscience and my bulwark. Without her I was a prey to misgivings and guilts. I was like a monk haunted by secret dreams of lechery, a servant of the commonweal tempted to wild tyrannies. Even though I did not yield to the temptations, I knew that they were there, and their attraction robbed me of faith in my noblest purposes. . . . I wondered if my doubts were written on my face like the tics and twitches of a scrupulous devotee. . . .

A small night wind rose and rolled up the low clouds from the delta. Then it began to rain—a soft, drenching dewfall that drove me inside for a solitary drink and a solitary dinner. Anne Beldon was dining with a friend from another Embassy, and George Groton was probably squatting in some pagoda, discoursing on the Dhamma with a man in a yellow robe.

It was just after ten, while I was working through a bulky document on the economic condition of South Vietnam, when Groton came in. He was breathless and drenched to the skin. He had been in a pagoda at the northern end of the city and had set out to walk home. He had forgotten about the curfew and had spent a perilous hour dodging the pickets and the mobile patrols. He was hungry, too, because like a good monk, he had eaten nothing since midday. I sent him upstairs to change and then asked the housekeeper to prepare a meal for him. Twenty minutes later, over a cold chicken and a bottle of wine, he gave me his first eager report.

". . . First, our fellow in the Embassy gave me a circular letter of introduction. It was written in French and it looked quite friendly. It said, 'This young man is a student of the Eight-fold Path and is therefore well disposed to us. He has the confidence of the American Ambassador, who also understands the Zen way. Please render him all courtesies and try to explain our position to him.' . . . So far so good, but down at the bottom he wrote something in Vietnamese. I asked him to translate it for me, and it turned out to be one of the propositions of *Nagarjuna* on The Examination of *Nirvana*. Roughly translated, it said, 'Since everything is relative, we do not know what is finite and what is infinite. We do know what is both finite and infinite at the one time. We do not know what is a denial of both finite and infinite.' . . . I asked him what it meant, and he said that it was customary in any correspondence to add a reminder of some spiritual truth of the Dhamma. I accepted that, but it worried me. I came to the conclusion —which I still can't prove—that he was using the quotation to indicate that he was not sure of me. . . . Anyway, he gave me the addresses of three small pagodas around the city which so far have been free from disturbances, or from police picketing. He also gave me the names of the abbots, and of other monks who understood and spoke French . . ."

He broke off and sipped his wine as if he were trying to find words to convey his impression. Then a little self-consciously he went on. "I thought I was fairly well prepared for this assignment, sir, but I wasn't. When I went into the first pagoda, it was like a Lutheran going into a Catholic church in Sicily. Everything was strange, baroque, overloaded with images and silk and incense and flower offerings. After Japan, where everything is spare and disciplined, I found the whole atmosphere distasteful, even vulgar. The first monk who took me in charge was quite young. But he was French-educated, and he told me exactly what he wanted me to know. There was persecution and discrimination by the Government. The Catholics could meet whenever they liked. The Buddhists had to get official permission. Buddhists were kept out of the senior positions in the Government. The deaths in Hué were calculated murders and not simply the result of riots and disturbances. The Buddhists, who wanted nothing better than a life of good works and contemplation, had been forced to organize for their own protection. . . . Several hundred monks and nuns were still in prison, and many had been subjected to beatings and tortures to make them confess a Communist allegiance. I have to say that he made a good case, but it sounded too much like special pleading. There was no tolerance, no understanding such as one comes to expect of religious persons. However, when he saw that I went along with his story, he took me into one of the rooms where the community were turning out leaflets and letters with a battery of typewriters and a French duplicating machine. They were doing it very efficiently, too. I asked to see the abbot, but he told me that he was a very old man who spent a great deal of his time in contemplation. I kept pushing him, however, and finally I did get to see the abbot. He was very old and very frail, and he talked almost in a whisper. The young monk sat with us all the time, and all I could get out of the conversation was that the abbot was far advanced toward *Nirvana* and wished to be spared any worldly distraction. . . .

"The interview lasted only five minutes, and then I was back under the propaganda barrage. I asked whether there was any truth in the accusation that the *Sangha* was being infiltrated by Communist agents. You'd have thought I'd kicked over a beehive. They were angry, insulted, horrified—and determined that I should not get out of the place until they had convinced me that they were all loyal Viets who were being oppressed by a Catholic mandarin ruling by a mandate from a Christian heaven. When they finally let me go, they made sure that I was accompanied by another monk who was obviously charged to keep me pure from contaminating thoughts!"

"A couple of questions, George. Were they hostile to the Americans?"

"No, sir. They made a great point of approving what they called our strong action against tyranny. They spoke of their good relations with the American press, and it was pretty clear that they have an open pipeline to most of the senior correspondents in the city. It was also clear that they were organizing communications between themselves and other pagodas and that they were doing it quickly and effectively."

"Any talk of neutralism or the French?"

"In the first monastery, no. But in the second I did talk with the abbot, and I made a strong point of asking to confer with him in private. He was a much younger man this time—in his mid-fifties, I'd say. He was very cool and very polished. We drank tea together, and he questioned me for a long time about my own background in the way of enlightenment. He was quite prepared to discuss the influence of Communist expansion on the future of Buddhism. He claimed that those who accepted the Four Noble Truths must regard Marxism as a transitory phenomenon, which would be first transfused and then transformed by the teaching of the Lord Buddha. He was prepared to admit the existence of 'young and disturbed monks' in the monastic system. But these, too, he claimed, would be gradually changed by experience and meditation. When I spoke to him about the suicides, he corrected me. Suicide was a notion repugnant to Buddhism. However, he quoted the Lotus Sutra, which calls upon all Buddhists to sacrifice themselves if their religion is endangered. I asked him if there were any potential martyrs in his own pagoda. He told me that there was one very old nun who was prepared to immolate herself but that he had counseled her against it. Then I asked him whether he thought neutralism was desirable. He claimed that it was implicit in the teaching of the Gautama, since all physical solutions to man's ills were as transitory as man himself."

"Was there any propaganda machine in this pagoda?"

"I was not shown any, sir. I had the impression that the abbot himself was a strong man who was trying to preserve his autonomy. Again, you see, it was very difficult for me to come to any rigid conclusion. Finally I asked whether he could recommend any monastery where I might spend twenty-four hours going through the exercises with the monks and trying to draw at least some spiritual profit from my visit. He named one and gave me a letter to the abbot. That's where I spent the rest of the time, and that's where I think I first hit pay dirt. . . . There was a Frenchman there, who claimed he had fought at Dienbienphu and then become disillusioned with the West and all it stood for. According to his story, he had embraced Buddhism out of spiritual conviction and had spent nine years in this same pagoda."

"Was he an agent, do you think?"

"Possibly, yes. I shared his sleeping quarters. I sat with him during the readings of the Scriptures, and he translated them for me. We prayed together and we talked for a long time, walking around the garden of the pagoda. He was very practiced and very knowledgeable. He gave me what sounded like an eyewitness account of the last days of Dienbienphu and his escape after three months as a prisoner of war. He was no intellectual, but he certainly had a grasp of, and a sympathy with, the fundamental attitudes of Buddhism. He talked of a Buddhist renaissance in Asia, but when I suggested that this had a political base he rejected the idea out of hand. He claimed that this renaissance was a spiritual phenomenon based on the need of all men for peace and on the declaration of the Pali Sutra. 'The Lord Buddha has himself attained peace and preaches peace to all mankind.' When I spoke of the demonstrations and the riots, he dismissed them as 'spontaneous demonstrations of a people still imperfect but yet seeking the perfect way.' The action of the Government was aggressive, brutal and foolish beyond words! I talked of subversion in the pagodas, and I was surprised to find that he agreed with me. But he dismissed the question as unimportant since the perfection of the way would ultimately wipe out the imperfection of those who walked in it. President Cung he called 'a descendant of the old militant Christians who came with a cross in one hand and a moneybag in the other.' "

"It's a very comfortable point of view."

"Too comfortable for the man who professed it, sir." He leaned forward eagerly and made emphatic gestures, so that his wine spilled on the table and he was forced to mop it up as he talked. ". . . That was where the false note began to make itself heard. The man himself —his name is Armand Leroux—was far too intense, far too French if you want to be convincing as an apostle of quietism. Finally I tried to pin him down to specific answers. Did the Buddhists have legitimate grievances? . . . They had. How could they be redressed? . . . Only by a Buddhist government with a proportional representation of the minority Catholics. How could such a government be installed? . . . Call off the war. Neutralize South Vietnam and make a deal for peaceful co-existence with the North. How could the deal work? On a basis of mutual economic interest —and, of course, the leavening influence of Buddhism. Then, because he was too well launched to be discreet —or perhaps because the indiscretion was well calculated!—he pulled the ace out of his sleeve. He said . . . No, wait a minute, sir! I wrote it down because it seemed very important." He fumbled in his pockets and finally brought out a tattered envelope, from which he read verbatim. ". . . 'What the Americans fail to understand is that North and South Vietnam have a common interest: a historic fear and hatred of their onetime conquerors, the Chinese. No matter that Ho Chi Minh is armed and trained by them, he does not like them any more than Phung Van Cung does. This is why he will not escalate the war: because then the Chinese would overrun the North and use it as a military corridor. So even if the whole of Vietnam were Communist, it would still be united against China. This is where the Americans are fools. They spend dollars and blood to establish a buffer against China when they can have one for nothing—if they make an accommodation with Marxism and a friendship with Buddhism in Asia. This is where Cung is a reactionary. He is a Catholic who wants to preserve the Church at the expense of the nation. But if the Americans push him hard enough, he may well try to make his own deal with Ho Chi Minh. And then we will have the same result by a slightly longer process. . . .' "

"And that was all, George?"

"That was all, sir. He seemed to realize he'd said enough, and deliberately turned back to the question of meditation as a road to *Nirvana*. . . . I did a lot of meditating myself, and then decided it was time to come back and talk to you."

"It's a lot to think about, George. Can you knock me out a report?"

"Yes, sir. But it has to be incomplete. When I've done it, I'd like to go back again to the pagodas and fill in more gaps."

"I'd like you to do that—now try to summarize for me. First, there is subversion in the *Sangha?*"

"Yes. Extent unknown at this point."

"So President Cung scores one mark. Next, there is an indication of Pan-Buddhism?"

"An indication, but no proof."

"There is evidence of strong neutralist opinion?"

"Very strong evidence."

"Another mark for Cung! You would say also that there is a conviction that Buddhism can come to terms with Marxism, and, ultimately, modify it?"

"That conviction, I would say, is strong and wide-spread. The more so, I think, because the Viet Cong never make any attacks on pagodas or on the persons of the monks. On the contary, they often make prayers and offerings in the villages."

"And a final question: What is your personal reaction to this first contact with the Mahayana?"

His answer was slow in coming, but it was very definite. "I felt confusion, distaste and mistrust. But then I have been accustomed to a refined and intellectual variant. So I have to mistrust myself, too, sir."

"We all do, George. The problem is that everyone else wants us to be certain of ourselves—as if we carried the philosopher's stone in our pockets!"

He looked up sharply at that, and his young intelligent eyes searched my face. There was anxiety in them and, perhaps, a hint of fear. "You talk as if you'd had a rough time, sir."

"Very rough, George. And it's going to get worse."

I gave him a quick account of the events of the last forty-eight hours and of my own grievous uncertainties. He listened in silence, and when I had finished he sat for a long moment, tracing intricate patterns with his fork on the stained tablecloth. Finally he said:

"Two things seem to be clear, sir. It's going to cost you much more to be strong in patience and decisive in action. There are so many points of view and so much conflicting information that you simply cannot afford to let yourself be rushed, no matter what crisis arises. . . . The second problem is our own statecraft. Because we're committed to a military action we're committed by the same fact to short-term solutions, which historically can't be the right ones. Support Cung or stage a coup to get another regime! Satisfy the Buddhists and keep the Catholics happy, too. Drive the Viet Cong north of the border and seal the frontiers of Laos and Cambodia! But even if we do all that, we haven't solved anything. You can't seal up ideas like an imp in a bottle. You can't fight the Viet Cong and ignore China, the millennial giant with an exploding population and, for the first time in history, unified aim. How do we live with her for the next hundred years? How does the rest of Asia live with her? What about the Buddhists? Subversion or no subversion, they exist like Islam and Catholicism and Hinduism. There are no short-term solutions there either. . . . You can inhibit or even abort a revolution, but you cannot stop the evolutionary process that prompts it. . . . From one point of view, you can laugh at all those shave-pates in the pagoda chattering around a cheap mimeo machine. From another, you can call them dangerous enough to beat them over the head and slap them in jail. But they exist! They exist as men, as a society and as a symptom of inevitable change. If we say that we want to modify the change, then I think we have a case . . . as good a case as China or Russia or Ho Chi Minh. But if we say, as sometimes we appear to do, that we want to determine the nature of the change and guarantee its finality, then we're out of court and damned to an expensive failure. . . . I'm sorry, sir. I'm tired and off balance. But I am concerned about this. And concerned for you, too."

I was grateful to him and touched with a deep pity for his youth and idealism. But how could I tell him the bitter truth that change was not only the outcome of natural growth, that it was the result of struggle as well —whether the Christians defined it as a battle between good and evil or the Communists called it a Marxian dialectic or the Buddhists displayed it as the Gautama subduing Mara under the palm of his hand. How could I tell him the extent of my own commitment to action and the short-term solutions? . . .

I sent him to bed and sat up late, working over my papers. I was still working when Anne Beldon came in, late, from her party; so we invaded the kitchen and made ourselves coffee and talked of banal things till midnight.

CHAPTER SEVEN

The next morning there was an attempt on my life. It was crudely conceived and clumsily executed—but it was very nearly successful. The time was a few minutes after nine, and Bill Slavich was driving me from my home to the Embassy. As we turned the last corner into Ham Nghi, a circular parcel wrapped in newspaper was tossed into the road in front of the car. Slavich swerved sharply to avoid it, and the next moment it blew up. The explosion caught us broadside, shattered the side windows of the car and sent us sliding wildly across the street, so that we cannoned off a lamppost and slammed hard into a parked camion.

Bill Slavich was cut about the face, and I had a few minor lacerations of the hands and wrists as well as a pigeon's-egg bump on my temple. There was the usual crowd, a swift sally of police who hustled me down to the Embassy and then the thing was over like a cut from a television thriller. Bill Slavich went into conference with the police and with Harry Yaffa while Anne Beldon fussed to clean me up for my visit to the Ministry of Foreign Affairs.

I make no secret of it. I was shocked and shaken. A phrase from a childhood litany leaped to my mind: "From a sudden and unprovided death, O Lord deliver us." Death had been very near and had, in truth, found me unprovided. I drank a pair of whiskeys in swift succession and was surprised to find that I could scarcely hold my glass. My face in the washroom mirror was gray and pasty. Then the swift chemistry of reaction began and I was angry and elated at the same time—

angry with those who demanded the risk of our lives
and yet had no gratitude for it; elated that I should
be able to present myself at the Ministry wearing the
scars of an attempted assassination.

By the time I was ready to leave, the foyer of the
Embassy was jammed with newsmen and photographers. This was front-page drama for them, and I was
very willing that they should enjoy it and make a profit
for me at the same time. Harry Yaffa had added his
own touch of theater by demanding a police escort to
and from the Ministry and extra police protection for
my house and the approaches to the Embassy. So,
carrying my own time bomb in my breast pocket, I was
driven to the Ministry of Foreign Affairs with outriders
and men at arms!

My conference with the Minister was short and
stormy. I handed him our note and waited while he
read it. He told me with cold anger that the application
of sanctions was an unwarranted interference in the internal affairs of a sovereign state. Which, of course, was
true, though I could not admit it. I reminded him curtly
that we could hardly be expected to finance policies of
repression which set us at odds with the whole Buddhist
world. That made him even angrier and he claimed that
we could not have done worse if we had paid our aid
money directly to the Viet Cong. It was the opening I
had hoped for, and I took indecent advantage of it.

"If that is true, Mr. Minister, then perhaps it was not
the Viet Cong who tried to kill me this morning?"

He was shocked at the suggestion, and launched himself into a passionate disclaimer.

"A monstrous thought, Mr. Ambassador! A personal
insult to me and to my President. We have our differences and our difficulties, yes! But at bottom we
are still allies, fighting a common enemy. I beg you,
put such horrifying ideas out of your mind. I give you
my personal assurance that there will be a full inquiry
by our security teams and that we shall not rest until
the men responsible are brought to justice."

"I accept the assurance gladly, Mr. Minister. But I

remind you that it is your Government which lends color to these ugly suspicions. The accusations in the National Assembly, for instance, your conspicuous absence from the funeral of our marines, your own suggestion that our policies favor the Viet Cong—how else am I to read these things if not as public declarations of hostility to me and to my country?"

It was the usual barbed talk of unhappy diplomats, and of course, it did nothing at all to change the truth of the matter. We held the big stick, and we were beating the Government over the head with it. So, in spite of my verbal victory, I felt less than proud of myself as I drove back through the bright morning.

The streets of the city were crowded. The sun shone bravely after a night of rain, and there was an air of comforting animation about the people as if, for all their travail, for all the sinister commerce of plots and subversion, they were determined to eat, drink and be merry as they might under the puritan rule of Phung Van Cung. Had I died this morning, they would still be about their business, untouched and uncaring. Only the Christians would have prayed for me, being committed to a belief in my fraternity with them in the Communion of Saints. For the rest, my memory would have been buried in an hour under the vast indifference of Asia. It was a somber thought, and it brought me at one stride back to the consideration which George Groton had proposed the night before: To what end was all our expense of money, diplomacy, work and human blood? Once again I recalled the dictum of Musō Soseki: "You are called upon to counsel and advise, and so, in fact, you may help to propose the ends that are later proposed to you. . . ." Already I had seen this happen. But in everything I had proposed I had limited myself to the short-term and the transitory. I had not yet been prepared to examine for myself those points of view which were in conflict with the current policy of the United States. Yet this surely was implicit in my commission, and if I did not address myself to it the swift and violent onrush of events would find me unprepared.

When I reached the Embassy, I found the place in a ferment. The switchboard was jammed with calls from other Embassies asking for details of the assassination attempt. The press were still calling for color and comment to add to their dispatches, and there was a steady coming and going of odd characters who conferred with Harry Yaffa and his minions. The drama was getting out of hand, so I issued an instruction to clear the premises as quickly as possible and return to the normal order of business. I called a meeting of my senior aides for two o'clock and then settled down to my own daily dispatches.

The news from the United Nations was informative. A Russian move to send to South Vietnam the old Indo-China Control Commission had been defeated. Instead the President of the U.N. Assembly had nominated Afghanistan, Brazil, Ceylon, Costa Rica, Dahomey, Morocco and Nepal as the countries to conduct the Buddhist inquiry. The Commissioners were expected to arrive within a week. I found a certain grim humor in the thought of a gentleman from Dahomey trying to make sense of Asian subtleties and the man from Ceylon being impartial about the wrongs of his co-religionists. However, the Commission was Cung's problem and not mine, and I was happy to leave him to cope with it.

Festhammer's cable was brief, but it carried a sting in its tail.

APPROVE YOUR ACTION ON SANCTIONS. APPROVE CONTACT OUTSIDE NORMAL DIPLOMATIC CHANNELS WITH OPPOSITION OPINION. HOWEVER, SINCE FINANCIAL SANCTIONS MUST ULTIMATELY WEAKEN WAR EFFORT, WE MUST CONSIDER A SUITABLE TIME LIMIT WITHIN WHICH EITHER A RECONCILIATION OF AIMS IS ACHIEVED WITH CUNG REGIME OR ALTERNATIVE ACTION IS RECOMMENDED. SENATE AND CONGRESS OPINION GENERALLY IN FAVOR OF SANCTIONS, BUT SENATOR GOLDING HAS RAISED STRONG VOICE FOR NEUTRALISM. HE

COULD PROVE RALLYING POINT FOR CUT-BACKS IN
AID BUDGET AND ISOLATIONIST OPINION GENER-
ALLY. ADMINISTRATION WOULD WELCOME ANY
NOTE OF CONFIDENCE WHICH YOU COULD INJECT
INTO PUBLIC STATEMENTS AND EMBASSY DIS-
PATCHES.

This was pure Festhammer, who always wanted to
have his cake, eat it, too, and then be given a pill to
cure his indigestion. I had enough problems of my own
without worrying over the bellyaches of some portly
Senator in Washington. Yet if enough Senators belched
loudly enough they could make a great wind, strong
enough indeed to flurry the palms and ruffle the gray
waters of the Mekong River.

Then, sandwiched between a situation summary and
a request for information on the financial returns of the
U. S. Operations Mission, I found another barb. This
was a short note from the desk of the Secretary of State.

The attached clipping was sent to us from our
Ambassador in Paris. The report could be pure
fabrication since it is unconfirmed by any of our
sources in South Vietnam. Would you please investigate and send us urgent comment.

The clipping was from a Socialist daily and was nearly two weeks old. It was signed Claude Gemelle, and it
purported to be the record of private and exclusive interview with President Cung. The concluding lines of
the text were circled in red ink.

Finally the President, with obvious bitterness,
said to me, "The Americans claim that I am pursuing a policy which must ultimately benefit the
Viet Cong and the Communist Party in North
Vietnam. I tell them, on the contrary, that it is
they who push me into the arms of Ho Chi Minh
and force me to consider desperate measures to
end the misery of my country." . . . When I

pressed him to explain further he refused, saying that his meaning was quite clear to anyone who had studied the situation in South Vietnam. And that was the end of my interview.

It was one of those cryptic passages on which a certain type of journalist builds a reputation for shrewdness and profundity, and it had obviously been edited to convey a double meaning. On the other hand, it bore a curious resemblance to the report which Groton had given me of his talk with Armand Leroux in the pagoda. It could therefore be a plant—part of a careful design of indoctrination to prepare the minds of the public for a political move. For that reason alone it deserved to be checked. I laid the clipping aside and made a note to discuss it with Yaffa and Mel Adams. I had Anne Beldon telephone my house and ask George Groton to join us at the conference and bring the basic notes on his talks in the pagodas.

When I had worked through the most urgent papers and drafted the day's cables, it was already a quarter to two, just time enough for a sandwich, a cup of coffee and a hurried preview of the agenda for the conference. I knew what I needed at this moment: a concerted exploration of all the possibilities open to us and a frank discussion of policies—even those which might seem at first glance inimical to our interests. Whether I would get it was another matter. The Service is notoriously thankless to men of original minds and strong convictions, and it is hard to ask a man to gamble a whole career on an unpopular proposition. I was not sure either whether any of my staff—with the exception of Groton—had enough confidence in me to hazard himself in my hand. The opening gambit was, therefore, the critical one, and I prepared it with considerable care.

". . . This afternoon, gentlemen, I want to engage you all in a theoretical exercise. I want to put before you a number of propositions and ask you to explore their consequences in open discussion. The conference will not be recorded and no one will be expected to assume any personal responsibility for any view which he expresses—however extreme it may be. If anyone wants to make a public defense of Ho Chi Minh or Chou En-lai he is welcome to do it. The purpose of the conference is to clear my own mind and give me a chance to take the broadest possible view of the situation in which we now find ourselves. One final point. There will be no set speaking order, and if you want to debate across the table I shall be happy for you to do it. . . . Here is the first proposition. The French propose that South Vietnam declare itself a neutral country. Suppose we agreed with their proposal. Could it be done? How could it be done? And with what consequences?"

There was a short embarrassed pause while they looked at one another and waited for someone to open the argument. Finally George Groton spoke:

"I'm the junior. So I'll start the ball rolling if you like. South Vietnam could neutralize itself tomorrow by a simple declaration and a request to the U.N. to guarantee its neutrality. We are then asked to withdraw. A bargain is struck with Ho Chi Minh to call off the war and stop the infiltration of troops and military supplies. The Government of South Vietnam is then free to enter into diplomatic and economic relations with both East and West. . . ."

"Then," said the military attaché, "Ho Chi Minh disclaims all responsibility for what happens in South Vietnam while secretly fomenting rebellion. The Viet Cong go underground for a while and emerge again as a local protest against local tyranny. Result, a civil war, like they have in Laos."

"Let's go along with the argument," said Mel Adams quietly. "There is rebellion. Cung is overthrown—which he well may be anyway. It is not at all clear that the next government would be Marxist. It certainly would not be pro-Chinese, because Vietnam does not want to be a puppet of China. Both halves of the country would have trained armies which could certainly be

united against Chinese military aggression. Even with
Marxist or near Marxist rule in Cambodia and Laos
and Vietnam there is no certainty of expansionist policies, against Thailand, for instance. I would guess that
the reverse might be true. The people are tired of war. I
think they would settle for economic betterment even
under a Marxist system."

"So you sell out three million Christians!" This from
the Second Secretary, a dour, craggy fellow with a crew
cut and heavy spectacles. "You sell out the million refugees who came south for resettlement after partition?
You abandon the self-help and education programs in
the hamlets and let confusion come again?"

"I don't think it's a question of a sellout at all," persisted Mel Adams stubbornly. "There would be confusion, yes, but it would be at least what we stand for—or
say we stand for—a chance for self-determination. As I
see it, the military elements are fairly evenly matched
and there is a strong ground for economic co-operation
between North and South."

"I think it's all a pretty theory," said Harry Yaffa
harshly. "You've got two elements—a local revolutionary movement and the enormous outside pressure
of China. Look at the stretch and strength of that pressure—from the Sea of Japan, to the Gulf of Tonkin, to
Outer Mongolia, to the Himalayas and the desert of
Takla Makan. . . . Do you think she can be contained
by a declaration of neutrality and a mixed bunch of
U.N. troops on the seventeenth parallel?"

"Do you think she can be contained by twenty-odd
thousand military advisers in South Vietnam?"

"Of course not. She's being contained by the Russians in the North, by the Seventh Fleet and the threat of
the atom bomb."

"All of which would still be there."

"Without the foothold we have now on the Asian
mainland."

The antagonism between the two men was breaking

out again and threatening to wreck the meeting. I interposed a question of my own:

"Could we ourselves remove the Chinese pressure by diplomatic recognition, removal of trade embargoes and voting for her admission to the United Nations? Could we then regard any local revolution as an indigenous growth, to be accepted on its own merits in due course?"

"No!" said Yaffa flatly. "Marxism is an expansionist philosophy."

"You can't kill a philosophy."

"So what then, sir? Do you accept it?"

"You may have to live with it."

"Peaceful co-existence? That's Khrushchev's gambit. But China doesn't accept it. China proclaims the old Stalin line—inevitable war."

"Stalin is dead. Mao Tse-tung and Chou En-lai are old men."

"But China still needs the rice bowls and she wants a seaway to Africa."

"Can she not have them by free trade with neutral Asian countries?"

"Can you guarantee that she would be content with that?"

"Hong Kong represents a working arrangement, at least."

The argument went around and around the table for another twenty minutes, and it was clear that we would never reach finality. So I posed a more local question:

"Given that we stay in South Vietnam—and that's a decision for Washington, anyway!—given our present problems with Cung and the Buddhists, at what point do we back a change of government?"

"The sooner the better," said Yaffa bluntly. "Unless you want the Buddhists to start a revolution of their own. Already there's word of a possible split in the Army and the formation of a third force to fight the Viet Cong and the President alike. It's a pipe dream, of course, because if they tried it the third force would be out of money and bullets in a month. Inevitably they'd join the Viet Cong."

"I say we back nobody," said Mel Adams. "We force the opposition to prove its own cohesion. And we reserve our own right to recognize or not recognize a new *de facto* government."

This provoked a new cross fire of opinions, and once again it was clear that my staff were fairly evenly divided between Adams and Yaffa. If anything, they leaned toward Yaffa as the man who had the more information at his disposal and must therefore be the more practical realist. It was a dubious proposition at best, and it troubled me that so many of my people were prepared to accept it at face value. Then George Groton stepped back into the argument with a real dilemma for Harry Yaffa:

"There's something I'd like to be clear on. We agree that any new government would lean heavily on Buddhist support and would probably be composed of a majority of Buddhist generals. Is that correct, Mr. Yaffa?"

"That's about the size of it. Yes."

"But it seems to me that Buddhist opinion in the pagodas is strongly in favor of neutralism. So are you not backing what you condemned at first: a neutralist, or potentially neutralist, regime?"

Yaffa flushed angrily and answered, "A neutralist Army regime would be a contradiction in terms."

"But Buddhism is naturally inclined to the reconciliation of opposites."

"That's theory. In practice it's quite different."

"How different? If the Cung regime is unsteady, it's because the Buddhists are rocking the boat. Couldn't they rock their own boat just as much—generals or no generals?"

It was a point well taken, and perversely, I wanted him to enjoy the victory. So I broke in again and passed around the table the clipping from the Paris press. I made no comment on it, but simply invited their opinions. Most were inclined to dismiss it as a provocative

generality, but Harry Yaffa frowned over it for a long-
ish while and then said:

"I'd like to think about this for a while, sir, and
check through my files. As a matter of procedure we
keep tabs on visiting journalists, and I may have something on this Claude Gemelle. . . . I've noticed something curious lately. Ever since the Buddhist trouble
started, the local correspondents have been very hostile
to Cung. So he's started feeding out comment through
visiting firemen: representatives of the foreign Catholic
press, magazine writers and stringers for odd journals
who drift in and out of Saigon, looking for features.
Cung's a man who talks freely but always measures his
words. So if he said this, or anything like it, I want to
know the real text."

"I think we may have a little information that relates
to it."

I asked George Groton to report on his visits to the
pagodas and especially on his talk with the Frenchman,
Armand Leroux. This provoked a new frown from
Yaffa and a lift of eyebrows from Mel Adams, but they
both listened in silence until Groton's narration was
done. Then Mel Adams shook his head.

"It's interesting, sir, but incomplete. I don't think we
can base any strategy on it."

"I know the information's incomplete," said Groton
eagerly. "But it seems to me we need to know much
more than we do now about the Buddhists. Especially if
we're being asked to change the Government to favor
their interests. I've read all the available reports. There
are too many gaps and some downright inaccuracies."

"I think, for a tyro, Mr. Groton has done a good
job." Yaffa's tone was studiously flat. "I think he might
continue to turn up useful information because of his
specialized background. However, if you let him go
ahead, Mr. Ambassador, he should be informed of the
risks."

"What risks in particular, Mr. Yaffa?"

"Armand Leroux, for one. He talks like a Frenchman, but in point of fact he's a Georgian—a long-time agent in this part of the world."

"Then why does the Government let him work unchecked?"

"Because he works for me, Mr. Ambassador—but he also gets paid by the French and the Russians. He shares the information he gets and collects a fee from all of us. But when a nonprofessional like Mr. Groton here begins to wander into the business. Armand Leroux might be very happy to collect a fee on him, too."

"Meaning what?"

"Kidnapping Mr. Groton. It's a favorite sport here. Great moral victory for the Viet Cong. They carry the victim around in a cage, or trussed to a pole like a pig to impress the peasants. . . . I'm not exaggerating. I'm not putting you off the project either. But I would suggest, Mr. Ambassador, that if Mr. Groton is going to continue we'd better give him some training—and a little protection as well. After this morning we can't rule out the chance of murder either."

It made sound sense, and I was not prepared to quarrel with it. I agreed—not without the afterthought that the arrangement might give me a pipeline into the secret activities of Harry Yaffa. There was one question still to be answered:

"Is there any connection, Mr. Yaffa, between the report in the Paris newspaper and the views expressed by Armand Leroux?"

"I don't know," said Yaffa dubiously. "But I do intend to find out. Leave it with me for a few days. I'll report to you as soon as I get something definite."

At that point, with a few words of thanks, I closed the meeting. I was wiser only in the knowledge that Yaffa and Mel Adams were the best professionals I had, that George Groton would probably grow to match them—and that I myself could never abdicate the rude solitude of executive decision.

Embassy cocktail parties are a necessary evil of the trade. They strain the memory, the courtesy and the digestion. They conduce to scandal, fallen arches and jealousies among the women. I have not met one diplomat who truly enjoys them—and yet no one has devised a better vehicle for that peculiar commerce of hints, harmonic overtones, unwritten warnings and out-of-court dealings which is the business dialect of diplomacy. Because one is expected to be bored, one can ignore what one does not wish to hear. It is demanded that one circulate, so it is always possible to slide out of a transaction or an argument. Because the party always takes place at the end of a business day, one has the right to be tired and to withdraw into a private corner to conclude a bargain or settle a dispute.

But even inside this framework of custom and convention there are certain interesting variations. The French, for example, cultivate wit and modish dress, but they are apt to be stodgy with canapés and drinks. The Indians serve uneatable food and are either waspish or embarrassingly earnest in conversation. The Swedes, when sober, are studiously formal, and the Japanese, who drink nobly at a geisha party, can turn a cocktail party into Kabuki drama at the flick of a fan. The Thais are pliant, good-humored and devilishly hard to corner, while the Americans are fluent, voluble and occasionally tone-deaf. The South Americans are so incredibly elegant that one wonders if all our aid funds are spent on dressing their wives or mistresses. But only the English have made a fine art of dullness and a whole literature out of the swallowed sentence and the urbane understatement. Their food is generally mediocre, their drinks underproof and their welcome tepid. One does not arrive; one lapses into the party. One does not talk; one chats. One is never cosseted, but never uncomfortable either, so that by the end of the evening it is all too easy to surrender to an illusion of domesticity and tell secrets of state to the cool charmer with the noble bosom and the Mona Lisa smile.

The English in the tropics have a special and seductive charm. By some strange genetic reaction from their dismal climate, they flourish while others wilt.

Their urbanity matches the subtlety of Asia, and the resolute Englishry of their surroundings has a tone all its own—like the Beefeaters of the Changing of the Guard. So, after a fairly dramatic day, I was not displeased to surrender myself to the hospitality of my British colleague. He was obviously not a heavyweight, otherwise he would never have been relegated to a post where British influence was minimal; but he was very practiced and very shrewd. He led me through the introductions quickly, put a drink in my hand, whispered something about a private talk later and left me to fend for myself with a poker-faced Chinese from Taiwan and an Italian who looked like Dante Alighieri.

I was, I found, something of a celebrity. There might be, and there were, many reserves about my diplomatic mission; but to have been bombed in a public thoroughfare—*ecco!* This was already a reputation! It was also a passport to the favor of the ladies, some of whom were beautiful and none of whom seemed available. Then, all too quickly, the gilt wore off and the mice began nibbling at the gingerbread.

The man from Malaysia inquired pointedly about American attitudes toward Indonesia and her policy of confrontation. The Thai made a guarded comment on the Buddhist situation and expressed a frank fear of neutralist tendencies in South Vietnam. The German wanted to know how he should interpret the withdrawal of military personnel and whether he should counsel German investors to stay out of Saigon. The Japanese was worried about finance because his people were building hulls for President Cung's Navy. The Laotian had some harsh things to say about Harry Yaffa and the CIA, while the Dane who ran only a legation talked about duck feathers (for stuffing the pillows of Europe) and mines in the Saigon channel (which might stop him shipping them out).

The Frenchman, who had obviously modeled himself on *le grand Charles,* stood aloof and ironic while the lesser breeds talked themselves out; then he led me into a corner and read me a well-prepared lecture on the mistakes of Dienbienphu and the illusion of a military solution for South Vietnam. Had he been more subtle and less patently superior, I might have been a better listener. Instead I gave him a discourse of my own on French business methods, the activities of French agents and the danger of subsidizing a new revolution after the sorry mess they had made of the first one. To my surprise, he took it quite calmly and then gave me a brief, blunt reading of my own horoscope:

". . . Let me tell you, dear colleague, what will happen. I will go further, I will make a bet with you—a hundred dollars! You think President Cung will bow to your pressures? He will not! He cannot! He is a Jansenist saint, vowed to defend the last foothold of Christianity in Asia. He mistrusts the Buddhists—not without reason. So he cannot ever come to terms with them —because they will not let him. What then? You will be forced to join with those who want to get rid of him. They will make you, oh, great promises—unity, discipline, all the rest. But they will not be able to honor the promises. Why? Because they will be too busy cutting up the cake among themselves. The war will drag on, six months, a year, and your own Congress will force you to break it off. You will still be forced to neutralize, but you will have to make a worse bargain than the one you can make now—the one Cung is already meditating, believe me!"

"It's a strange thing. I've heard that same story three times in as many days—but always from a French source."

"So the source is tainted—is that it? *Eh, bien!* The bet still stands if you want it."

"I'll take it. . . . And I'll check the report, too."

"You will lose, my friend. Because you have to lose. Oh, I know we have made our own mistakes here! We have paid dearly for them. But you are slower to learn even than we were. No one can stop revolution in Asia. It grows out of the ground like the trees in Angkor Wat —the trees that ate the city and toppled it in ruins. You may defer it a little, but in the end you will have to come to terms with it. . . . Remember! The armies died and the elephants died and all the armor rusted, and in the end the trees ate the city!"

With that he turned away and left me looking out at the garden and the hostile shapes of the mango trees. Then the bland voice of my host cut into my reverie.

"Intelligent chap, isn't he? Quite pleasant when he wants to be. But perhaps a little too intense, wouldn't you say?"

For the next five days I lived in another world: the world of the fighting man, the infantry soldier, the bomber pilot, the helicopter crews and the lone, jungle-lean veterans of special operations. I traveled in transports, armed helicopters and jeeps. I tramped through red mud and farmyard offal and the sand of mountain rivers. I flew with a fighter escort just south of the seventeenth parallel and looked down, over the mountaintops, into the stronghold of Ho Chi Minh. I skirted the borders of Laos and Cambodia, where the rivers run westward until the mighty Mekong breaks eastward into the South China Sea. The place names built themselves into a weird Oriental melody over the beat of the engines—Huong Hoa, Bau Don, Budop, Quan Loi, Tanchau, Chaudoc and Mui Ca Mau.

Everywhere I went I was hedged by armor—in the air by fighters, on the ground by infantry and armed troop carriers and hovering whirlybirds. General Tolliver was taking no chances. I was the representative of the United States, the named man of the President—a rich prize for any guerrilla chief bold enough to attempt my capture. In the helicopters they dressed me in a flak jacket and put a steel plate under my backside to protect my spine and my genitals against ground fire striking upward through the thin metal skin of the chopper.

I stood in a captured field post and inspected the pile of weapons, from China and Prague and Russia, and more sinister still, from our own ordnance factories. I saw the bodies of the Viet Cong laid out in the sun, with the flies feeding on their wounds. They were small, brown and tattered, but muscular and well fed. Their field reports, taken from their bodies, were accurate and professional. They were hardy soldiers, skilled in the tactics of this shadowy war.

In a mountain village surrounded by primitive tribesmen and their bare-breasted women, I talked with a junior-grade lieutenant who was training them in search-and-clear operations against the northern raiders. With Tolliver always at my side, I padded through fortified villages ringed with ramparts of mud and walls of spiked bamboo. In their rough dispensaries children were being inoculated against smallpox and cholera, while young Americans, scarcely out of college, taught them to bury their offal, drain their swamps, grow sweet potatoes and cultivate red squill to kill the rats that infested their crops.

I learned at first hand the problems of a divided military command, the jealousies of local headmen and provincial governors and the frustration of field officers whose front line was the next paddy field and who might wait for ten hours for reinforcements because village radio networks failed to function or because the local militia would not move at night for fear of wandering spirits!

In Cai Nuoc, I saw the grisly relics of a Viet Cong attack, a pile of burned bodies—men, women and children—and twenty-five battered survivors from a garrison of a hundred men. It was a brutal lesson on the nature of this war and a damning indictment of political intrigue and ineptitude. Small wonder that the villager and the peasant were ready to make their own accommodations to the situation—and to hell with the generals and the mandarins!

Yet this was only part of the story. For all his personal shortcomings, Phung Van Cung had laid down, in less than ten years, a massive framework for the reconstruction of his country. Even now, under the stress of war, the framework still held together. Agriculture was being improved, commerce and industry were expanding. Social medicine was being taught in every hamlet, and public communication by radio and newspaper and village duplicating machine was bringing the country folk into closer touch with the twentieth century. Granted that his methods were harsh; they were no harsher than those of his onetime collaborator, Uncle Ho. Granted that there were corruption and peculation in high places, public administration at the township level was based solidly on the family system and was, for Asia, remarkably efficient. Properly trained and equipped, led by disciplined officers, the Viet was a good fighter. He did not lack courage, only the confidence in his field commanders and in the good faith of his General Staffs. He was a good improviser, too. I saw carbines and pistols, and even a Lee-Enfield copy, tooled in village smithies. I found matter for pride, too, in the quality of our own fighting men and in the dedication of the members of our Civil Aid teams and the scattered units of our Operations Mission who shared the life of the people, and brought them, at singular risk and hardship, the knowledge of a more evolved technology.

Each night after mess I sat with General Tolliver and his local commanders and reviewed with them the events and impressions of the day. It was a chastening experience to hear the talk of these men—veterans all —and to feel their sympathy and understanding for the folk whom they had come to serve. They were not cynics—though God knows they had reason to be! They had complaints: that military operations were hampered by political pressures; that President Cung disliked casualty lists and was unwilling to mount strong and persistent attacking operations; that night operations were discouraged and that provincial governors were reluctant to collaborate with military commanders. But to the common folk they were warm and welcome, and they spent themselves in efforts far beyond the military contract.

Tolliver himself was reserved at first, having a healthy mistrust of all politics. But, as our progress continued, he warmed to me, and I to him. He had his own private resentment: that he had been forced too many times to make military prophecies to satisfy the Pentagon and visiting Senators. In his view all such prophecy was meaningless. So long as we were prepared to pump in men and equipment, so long as we had air power and the Seventh Fleet, we could maintain a military operation in South Vietnam for a long time. But there was no end in sight, no major decisive action to be mounted; and certainly there was no hope of victory. He made an interesting point, which I recorded in detail in my notes.

". . . What people forget is that we are up against one of the greatest military strategists of modern times, General No Nguyen Giap. This is the man who staged —yes, literally staged—the collapse of Dienbienphu. He knew the traditional French weakness for a set-piece battle. So he let de Castries assemble twelve thousand men along a river valley with two airfields in the middle. They had everything they needed—air communication, heavy artillery, tanks . . . the whole works! They knew, too, that Giap had no artillery and was short of supplies. So it looked like a pushover. The single, classic, decisive action—and boomph! it's all over! But the French didn't reckon with the Chinese. They gave General Giap two hundred field guns. Giap had them dismantled and carried piece by piece on the backs of men who hacked paths out of the jungle and walked sometimes fifty miles a day. To get food for his troops Giap set up a relay run of Chinese coolies, each with a bicycle loaded with bagged rice. . . . They set up the guns on the ridges around Dienbienphu, they tunneled under the French outposts and they laid a ring of sixty thousand men around the valley. Then the rains came and the French couldn't move! In fifty-six days it was all finished. . . . Now that same Giap is conducting the war against South Vietnam. For him it's the same war because Phung Van Cung is just a running dog of imperialist America! But Giap's too shrewd to rely on the old strategy. He knows we won't fall for it either. He's even bold enough to announce his new one. You heard it on Hanoi radio last night . . . 'The enemy will move slowly from the offensive to the defensive and will be caught in a dilemma: he has to drag out the war in order to win it, but he does not possess the psychological or the political resources to fight a long-drawn war!' . . . You notice the way he puts it. He knows our physical resources are almost unlimited. But politically the country is shot to hell. . . ."

"And that's why Phung Van Cung is always talking about the psychology of the people."

"Exactly . . . and the real tragedy is that we can do very little about either the psychology or the politics. Because we still don't understand them perfectly."

"But Cung understands them?"

"The psychology, yes. But the politics will beat him."

"Then who can lick the politics in time?"

"Not the politicians," said Tolliver with a grin. "Look at us! The last battle of our own Civil War is still being fought on the issue of desegregation! And who's holding up the fight? The same kind of people as you've met here, politicos, grafters and carpetbaggers! . . . Let's go to bed, Ambassador! We head back to Saigon at sunrise."

That night I lay wakeful, listening to the honking of frogs in the nearby rice paddies and the measured, reassuring tramp of the sentries. I had hoped that my tour of the combat areas would give me a new line of thought on the crisis. Instead I found that all the lines converged on the same person and the same problem: Phung Van Cung, and whether he could hold power long enough to complete the work he had begun so well.

I had seen his problems at first hand now. I had seen, too, the monumental shape of his plan for the country. He was a building man, and in the field it was far easier to admire his work than in the confines of a sophisticated and disillusioned city. In the country, too, the conflict between Buddhist and Christian was less apparent. In some places there was no conflict at all because of the simplicity, the ignorance and, occasionally, the charity of monk and missionary alike. One thing, however, had become very clear to me. Unless Cung himself were prepared to display himself to his own people, to focus their loyalties on his own person, then all his apparatus of control and development would avail him nothing. He might immobilize for a while the strong men who opposed him, but he could build nothing on second-rate officials who had no appeal for the country communities or the disparate races who made up the population.

What then? I was the man who held the scales in balance. I was prepared to throw my weight in Cung's favor. But he mistrusted me and rejected my counsel. And over us all hung the shadow of General Giap, the master chess player who looked down from the North and saw the game whole, knowing who were the pawns and who the foolish bishops and when the castles would fall to his patient strategy.

Legally my position was clear. I had no right at all to pass judgment on Phung Van Cung, nor to make any determination of his political future. In fact, the pressure of events and circumstances was forcing me into the position of an arbiter of his destiny. All at once I was judge, jury, prosecutor and counsel for the defense. I was his banker, yes. But what more might a banker demand than fair collateral for his money? I was his adviser, but if he had no liberty to reject my advice, then I was the usurper. . . . And yet, and yet . . . I was none of these things. I was the paid servant of my country, the agent of her policies, good or bad. But my President had told me, "You are more than a servant and more than an agent. You are my eyes and my ears and my tongue. I trust you to act for me and to accept either the honors of success or the penalties of failure." So I was back in court, with the fate of a man and a country hanging on my verdict.

Far away across the marshes I heard the rattle of gunfire. Then there was quiet again, stirred only by the honking of the bullfrogs and the comforting tread of the sentries inside the barbed wire.

CHAPTER EIGHT

I arrived back in Saigon with a bag full of notes and a fund of new confidence. Now at least I could weigh the information that was given me, and weigh the men who gave it as well. There had been no major moves during my absence, but the curfew had been lifted and a large number of students and monks had been released from detention. Radio Saigon and the Government-controlled press had made a series of attacks on our sanctions, but these were simply echoes of Cung's speech in the National Assembly, and I was not disposed to make any reply. The airlift of administrative personnel had already begun, and was expected to be completed within two weeks.

President Cung had kept his promise and sent me a long document on Communist subversion in the pagodas. I read it very carefully, and found it a competent if not wholly satisfactory compilation. There were enough facts to demand caution and justify surveillance, but there was too much conjecture to justify large-scale repression of the whole *Sangha*. Too much emphasis was laid on the riots and the public gatherings, which were prompted as much by police brutality as by subversive activity. The charges against Harry Yaffa and the CIA were expounded at great length, but the evidence in support of them was sketchy, to say the least; while some of it was clearly based on confessions extracted under duress.

I handed the report to Mel Adams, who came to the same conclusion. Harry Yaffa read it, too; but he had a different opinion.

"It's been doctored, Mr. Ambassador! Cung and his boys know a great deal more than they admit. They're deliberately vague about our activities, and the agents they mention are the least important."

"Then why bother sending me the report at all?"

"That's clear enough, I think. Cung made the promise to send it, and he had to honor the promise or lose face. It's my guess that his security people kicked up a fuss because a true report, in my hands and yours, could compromise some of their own people. Their security system is a multilevel affair, too, and they would lose more than they gained by listing all the available information."

"I promised, as you know, to send a copy of that document to Washington. Any objections?"

"None at all, Mr. Ambassador. But I'd like to add a few comments."

I had no objection to that either. I was more interested to find out what new information Yaffa had for me. It was a good deal more than I had expected in so short a time.

". . . First of all, George Groton flew up to Hué the day after you left. I got him an introduction to the principal abbot there—strangely enough through the Rector of the University of Hué, a Catholic cleric who resigned after the first shootings and is now under a kind of house arrest in the Archbishop's residence in Saigon. Groton spent two days in the pagoda, and there he heard a whisper about an organization called the South Vietnam National Liberation Front. This tied up with some new information out of Cambodia. We've known for some time that Sihanouk has been in touch with Vietnamese exiles in Paris and, with the help of the French, has been trying to set up a neutralist party. Now we have a name for it."

"The French again!"

"That's right. But so long as they stay under cover and let the Cambodians do the negotiating, a neutralist organization might well gather some local strength."

"What about the Communist influence in Hué?"

"Not too much evidence. Groton reported a strongly nationalist feeling, which is natural enough, because Hué is the old cultural capital of the country. There is, however, a highly organized opposition to the Cung regime and very active propaganda for a coup."

"Led by whom?"

"General Khiet, the corps commander in the delta. He was born in Hué, and comes from an old and respected Buddhist family."

"Groton's doing well then."

"Very well."

"Where is he now?"

"In Cambodia, sir. We gave him a civilian passport and a tourist visa and suggested he might like to look at Angkor Wat and then do a little talking to Buddhists in Pnompenh. He might get onto one of the pipelines that lead back into this country."

This was beyond the terms of my original brief, but I could hardly object to it without seeming to show a special favor to Groton. So I let the matter drop.

Yaffa went on, "I've also checked out that news report from Paris. Claude Gemelle is a freelance who drifted in here about a month ago and stayed a week, interviewing various people. He's not a known agent. Some of the people he interviewed are friends of ours, and his reports on them are substantially accurate. So the chances are the Cung report was accurate, too."

"Accurate but still vague."

"That's right, sir."

"Could it, in your view, bear the meaning that Cung is prepared to make a deal with the North if we push him too far?"

"It could."

"Is there any way, short of a frontal attack, that we could get him to repeat the statement?"

"I've been thinking about that, too. But he certainly won't repeat it to any of the local press . . . And you can be sure he won't make it to a diplomat."

"I'm not so sure of that."

"How come, sir?"

I told him of my cocktail conversation with the Frenchman, and he frowned unhappily.

"It doesn't tie up, Mr. Ambassador. Not with the Cambodians and the exiles and the National Liberation Front."

"It might, you know. Look at Cung's position! He is threatened by a revolt of the generals. There is more than talk of a third force to split the Army. Then there's a neutralist move started in Cambodia and Paris. It's a three-pronged threat, so Cung might well decide in desperation to make an approach to the North while he still has bargaining power."

"But if the French know that, and approve it, why are they backing the exiles and the Cambodians?"

"A maneuver—a feint, if you like! More pressure on Cung to drive him to a decisive move. Any kind of alliance between North and South gives the French an economic and diplomatic advantage. . . . I don't think we should rule out the possibility."

"If it is true," asked Yaffa thoughtfully, "if Cung is meditating a deal, where do we stand? Do we let him make it or do we give the password and precipitate the coup?"

"That's a matter of high policy. I'd have to refer it to Washington. My guess is they would opt for the coup. They've spent too much and committed themselves too far to agree to a handshake deal with Uncle Ho."

"Then I'd better make this the number one project for all our people."

"Do that, Mr. Yaffa. But impress on them that I must have facts. I cannot make or recommend any more on conjecture."

"I know that, sir. We'll do the best we can."

And there, perforce, the matter rested. There were five days' papers on my desk and a long report to be written on my tour. Anne Beldon and I worked through the afternoon and into the night, and the mountain of paper was still only half diminished.

It is hard for me, after all that has happened, to describe the relationship that grew between us in the long privacies of our work. She is still in the Service, and I would not wish her exposed to scandal or detraction. And yet she is part of this chronicle. There are some women to whom, even in passion, one can never dare to reveal oneself because they demand instantly a possession and a proprietorship of the soul as well as the body. When they are refused it, they become sour and shrewish, because they have no sweetness in themselves. There are others for whom giving is the true nature of love, and these are the only ones with whom it is possible to enjoy an intimacy while maintaining a professional relationship. The cynics may smile if they will, and the gossips may whisper behind their hands; but when one has known a deep and satisfying love— and both Anne Beldon and I had known it—one is reluctant to commit oneself to the consequences of a sudden passion. In public we were formal with each other. In private we were easy, and grateful for the comfort of companionship. We did not skirmish with words, nor flirt with the subtle gestures of affection. There was too much risk in that for both of us, though the risk was never mentioned.

Since Gabrielle's death I had grown niggardly with my confidence, but I opened myself to her and she responded frankly. I told her of my dilemmas and my fears of myself, and she was wise enough to admit that she was afraid for me, too. I talked of my affection for George Groton, and she understood the craving of the childless for a continuity of themselves. She had it, too, though she had learned to master it, knowing herself so much more vulnerable. It was this affectionate maturity of heart and mind which drew me to her most strongly. She had what I believe the moralists call a formed conscience—a tolerant, easygoing acceptance of the follies of the world, but a clear view of the ones she had committed herself and was determined not to commit again. She had a quick humor, and a quick temper, too, which most of the time she managed to hold in check. She was never coy, though she never lapsed into that coarseness of speech which many women of the world affect.

Had she had lovers after the death of her husband? I never asked her. Was she in love with me? Yes—though when I found out it was already too late. Was I in love with her? I know now that I was, and I damn myself for all the lost hours, and the words unsaid, and the decorous, mezzotint memory which is all that is left to me now. And yet a widower of fifty-eight, an Ambassador and envoy embroiled in high and hazardous policy to play kiss-me-Kate and mumble-me-tumble-me in the Embassy drawing room! It would never have done for the Duke, sir! But nobler fellows than I and far better envoys and brilliant Presidents had chosen otherwise; and were my bay leaves the greener or my triumphs less hollow because I had refused to pick the roses by the path? A man of my age should never flirt with love. Take it or leave it! Because tomorrow is always a day too late! . . .

Immediately after my return from Saigon there occurred a whole series of unconnected incidents, each of which produced a chain of fateful consequences.

On Sunday morning, the day before the arrival of the United Nations Commission, an elderly Buddhist monk stepped out of a car in front of the cathedral and burned himself in full view of the congregation coming out from ten o'clock Mass. Result: more disturbances, more arrests and an end to Cung's precarious truce with the Buddhists.

On Monday night in Cholon a grenade was thrown into a bar frequented by Vietnamese and American servicemen. Three bar girls were killed, one Vietnamese paratrooper and two U.S. marines. In addition there were more than a dozen wounded. One marine staggered into the street with a belly wound and was hurried into a Chinese dwelling, where some prompt and skillful first aid by the women saved his life. Result: a

call to me from Tolliver's public relations office and a
suggestion that the Embassy should make a gesture of
thanks. The dwelling was the house of Number One
Chinese, that anonymous and elusive personage of
whom Mel Adams had told me on my first arrival in
Saigon.

In view of the importance of the family and in the
hope of making at least a partial entry into the hermet-
ic community of the Chinese, I decided to make the gesture myself. I wrote a letter, which was delivered by
hand, expressing my thanks and the thanks of the Government for the act of mercy. I asked leave to call on
the head of the family and offer a token of our gratitude. The same messenger brought me back a beautiful
piece of brushwork, which, in the most exemplary
Mandarin, invited me to drink tea at four the following
afternoon.

I chose my gift with some care. It must be simple,
precious and yet not too expensive lest it provoke distaste, embarrassment and a too large return. I settled,
finally, on a piece from my own collection: a beautiful
water bowl of jeweled faïence, made by Nomura Ninsei
of Awata in the seventeenth century. Armed with my
gift and a two-hour study of Embassy documents on the
Chinese minorities in Vietnam, I set off, with a new
driver and Bill Slavich riding shotgun in the front seat.
He was taking no chances of another attempt on my life
in the crowded quarters of Cholon.

Number One Chinese received me with antique ceremony. He was an elderly man, dressed in a scholar's
robe. He was grave, composed and endowed with the
natural dignity of the patriarch. He made me the usual
speech about the honor done to his unworthy house and
received my gift with serene approval. He introduced
his sons and his grandsons and then dismissed them.
Tea was brought and served in ceremonious style.
Then, with compliments and circuitous approaches, we
began our talk.

My host deplored the violence and trouble of the
times. He regretted the attempt on my life and the inju-

ry to innocent people from terrorist attacks. From that we passed to the special problems of his own people, and he exposed them to me in their historic context.

". . . For a thousand years, Excellency, this country was a province of China. Although the culture of this country was formed by China, we are still regarded as traditional enemies. The first history of Vietnam was written by Chinese. We introduced the plow and the water buffalo. We shared our language and our learning: our officers married Vietnamese women. Even when Lé-Loi founded the Vietnamese dynasty which lasted for three and a half centuries, he founded a mandarinate, based upon the Chinese model; and this system lasted until the French took over the country. . . .

"During the Japanese war nearly half a million of my people came here as refugees or immigrants, and there has always been mixed marriage between our women and the local men. We became, as we usually do, traders and bankers and, under the French, we retained Chinese citizenship and the right to appeal to China for the protection of our special rights.

"In 1956 the Government granted us all Vietnamese citizenship. But this was less a grant than an enforcement. If we did not accept nationality, we could not engage in commerce, industry or agriculture. We still had some self-government under the Regional Administrative Associations . . . but these were abolished in 1960. Our schools were placed under Government control and forced to teach the Vietnamese language. . . .

"I myself see these things as a natural growth of nationalism in Asia. Similar things have happened in Thailand and Indonesia and Burma. I do not see any profit in fighting them, but I have had a difficult time teaching my people the art of accommodation. There is much criticism and discontent. There is also evasion of the law. . . . And because China is now a Communist state, the loyalty of my people is always in question. . . ."

It was a frank, if incomplete statement of a minority problem which plagued the whole of Southeast Asia. It made no mention of the political attitudes of young and frustrated Chinese students and of the enormous appeal of a united and resurgent China. It said nothing about illegal migration and the infiltration of Communist agitators. There was no mention of squeeze and cumshaw and poitical payoffs all around the board. But I knew of these things and Number One Chinese knew that I knew them; so face was preserved and I was able to ask a less tendentious but no less important question.

"You are the leader of this community. From all I have been told, you have done a great service in keeping it united, controlled and free from a too dangerous political involvement. I should like to know your own personal opinion of President Cung and of his political policies."

He considered the question for a moment, then he asked:

"We are drinking tea in my house. Therefore this is a private and confidential discussion, no?"

"Of course."

"Then let me say, Excellency, that if our President were less French and more Chinese in his outlook he would do much better. Like the French, he is well versed in the apparatus of authority. So are we. But we understand that the apparatus is only as good as the men who run it. And that, in the end, it is the people who must be placated. I have my own apparatus, too— the family groups, the secret societies, the welfare associations; but if I, who am an old man, am still able to rule, it is because I am always available to the people. . . . This, you see, is the President's weakness. He is not known. Every rogue in office claims to speak with his voice, and how can the people tell the difference?"

"Is he honest?"

"I know he is. I have made bargains with him and he has kept them. He has sat where you sit now and we have planned good things for my people—hospitals, school improvements, protection from police graft, opportunities in the civil administration. I have helped him to form the Vietnam-China Cultural Association and to arrange economic co-operation with Taiwan. I have never asked him for more than he could promise. I have never promised more than I could perform. So we respect each other. We are not friends. But he is welcome in my house at any time."

"How do you regard his action against the Buddhists?"

He shrugged and buried his long hands in the sleeves of his scholar's robe.

"I am an old-style Confucian. I mistrust all religions because I find that all, without exception, carry within themselves seeds of discord and violence. Sometimes they produce holy men—but these are always the ones who dedicate themselves to service and to good works and not to argument. I think the President has made many mistakes, but these have been compounded by those who see a political profit in them. I think he may make more because isolation breeds suspicion and suspicion makes for harsh action."

"And what do you think of our policies in Asia?"

For the first time he smiled and answered my question with another. "Do you wish me to be polite, Excellency, or to tell you the truth?"

"The truth."

"Then the truth, as I see it, is this. Seven hundred million people cannot be ignored. Neither can they be shut up inside a cage and refused a normal commerce with the rest of the world. They are too old for this— too experienced and too proud. My ancestors came to this country in the time of the Mings. They served as mandarins under Lé-Loi. And I am still here—Number One Chinese—in the second half of the twentieth century. This is a monumental continuity and it cannot be broken either by revolution from inside or by pressure from without. . . . This is not a political question —a temporary argument between Confucian or Marxist or American Democrat. This is the whole history of Asia which writes and rewrites itself every day as the sea writes on the sands. . . ."

We talked a little longer, but all was said that could

be said. When I rose to go, he handed me his own gift
—a small disc of translucent jade, nestling in silk in a
sandalwood box. There were characters on it, intri-
cately and beautifully carved, and Number One Chinese
translated them into the Confucian Analect.

"He upon whom a moral duty devolves should not
give way even to his master."

Two nights later I went to dinner with my Australian
colleague. He was pleased to call it "a domestic kind of
occasion." I expected a dull evening, but I owed him a
courtesy and I was prepared to endure it. To my surprise, I found myself in a small company of witty and
irreverent people who, with perfect good humor, washed
the starch out of my collar and made me feel human
again. There was my Danish friend—he of the duck
feathers and the shipping problems; the head of the
Australian Military Mission, who had spent better than a decade in guerrilla warfare in Burma and
Malaya, but whose talk was of gemstones and Pali
manuscripts and exotic colonials who still cropped up
in outlandish places. There was an attractive brunette in
her early thirties who made the income of a minor Picasso painting the notables of Thailand; and my colleague's Swiss wife, who, to judge by the meal, was a
chef of the Cordon Bleu. I found myself placed between
the wife of the Dane and the English spouse of the
guerrilla expert; while opposite me was a jowly, good-
humored character who turned out to be a peripatetic
novelist of considerable reputation whose books I had
never read.

For once there was little talk of diplomacy; and I
found myself challenged out of my solitude to contribute to the talk that ranged from French cooking to
celadon porcelain, Karl Barth, the exorbitant price of
bad art and the follies of a pair of famous film stars. My
host was content to let the evening take its own course,
and the author was a very practiced listener who started
the hares and let the talk chase them in a dozen direc-
tions at once. I asked him what he was doing in this

comfortless neck of the woods, and he told me that he was engaged in a study of the Ecumenical movement and the relations between Christian and non-Christian religions. He was a Catholic, and the recent events in South Vietnam had disturbed him deeply. He had come to make his own inquiries. He was an Australian by birth, and the Embassy was handling his introductions. He was also much read in France, and President Cung had agreed to give him an interview and to pass him on to other official sources of information. He was appreciative of the courtesy but shrewd enough to see that Cung might wish to use him to offset the report of the United Nations Commission. I asked him whether he proposed to publish any of his information. He answered that he was a novelist and not a journalist and that a novel might take two years to grow. Besides, he was chary of reportage and unwilling to lend his name to hasty assessments of a complex situation. After a surfeit of international reporters and weekly oracles, I found his point of view refreshing. I cornered him over the coffee cups and asked him point-blank whether he would do me a favor.

"If I can, certainly."

"When is your interview with President Cung?"

"Ten thirty tomorrow morning. Why?"

"Would you be willing to ask him a question which I'll give you?"

"Yes."

"Would you be willing to report his answer to me?"

"No, I'm afraid I wouldn't." His answer was very polite, and he smiled as he gave it. Then he added, "I'm jealous of what I am, you see. I'm not an agent. I'm a friend of the United States. I've lived there. I like the people and the country. But what you ask puts me in a false position. . . . Now if I could bring my own Embassy into the discussion . . . ?"

"Why not? I imagine Manson is as concerned about this as I am."

I signaled to Manson, who came across to join us. I

told him of my request and of our author's objection to it. Manson said agreeably, "The question is of mutual interest. The answer is important to us all."

"Fair enough," said the author. "Now what's the question?"

"Does Cung propose, now, or at any time or in any circumstances, to enter into relations with North Vietnam?"

There was a moment's pause. Then Manson nodded agreement, but added a rider. "Perhaps you'd better explain the meaning of the question, Mr. Amberley."

"And what hangs on the answer, too," said our literary friend evenly. "I'm quite prepared to accept the responsibility for an accurate report. But the consequences are something else again. So I'd like you to be honest with me."

He was too canny and too well informed to be taken in by a half-truth, so, gambling on Manson's own judgment of his guest, I told him the story up to the point of my conversation at the British cocktail party. Manson proved a good ally. He said that he, too, had heard the same kind of talk and would be glad of some confirmation. The novelist listened in silence and then pondered the proposition a few moments. Finally he gave us a guarded answer:

"I see what you need and why you need it. I have a duty to my own government and a friendly attitude to that of America. But it seems to me that if I get a certain answer it could precipitate a certain action. Am I right?"

"Yes."

"What if I deliberately misreported my talk?"

"I don't believe you would."

"Or misconstrued it?"

"I think you are too intelligent for that. But, in any case, no action could or would be taken on a single testimony from a non-American source. The CIA would check out your report from its own informants."

"Then I'll put your question to Cung and try to be

clear on his answer. I'll let you have a written transcript of my interview by five tomorrow."

"Thank you."

He shrugged, took a swallow of brandy and gave us a crooked grin.

"When I was younger I used to believe in the total disinvolvement of the artist. Now when I'm known enough and rich enough to be detached, I find myself involved every day in a moral decision. This is a curly one. If I'm wrong I shan't easily forgive myself."

"Yet you decided quickly enough."

"I have some advantages, Ambassador. I know what words mean and I have respect for them. I play a solitary trade. I look at the world with my own eyes. I take my own risks and pay my own forfeits. I understand what damnation means—and I learned long ago that you can never borrow another man's absolution."

The next morning the Cambodians were on my doorstep with an angry protest and a demand for reparations. A Viet Cong unit had been pursued across the southern border by infantry and helicopters. A Cambodian village had been laid waste by rocket fire, and a number of villagers had been killed and wounded. I promised to investigate the incident, and after forty minutes of terse exchanges they left.

It was another of the bitter paradoxes of this cankerous war. In fact, the neutrality of Cambodia had been violated; but also in fact, the Cambodians breached their own neutrality every day by allowing the passage of arms and men down the Mekong River and by offering shelter to the raiders who slipped back and forth across the border at will. The real victims were the village folk, grandmothers, children and peasant farmers, who were buried now, whose only epitaph would be a pile of newspaper clippings and files of diplomatic correspondence. Yet in one small village the dragon's teeth had been sown again, and the crop would sprout, inevitably, into armed men. . . .

At midday Harry Yaffa came in with two reports. One was from the CIA in Hong Kong. A Vietnamese there, a former Palace official and a known proponent of the "third force," had been under surveillance for some time. He had finally made contact with officials of the Bank of China and immediately afterward had established with the French Bank of Commerce a credit of half a million sterling pounds. Two days later he had given to an American correspondent a highly colored account of Palace intrigues and dissensions in the High Command and offered him fifteen thousand U.S. dollars to get his wife and family out of Saigon within six weeks.

The second report came from Vientiane, in Laos, where a minor official of the South Vietnam Ministry of Foreign Affairs had met and talked with a known agent of North Vietnam. There was no information on the subject of their talk; but two hours afterward the agent had left the capital in a plane chartered from a French opium runner.

In the intricate pattern of plot and counterplot the two incidents might bear a dozen interpretations, but Yaffa was convinced that they matched best with our own conclusions: that there was a move to split the Army by forming and financing a third force which would later be forced into the Viet Cong camp; and that Cung was involved in tentative discussions, at least, with the Government in Hanoi.

When I told him of my talk at the dinner party, he was quite excited and asked me to call him the moment the report was filed. Our wandering novelist proved as prompt as I had hoped. At five o'clock exactly he presented himself at my office with a carbon transcript of his interview with President Cung. The original, he told me with a grin, had been lodged with the Australian Ambassador, so that international courtesies might be preserved. When I asked him to wait and give me some comments after my reading, he declined courteously. He had undertaken to record a dialogue. His report contained one comment and a summation. He was not prepared to go further. This being a very reasonable point of view, I thanked him and let him go. I envied him his independence and his right to limit his own responsibilities so precisely. My own charge was almost unlimited, but I had no right at all to dispense myself from it.

The transcript I found an admirable document. It was simple, concise and limited strictly to the terms of reference. I reproduce it in this chronicle if only to show the clarity with which the final issue presented itself to me.

Q. It is clear that the Buddhist question is still unresolved. Do you expect any more Buddhist demonstrations and acts of martyrdom?

A. If they occur we shall know how to deal with them. But the American attitude conduces to this kind of fanaticism. . . . The Americans are destroying the psychology of our country. They do not understand us. We understand our own people. How they think, and how they react. The Americans talk about democracy, but the democracy they talk about is of no use to this country.

Q. What do you consider is the best form of government for South Vietnam?

A. What we have now. A strong central authority, which can fight the war and develop the country. . . . If this is dictatorship, then we need dictatorship, but we are laying the foundations of democracy in the countryside. . . . The city [Saigon] means nothing to us. If necessary we shall abandon it altogether, and organize it into strategic hamlets, as we have done in the country. The people in the city are discontented, spoiled, intoxicated by Western individualism. Our people have to develop within the framework of the family and the community, and the limitations of their history, their economy and the social order. This is what we mean by personalism.

Q. Even if one accepts the *natural* limitations imposed by history and the social order, are you not imposing unnatural and artificial limitations? For exam-

ple, by the repressive measures against the Buddhists
and the students?

A. Of course we impose limitations. The Buddhist
monks don't want to fight, so why should they have the
right to interfere with the course of the war? The *Sangha* is only a small part of the nation. Why should it
have the right to determine the whole course of our
history? The students, young men and women, should
be ready to share in our struggle against the Viet Cong.
Why should they claim the right to disrupt it by dis-
loyal demonstrations? The American attitude foments
these things. If we are to have a victory, the people
must be disintoxicated.

Q. It is obvious to everybody that although American soldiers are being killed in your war, although you
are fighting it with American money and weapons,
there is now open hostility between the regime and the
United States. What steps can, or should be, taken to
heal the breach?

A. The steps are clear. Let the Americans give us
arms, money, helicopters and military transport, and we
will fight the war ourselves. This is our war, not theirs.
It is I who plan the strategy. It is I who am responsible
for building eight thousand strategic hamlets. Yet every
time I want to use a helicopter, I have to ask permission of the Americans.

Q. You want the Americans out of the country?

A. Exactly.

Q. If you had everything you wanted—arms, money,
transport and the Americans out of the country, how
long would it take you to win the war?

A. Two or three years at the outside.

Q. And if the Americans stay, how long will it take
you?

A. God knows.

Q. When you have won the war, what sort of relationship do you see with North Vietnam?

A. [In angry tone] In this very room American
officials have accused me of maintaining relations with
Ho Chi Minh. I told them that the Americans have

done everything possible to force me into his arms, but I have remained loyal to my aims and to the country.

[This was followed by another long tirade against the methods and the policies of the United States.]

Q. Let's look at it another way. As the master strategist of the campaign, you must be interested in what is going on in the North, if only from an intelligence point of view.

A. Of course.

Q. How do you see the situation of Ho Chi Minh and North Vietnam?

A. There are three main groups in his Communist Party. There is the Army, which depends on China for arms, supplies and training. There are those who follow the soft line of Moscow, but they are of little importance. There is another group of those who became Communists for reasons of nationalism before and after Dienbienphu.

Q. Obviously this must be the group which interests you most of all.

A. Naturally.

Q. Have you succeeded in penetrating their ranks? Do you have any relations with them from an intelligence or other point of view?

A. Yes. But it was not I who took the initiative.

Q. Let us presume that the Americans do not give you what you want, that they continue their sanctions and their open opposition to your policies. What then?

A. Then I must take whatever steps are necessary to end the long agony of my country.

Q. Would those steps involve a deal with Ho Chi Minh?

A. Politics is the art of the possible. I have to examine all the possibilities—and that is what I am doing now.

COMMENT. At this point President Cung dropped the subject abruptly and launched into another long dissertation on personalism, and on the mistakes and machinations of the Americans. I managed to ask one more question before I took my leave.

Q. What do you think of Mr. Maxwell Amberley?

A. There is no trace of morality in what he is doing. At least with his predecessor there was a moral point of view. In this man there is no morality and no trace of religious thinking.

SUMMING UP. My final impression of the interview was that Cung wished to use me as a disseminator of his own strong anti-American feeling. It was also clear that the question of possible relations with the North was a not too veiled threat of what might happen if the regime did not get its way—the neutralization of South Vietnam by a quid-pro-quo deal with the North: "We'll get the Americans out if you call off the war." I have no means of judging whether Cung really believes that such a deal is possible, or that he could survive it once it was made. . . .

I called Harry Yaffa to my office and handed him the typescript. He read it in silence, then laid it down on my desk in a gesture of finality.

"I think that does it, sir! It comes out loud and clear and it jibes with all our other information. We've got the generals in revolt, a possible mutiny in the Army and a clear threat from Cung to play his own game out in left field. . . . I say we have to move—and quickly, too."

"I agree that we may have to, but Washington has to decide this one."

"Are you going to file a report?"

"In forty-eight hours. But I have to do two things first."

"What, sir?"

"First I want this transcript circulated to all Embassy sections and to Tolliver and his people as well. Then I want a full-dress conference here tomorrow evening. In the meantime I'm going to call on Cung and face him with this information."

"Is that wise?"

"It's necessary."

He shrugged dubiously and gave me a tart reminder: "In that case, sir, we'd better protect the man who gave it. We should get him out of the country fast."

"I'll leave that to you, Mr. Yaffa."

"I'll warn the generals, too, in case Cung decides to stage a sudden crackdown. It's a question of their necks, you know."

"I know it. Do what you think is necessary."

When he had left, I stood pondering the words on the jade talisman and watching the light fade into a swift darkness.

I worked late that night and slept badly afterward. I dreamed that I sat, naked and alone, in an open space as flat as a billiard table. There was light, but I could not see what gave the light. Against the light, black and distant, there were tall rectangular shapes, like theater flats. As I watched, I heard a faint plectral music like the sound of samisens or biwas. As the music played, the shapes began to dance, tiltwise, spinning now on this corner, now on that. The music grew louder. The dancing shapes came closer, until, at a moment of unbearable climax, the shapes surrounded me, then locked themselves together, enclosing me in a room, a room without a roof, so that I could still see the light overhead. There was silence now—silence and light and myself cross-legged on the floor, looking up at the light. Then, by minute degrees, the walls began to move inward. At first I thought it was an illusion of the stillness and the tension of contemplation. I looked at the wall in front of me. It was quite still. I looked over my shoulder and the wall behind was closer. While I was watching, the walls to front and right and left moved toward me. I looked up. The light was smaller. Terror caught hold of me, and I sat, stiff and rigid, eyes fixed upon the narrowing light. The walls grew closer, the light diminished inch by inch, until I felt the first pressure on back and elbows and knees. The pressure grew stronger, I could feel the bruising of flesh and muscle. The light grew smaller and smaller, and then suddenly I screamed in pure terror, and woke, parched and sweating, to a room full of moonglow. I looked at my watch. It was four in the morning. The terror of the nightmare still clung about me, and I dressed myself in clean clothes and worked in my study until breakfast time.

I needed no Joseph to interpret my dreams. I knew exactly what they meant. I, judge, jury, prosecutor and defense counsel, was about to stand trial myself. Soon, very soon, the evidence would be in, the pleas made, and verdict would be passed on Maxwell Amberley, envoy extraordinary. Stripped of the costume of his office, he would stand, in open court, to hear impartial judgment. And after the judgment would come the sentence—a lifetime of confinement in the solitude of the secret self. . . . It was nonsense, of course; nonsense to be dismissed by the first sunlight and the first cup of coffee. Maxwell Gordon Amberley was not on trial. He was the man who sat in the seat of the mighty, with the power of life, death and dominion. He would be just, of course, and even merciful; but he was a man charged to decide, neither bowing to fear nor inclining to favor. He would be magnanimous, but prudent. He would admonish, but without rancor. Great affairs had been entrusted to him, and he would behave greatly, an arbiter of all the yesterdays and an architect of glorious tomorrows. Amen! . . . And another cup of coffee, please, Anne. I have a big day ahead of me!

My meeting with Cung was set for eleven in the morning. At nine thirty my masseur came in, and I lay for an hour under his soft, strong hands, while the tension drained out of my muscles and I set my thoughts in order for this final conference. It was the final one; I knew that. Time was running out for both of us. The wheel was already spinning, the croupier was making his last parrot cry: *"Rien ne va plus!"* The little ball was bounding from red to black and back again; and we were both playing against the house, and against each other.

One thing I had determined. I would be absolutely honest. I would not use the guarded language of the trade. I would say all the truth that I knew. I would admit my mistakes. I would confess, where confession was justified, to ignorance and incapacity. And when the time came to act, I would not shrink from that either. . . . Alas for my puritan rectitude! There was only one thing I could not admit. My bets were on the board, but I was the house, too; and the house had to win, if not on clean-sweep zero, then on the percentage. But what would you, gentlemen and players all? You kicked out the French. The Japanese went bankrupt. You didn't like Chinese fantan. So I was the only game in town! . . . My skin was oiled, my muscles flexed easily. My mind was clear and I had forgotten the nightmares, and in this courageous vacuity I set out for the Palace.

Cung received me with green tea and cool courtesy. This time he made no preambles, but challenged me openly:

"You have something to say to me, Mr. Ambassador? I am ready to hear it."

My own prologue was well prepared, and I recited it as simply and as calmly as I could.

"Our last talk, Mr. President, ended in a stalemate. Now we are come, each of us, to a crisis. I want to end the crisis if I can; I will go as far as possible to do that. Last week I made a tour of the battle areas. I saw, at first hand, how much you have accomplished for this country. I acknowledge your achievement freely. I admire it greatly. I admire you, too, though we have been at odds with each other. I respect your single-mindedness and your personal integrity. I will admit the mistakes of our own policy; I confess my own shortsightedness in many particulars. On the other hand, I expect that you will admit the difficulties and the problems of our equivocal position in this country, where we may advise but not fight, where we must pay but not control, where we have no voice in your Government and yet must share the blame for its mistakes. I hope I make myself clear, Mr. President?"

"Admirably clear, Mr. Ambassador. Please go on."

"But to admit all these things changes nothing in my present situation or in yours. Let me show you the true shape of things, Mr. President. Your senior generals are in revolt and plotting to overthrow you. Your Army—a section of it at least—is on the point of mutiny. Your administrators are ready for defection. The Buddhists are hostile to you, the Catholics divided between their allegiance to Rome and their hopes in you as a national deliverer. You have failed to attract the common people either to your aims or to your person. You have insulted and alienated us who are your friends—and yet you will make no concession, no gesture even, toward a settlement. More than this, knowing yourself isolated, you make a threat—a repeated threat, Mr. President—that you will embark on another dangerous venture: a pact with Ho Chi Minh, which you hope will give you a security which you have been unable to earn by arms, diplomacy or simple loyalty! I am here today to tell you that we are nearly at the end of this road together. There is still time to turn back and take another path. But if you refuse to turn back, then you walk alone—and there is small guarantee of your survival!"

To his credit be it said that he took it very calmly. He sat a long time, silent, eyes hooded, staring down at the backs of his manicured hands. When he spoke it was in the dry fashion of a lecturer, dedicated to the persuasion of pure logic.

"I appreciate, Mr. Ambassador, the frankness of your opening words, and I believe in the sincerity of your compliments and of your intentions. So I will try to be frank with you. You tell me of revolts and plots and dissensions. I know they exist. I know better than you the people who take part in them. But look around you! Who is in control here? I am! Not easily, I admit! Not without anxiety. But I am in control. And in the combat areas, whose orders direct the course of the campaign? Mine! You will admit that, I think."

"I admit it. But there are . . ."

He held up a hand to stay me. "No, wait, please! You tell me you are convinced of my honesty and my single-mindedness. Can you say the same of General Dao or General Khiet or my friend Tho, up in the North? What do you know of these men but what they have told you of themselves or what you have heard from others? They are good soldiers, yes! But economists? Public administrators? Financiers? Educators? I have lived with these men, plotted with them, too, against the French and the Japanese. I know them! I tell you, Giap in the North would make fifty of them—and you think you can build a government out of them! Would you let General Tolliver do your job, or elect him President of the United States? Look at their bank accounts and look at mine! I am poorer than they, believe me! You will find none of your dollars sticking to my fingers. But to theirs—too many! What do you want, Mr. Ambassador? What do you want?"

"A settlement of differences. Between you and the Buddhists, between you and the generals! I am willing to offer my services as mediator if you wish."

"I try to tell you, Mr. Ambassador, this is the Western way. It is not ours. They would love you to mediate. They would be bland and reasonable, and all the time they would be saying, 'Cung is already beaten. He has had to call in the Americans. So today we ask for his thumb and tomorrow we take his arm!' "

"Even that might be better than mutiny and rebellion!"

"No!"

"Why not?"

"Because one concession breeds another threat, and another after that. Better one trial of strength than a slow wasting."

"You may not survive it."

"If I go down, Mr. Ambassador, America goes out of South Vietnam. Not immediately, perhaps, but, sooner or later, yes! You are strange people. You eat up friends like grapes and spit out their skins because the taste is too sharp."

"Then tell me something, Mr. President. What do you want to do?"

"It's very simple. I want to fight. I want to finish the war and build a peace for my people."

"We are here to help you do it."

"That is what you believe. In fact, you hand us a gun and then destroy our will to fight. You intoxicate the people with your Western ideas of individualism and of a freedom for which we are not prepared."

"So I repeat the question. What do you want?"

"Give me the guns, the money, the transports, the aircraft, and I will finish the war very quickly. But you and your people must go!"

"We can't. You know that. We are committed too far."

"So, at bottom, you are like the French, who must maintain a foothold in the living room to prove they are friends. What is this but old-style colonialism?"

"Something else, Mr. President. I've seen the guns we gave you turned against your own people. Can we shut our eyes to that?"

"But you will shut them, will you not, when the generals come to kill me with those same American guns? Or will Mr. Harry Yaffa be there to pull the trigger?"

"This is a fruitless argument, Mr. President. It ignores the facts. You cannot survive without concessions. Yet you won't concede, you won't negotiate, you won't accept mediation. You want our guns and our money and you don't want us. . . . That closes all the doors—except one."

"And what is that?"

"You could abdicate—or accept a Committee of Government with yourself as Chairman."

"Abdicate!" He was genuinely amazed. "Do you ask your President to abdicate because the Republicans disagree with his policy?"

"In point of fact, we do—every four years!"

"I will not do it! Never! I will not retire like Bao Dai and see this country destroyed!"

"So all the doors are closed, except the one you are trying to open secretly—a door to the North!"

"Does that shock you, Mr. Ambassador?"

"It shocks me profoundly. I find it a monstrous folly!"

"Why a folly?" His smile was quite gentle and

pitying. "I have survived the Americans. I shall survive these venal generals of mine. Why should I not survive an alliance with Ho Chi Minh? At least we talk the same language."

"Is this what you wish, for God's sake?"

"No. It is what you may force me to accept."

I battled with him for another hour, but I could not budge him. He would give nothing, change nothing, negotiate nothing. Finally he asked me:

"Now what will you do, Mr. Ambassador?"

"I shall report to Washington and await instructions."

He shrugged, walked over to the bookshelves and ran his finger along the titles until he found the volume he sought. He leafed through it and then turned back to me, smiling.

"You are a lover of things Japanese, Mr. Ambassador. Here is something that may interest you: Three great men of Japan were faced with a reluctant cuckoo. Nobunaga said, 'I shall kill the cuckoo if it will not sing.' Hideyoshi said, 'I shall invite it to sing.' Iyeyasu said, 'I shall wait for it to sing.' . . . And there is the riddle, Mr. Ambassador. Which one was right? . . . And which one are you?"

CHAPTER NINE

At seven that evening I held a crisis conference in the soundproof briefing room at the Embassy. It was a command performance, in which each man must know his music perfectly and play it, note by note, truly, to the last bar. I was the conductor, who must have the whole score by rote—every last grace note, rest and cadenza. I must direct, discipline and interpret. I must make meaning and harmony out of what otherwise would be nonsense and barnyard cacophony. I had faced this orchestra before, on the day of my arrival. They had been wary then, and reserved. Now they were different. They had seen me beat out the rugged score of the Saigon Symphony. They knew the score was bad and the performance ragged, but at least I had picked up the rhythm and held it against hisses and catcalls and a shower of turnips from the circle; and tonight they depended on me more than ever.

As I waited for them to settle and arrange their papers, I diverted myself with this fanciful conceit of the orchestra and the conductor. But, like every metaphor, it was built upon a concordance and a contradiction. And the contradiction was this: that even when I rendered the score note-perfect, I still could not guarantee its integrity because my rendition must always be personal and particular. An emphasis here in the woodwinds, a muting of the horns there, a vibrato in the fiddles, an extra bounce in the tympani, and change of pace and a special tinkle on the glockenspiel—and the composer shifts restlessly in his grave! But who can say that the maestro lies, because it's all written in the score; and, besides, the audience listens but cannot tell a crotchet from a glissando. So tap on the music stand, quiet the whispers and let's hit the first chord right on the nose!

". . . You know why we are here, gentlemen. We are in a political crisis, and we may soon find ourselves in a military one. I have to make a report to Washington, recommend a course of action and then execute their orders, whether they accord with my recommendations or not. . . . Everything said here tonight goes on the record for Washington. You have a duty to offer your opinions, just as Washington has the right to accept or reject them. . . . Now, let me show you where we stand. . . ."

I gave them, first, my own report, up to and including my latest interview with President Cung. I had Tolliver's staff experts deliver a military briefing and

Boettiger from the Political Section make a situation summary on Thailand, Laos, Cambodia and South Vietnam. Yaffa spoke for the CIA. Hennebury from the Operations Mission reported from the point of view of those engaged in civil aid enterprises with the Government. Finally I summed up the alternatives:

". . . So it seems to me we have a clear choice. Either we sit quietly and allow events to happen under their own momentum or we intervene with a clear indication that we would welcome a change of government and would be prepared to bankroll the successful contender. In the simplest terms, it's a choice between Cung and a military junta. So, for the record, gentlemen, your opinions, please! . . . General Tolliver?"

"If it's a choice between waiting and acting, Ambassador, I say we have to act. I've got upwards of twenty thousand men and a hell of a lot of strategic material scattered all over the country. A mutiny in the Army or a revolt of the generals could leave them exposed and vulnerable to the Viet Cong—or even to faction fights among the South Vietnamese. I don't think any of us can accept that risk. If you want to pin me down to a choice between President Cung and the generals, I have to choose the generals because I think Cung is losing influence every day. Sooner or later he'll be pulled down. Better now, while the Army is intact, than later, when it may have been split by mutiny."

"Thank you, General. Could we hear now from the Operations Mission? Mr. Hennebury?"

"I'm afraid I have to take the same view as General Tolliver, if for slightly different reasons. We've spent the best part of ten years building an economy in this country and helping the people to organize industry, agriculture, commerce, public works, education and all the rest. We've got a lot of people out in the field, too, and they have to be protected. But, more important, I don't think we can risk handing over all this real progress, all this evidence of American cooperation and goodwill, all this productive capacity, to a rickety alliance between President Cung and Ho Chi Minh. If a new regime gives us less risk and more time to consolidate and re-educate, I think we have to decide in favor of it."

"Mr. Boettiger?"

"From my point of view, the choice seems too harsh and too rigid. In a purely political sense there is still a lot of working life in the Cung regime—if Cung would negotiate. Unfortunately, we can't be sure what kind of a political sense will show up in a junta of generals. So, again on a purely political level, we'd rather have the devil we know. . . . The other side of the picture is, of course, that Cung won't negotiate and that rebellion is already being planned. So reluctantly, we come down in favor of a change of regime. . . ."

"Mr. Yaffa?"

"It's the job of the CIA to balance the risks of any political action. It's our view that the risks in the Cung regime are bad ones, and they get worse every day. A military junta led by General Khiet would have the initial support of the Buddhists, the trade unions and the Army, which is a whole lot more than Cung can command right now. So we advise for support of General Khiet."

"Mr. Adams?"

Normally Adams was a fluent and ready speaker, who always had his facts ready and made a pretty trick of fanning them out for the audience like a conjurer with a deck of cards. But tonight he was slow to begin. I noticed that he looked yellow and tired, and I wondered if he was coming down with malaria or hepatitis. At ordinary times his voice was clear and crisp but tonight there was a rasp in it and a hint of suppressed anger.

"You have told us, Ambassador, that we have a duty to offer our opinions. Mine, I'm afraid, will be an unpopular one. But I propose to discharge my duty as it has been pointed out to me. So here, in order, are my views. I want to read them so that there will be no doubt of my meaning.

"Item one: I think the Ambassador is making a

The final section of the report is a summary of my conclusions and recommendations.

. . . It is clear, therefore, that any decision we make involves doubt, risk and danger, since all our calculations are based on incomplete knowledge and an unstable equilibrium of forces. Yet, if we defer decision, events may outrun our capacity to deal with them. . . . Therefore, with deep misgiving, but in default of any other clear course of action, I am forced to present to you these alternatives. Continue to support the Cung regime and risk mutiny, disorder and tactical isolation, or back the generals and give the country a breathing space to sort out its internal dissensions and restore a semblance of unity.

It is my personal view that President Cung is now beyond the reach of counsel and that we cannot work with him any longer, and we certainly cannot be party to his present or projected policies. General Khiet and his colleagues have given assurances to Harry Yaffa that they will endeavor to protect the person of Cung and his officials in the event of a coup; but they make no promises, nor do I think they can, because Cung himself may decide to make a last-ditch stand with whatever forces are still loyal to him. So, in a situation fraught with risk, I think we have to accept this risk, too.

Finally, I must repeat what I have said in earlier communications. I, too, am one of your risks. My assessments may be wrong, but they are made on the basis of available information. I await your instructions, and I shall carry them out to the best of my ability.

Maxwell Gordon Amberley
Ambassador

So at last it was done. I read the final draft carefully

and signed it. I looked at my watch to note the time on the message form. It was just after one in the morning: the thirteenth hour, which is no hour at all, but a sinister suspension of time, a syncope between illusion and reality. I handed the message to Anne Beldon and made a pale joke.

"What I've written, I've written. Send it off, Anne, and let's get the hell out of this place!"

She stared at me for a moment, anxious and puzzled, then she turned and left the room. I lit a cigarette, but the taste was stale and unpleasant and I stubbed it out. Then I went into the bathroom and washed my hands.

That night I dreamed again. The setting was the same: a flat, empty plain, full of light. This time, however, there were no dancing shapes and no walls. There was the glowing sky, the flat earth and me. I was dressed in *yukata* and *tabi,* and I sat cross-legged, hands folded in my lap, in the attitude of learning. I knew that I was waiting for Musō Soseki, and that when he came he would have a great secret to impart to me. No matter that I was alone; no matter that he delayed a long time. Patience and discipline were a small price to pay for a secret wisdom.

I closed my eyes and set my mind in the attitude of an empty vessel, waiting to be filled. I knew that my master would approve this and commend me for it. After a long time I opened my eyes, expecting to see Musō seated before me. The land was empty as ever— except for a small brown bird who stood very close, watching me out of dull eyes like dusty beads. We looked at each other for a wordless minute, and he cocked his head, now on this side, now on that, as if trying to make sense out of this vision in a dressing gown and white cotton socks.

I was lonely and I tried to talk to him, but he would not answer. This, I knew, was very reasonable, because either he did not know my language or he had nothing useful to say. Then I asked him to sing. He stood there in silence, studying me. I whistled a little tune and beat time to it with my hand. He would not sing and he would not dance. After a while my mouth was dry, so that I could not whistle any more. I pleaded with him, which is a very great thing for an Ambassador to do, he being an important personage. Still the brown bird would not sing. So I decided to go back to my contemplation and ignore him. But when I opened my eyes again he was still there, silent and quizzical. I pleaded with him again. He would not sing. I whistled a jig tune for him and beat time with my hand to encourage him. Still he would not utter a sound. So I raised my hand and brought it down, slap! on his cocked head. I felt his bones break and his body twitch between my hand and the flat earth. But when I lifted my hand, there was nothing there, not even a feather. So I began to cry, softly and plaintively, because I was all alone and there was not even a bird to sing to me. . . .

I came down to breakfast red-eyed and aching in every bone. Anne Beldon had already left for the Embassy, but the housekeeper told me that Mel Adams was waiting for me in the drawing room. I was too tired to be angry with him again, so I asked him to join me at table. He, too, looked as if he had not slept very well, but he seemed calm and composed. He shared my coffee and smoked a cigarette while I toyed with my breakfast; then he told me why he had come.

"I wanted you to know, sir, that there was nothing personal in what I said last night. You've always been very kind to me. I respect you and I'm grateful to you. But last night was an official occasion. We were asked to stand up and be counted. I had no choice but to give a true testament."

"I understand that, Mel. I wasn't very happy with the way you gave it. I'm still not happy. I think you might have let me down more gently."

"That's why I'm here this morning, sir: to apologize for my brusqueness. I could have phrased things more gracefully. I could have chosen a private occasion to prepare you for what I was going to say. But I guess I was afraid."

"Afraid of me, Mel?"

"No, sir. Of myself, more like. Of the subtleties and the courtesies of this business that make it so easy to hedge yourself and remain the safe dissenter. But in this I didn't dare to stay safe any more. I had to burn the boats and the bridges and stand on what I knew I believed."

"And you do believe it, Mel? Sincerely?"

"I do."

"Do you want to argue it out with me?"

"No, sir. Right now I'm like Martin Luther: 'Here I stand—I cannot do otherwise.' . . . But I'd like you to accept my apology."

"I accept it. I hope you believe that I also am sincere in my belief."

"I do."

"What now, Mel?"

"Would you mind telling me what you recommended to Washington?"

"To back the generals."

"Then you don't mind if I apply for transfer."

"I think you must, for your own sake. I'll endorse the request."

"Thank you, sir. You're going to be busy for a while. I don't want to shirk any responsibilities. I'm quite prepared to continue working."

"On all counts, Mel, I think it might be wise if you got sick. I'm sure you could get a diplomatic bellyache that would keep you home for a while."

"If you think it proper, sir."

"I think it's expedient—as Harry Yaffa would say!"

He laughed at that, and the tension between us eased. I poured him more coffee and took one of his cigarettes, and we sat for a few moments, smoking in silence and looking out at the mynah birds pecking at worms in the damp lawn. Then Adams said hesitantly, "If I'm not quite out of court, I'd like to make a proposal to you."

"Go ahead."

"If Washington decides to back the generals, I think you should make a deal with them: Cung is to be taken alive and handed over to our Embassy officials for safe conduct out of the country."

I weighed that one for a few moments and then rejected it. "We can't do it, Mel. The uprising then becomes an American-sponsored affair."

"Which it is!"

"But which nobody can prove it is, unless they have all the knowledge we have! But if we accept delivery of Cung and carry him into exile, we look like the British carting Napoleon off to St. Helena. Old-fashioned imperialism with a vengeance! How do we wear that one?"

"Is it harder to wear than assassination?"

"Assassination is a risk but not a certainty. I don't think the generals want to kill Cung any more than we do."

"But they'd sure as hell prefer him dead."

"That's still a perhaps."

"Please, sir! What I'm trying to do is protect you and the Embassy—and the country, too, from just that perhaps!"

"You can't do it the way you suggest."

"Then let me put it another way. If Cung came to us and asked for sanctuary in the Embassy, would we give it to him?"

"Yes."

"Would we press for his safe-conduct out of the country?"

"Yes, but we could not guarantee it."

"Well . . . ! I guess that's plain enough, sir." He pushed back his chair and stood up. "Thanks for the coffee. And I'm glad we're not enemies. I'll go to the Embassy and tidy up my papers. Then I'll call the doctor about this bellyache."

When he had gone, I sat a long time over the lees of the coffee, measuring myself against the stature of Mel Adams. In one sense, his critics had been right when they rated him too dry a man for Ambassadorial rank.

He lacked the executive drive, the streak of amorality and opportunism which makes a first-rate negotiator. He was too clear a thinker to be seduced by the transitory triumphs of the trade. He had too firm a grasp on principles to practice happily the art of the possible. He lacked the detachment, or perhaps the cynicism, to measure cost against profit even when they both were reckoned in human blood. In the floating world of international diplomacy he might even be dangerous—like a recluse saint, ignorant of malice, preaching a children's crusade against the powers of evil, while sutlers and camp followers crowded like vultures to batten on the innocent.

In another sense, he was too rare a man to lose. Patriots were disprized in our naughty times. They were foolish lovers, jealous of those who traduced the honor of milady. They were fond knights who, even were she light and venal, would still defend the memory of her pristine virtue. Without these fond ones we, the worldly and the wise, were poor indeed. We burned no bridges, but—God knows!—we sold them often enough. No martyrs, we; because martyrdom was always messy and never expedient, except for the peddlers of relics and legends. We shouted no truths from the rooftops, because, like jesting Pilates, we turned away from truth to penny prophets and readers of teacup dregs. . . . our only regret was that we had but one life to give for our country. So why the hell should we gamble it on a sucker play?

Out on the lawn the mynah birds were still pecking over the grass, because later, when the sun came out, the ground would harden and the forage would be thin indeed. Which was why the early bird was the one that caught the worm and why true patriots were a problem in the demimonde of diplomacy. I never felt more like a denizen of the half-world than when I arrived at my office that morning and found an engraved invitation from the Ministry of Foreign Affairs to a Presidential dinner in honor of South Vietnam's National Liberation Day. There was a bitter comedy in the fact that, as the senior diplomat, I should be expected to propose the toast to President Cung, while his Foreign Minister would propose the toast to the President of the United States. This was pure Toulouse-Lautrec, and I wished he were alive to paint it. No matter that the surgeon had just left and the pimps were carving one another in the back alleys, the trade must still go on in the House of All Nations! Look now! We squabble a little and betray a little, and sometimes someone gets pushed out of a window; but we are still friends, aren't we? The music plays, the ladies are dressed like princesses, and there will be champagne for supper and speeches and maybe a little dancing before bedtime. At least we would have dancing, except for the war and the regulations and the threat to our morals! But the speeches will be good: ". . . In spite of our occasional differences we are still friends and allies in this struggle against Communist tyranny. . . . Your noble President . . . My noble President . . . My noble backside!" And even while I made the speech I would know it was a lie. Cung would know it and General Dao, resplendent in his decorations, would smile into his champagne and recognize me as one of his own.

The invitation was still in my hands when Harry Yaffa came in to ask if there was any news from Washington. I told him it was still much too early and that, in any case, the best we could expect would be a holding order while my report was taken under advisement by the State Department, the Pentagon and the White House. However, he did want something settled immediately. If Washington was prepared to back the generals, how and when would the word be given? I tossed the invitation card across the table, and he grinned as he read it. He had a refined taste for such ironies, and I thought that if I must endure them I might just as well find some pleasure in them for myself. I told him:

"That's when the word will be given, Mr. Yaffa—if it is to be given at all! And the word will be 'A toast to the gallant people of South Vietnam!' "

He threw back his head and laughed in pure delight.

"Beautiful, Mr. Ambassador! Beautiful! A public occasion. At least two of the generals will be there. Maybe all four, depending on whether Cung wants to seduce them or frighten them that week. It couldn't be better!"

He went off into another peal of laughter. He was still laughing when Anne Beldon came in, frowning and obviously in a foul humor. She dumped a pile of correspondence under my nose, picked up another pile from my tray and went out, closing the door twice as hard as usual.

Harry Yaffa shrugged and gave me a sidelong look. "The moon in perigee, eh, Mr. Ambassador! She's not very happy this morning."

"She's been working late hours. I imagine she's tired, like the rest of us."

But I knew she was angry with me, and I longed for the time and the words to tell her how much I needed her understanding. But Yaffa had other things to discuss with me, and for the first time I was glad of his company and prepared to be cordial to him. I wanted no more prompters and accusing confessors. I was back among the professionals who did not turn a man into a Judas goat because he made the best bargain in a bad market.

Yaffa leaned back in his chair and preened himself a little. "On the question of what happens to President Cung after the coup, I think we've got ourselves a deal. . . . I didn't raise it at the conference yesterday because, frankly, the way you've got me boxed in, Mr. Ambassador, I'm still not prepared to guarantee anything. But this is how it lies. I've spoken to General Khiet, to Dao, Tho and the fourth man, Thuyen. All of them agree that they don't want to be saddled with an assassination. But, more than that, they have a deal among themselves. The fourth general, Thuyen, who's the artillery expert, is a cousin of Cung's on his mother's side. When he was invited to join the conspiracy, he made it a condition that Cung's safety should be guaranteed by the rest of the junta."

"Harry, that's the best news I've heard in three stinking weeks!"

He purred happily under the compliment, but held up an admonitory hand. "I thought you'd be happy, sir. But you do understand, there's no certainty in the thing because Cung himself is not a party to the deal. If he decides to fight it out, then no one can be sure that he won't get hit by a bullet."

"That's clear enough. But orders will be given that he is to be taken alive if possible?"

"The generals are agreed on that. I don't know, and they won't tell me, what orders will be given or how they will be framed. I think it's better we don't know anyway."

"I agree. But you're prepared for me to put this on the record with Washington?"

"Of course."

"Let's do it now."

I called Anne Beldon and dictated a supplementary passage to Festhammer:

FURTHER MY REPORT CIA NOW INFORMS ME THAT JUNTA GENERALS ARE AGREED ALL EFFORTS WILL BE MADE TO TAKE PRESIDENT CUNG ALIVE IN EVENT OF COUP. THIS AGREEMENT MADE AS A RESULT OF PRESSURE BY GENERAL THUYEN WHO IS RELATIVE OF CUNG FAMILY. THIS IS BETTER THAN WE EXPECTED THOUGH THERE IS STILL NO GUARANTEE AGAINST ACCIDENT OF WAR. WISH ALSO TO COMMEND YAFFA, WHO HAS USED BEST EFFORTS IN THIS MATTER AND DISCHARGED DUTY EFFICIENTLY. AMBERLEY.

When we were alone again, Yaffa said soberly. "You know, Mr. Ambassador, I underrated you. I hope you'll let me say you're a much bigger man than I thought."

"Thanks for the compliment, Harry."

"No, I mean it. This is a rough business. It sorts out the men from the boys very quickly."

"What brought you into it, Harry?"

He gave me a quick inquiring glance, then shrugged and relapsed into his attitude of ironic amusement.

"I'm a natural-born intriguer, I guess. I like what I do. I don't have very much respect for human nature, or myself either for that matter. Man's a half-civilized animal at best, so he needs a policeman to keep him decent on the street and fellows like me to watch the aces up his sleeve when he plays international poker. . . . Me? I'm a good watchdog because I don't have any illusions about anything. If your best friend isn't interested in the family silver, the odds are he has a yen for your wife. People are as honest as they can afford to be; and when it comes to sex, power hunger and what they need for kicks, they're not honest at all. I'm an oddball myself, so nothing surprises me, nothing shocks me and I'm always ready to hedge my bets. That makes me a good agent, if not exactly the man you'd like your daughter to marry!"

"And do you trust yourself, Harry?"

"Further than I'd trust anyone else, because I know myself better then most—even if I like myself less."

"It's a bleak philosophy."

"It's a bleak world, Mr. Ambassador. But in my own way I get a kick out of it. When there aren't any more kicks, I'll buy out." He gave a small dry laugh. "It's one of the advantages of my business. I know a lot of easy ways to die!"

When he had gone, Anne Beldon came in to take dictation. She looked pale and tired, and her manner was studiously formal. We worked for nearly an hour; then, when we broke off for coffee, I asked what was troubling her. She was too direct to evade the issue, and she answered simply:

"You shouldn't ask me that question, Mr. Ambassador. It puts me in a false position. I'm a secretary. I'm paid to do my job without comment and keep my opinions to myself."

"Are you troubled by what's been happening? By my recommendation to Washington?"

"That and other things."

"Then I'd like to know your thoughts."

"You have no right to know them."

"That's true. But let me tell you something, Anne. I'm very fond of you. I lean heavily on your help and, well, your care of me. I'd like to think you could trust me enough to give me your confidence."

For a moment I thought she would burst into tears, but she controlled herself, and after a moment's hesitation, she told me:

"I'm ashamed, that's all. I'm ashamed of the crude and callous way we dispose of people's lives and destinies, as if—well, as if they were cattle being herded from one field to another. Oh, I know it's politics and diplomacy and military necessity and all the rest! But who, in all this, thinks about the people or speaks for them? . . . My girl friend who had a baby last night while her husband was away fighting in the delta; the boy I used to coach in English, so he could read our textbooks and win a medical scholarship to America; the little French nun who takes my old clothes and remakes them for the girls in the V.D. hospital—where were they last night when you were all talking about a deal with the generals?"

"They were there, Anne, believe me!"

"But who spoke for them? Only Mel Adams—and nobody listened, and nobody cared."

"That's unfair, and you know it."

"I wonder if it is. We came back here and you dictated your message to Washington and I still didn't hear a word about what the people need, what they fear, what they long for—just a little quiet and a chance to see their sons grow up without ever hearing a gunshot or seeing an armed man on every corner."

"Are you disappointed in me, Anne?"

"Yes, I am. I expected—oh God!—I don't know what I expected! But you were so steady, and you seemed so patient and wise that I thought you'd never give way to all this pressure. When you talked to me at night about Asia, and the patterns that persisted under all the changes, and the continuities that made a mockery of time. I hoped so much—too much, perhaps! When you showed me the jade talisman from Number One Chinese and read me the words on it, I thought, Here is a man who really understands and wants to serve people instead of policies! . . . But you didn't. And now Mel is gone, and there's no voice at all for the one-day baby—only for the goddamn generals!"

She was weeping now, and I went to comfort her; but she drew away from me sharply.

"No! Don't touch me, please! I won't cry any more. I'll wash my face and be a good secretary. And I'll hate these dirty days forever and ever!"

I was quite unarmed for an argument like this one, so I came out of it very badly. Besides, the time for argument was long past and I had neither wish nor energy to go wandering again around the maze. Yet Anne's outburst disturbed me deeply and dredged up again all the secret doubts and guilts which lurked at the bottom of the mirror pool. What did she expect of me? A mad charge against the windmills, so that she could pick me up and put plasters on my bloody pate and croon over a draggle-tailed hero? Was I a monster because I understood the true nature of society: that the knowing must decide and the strong must act, because unless they do there will come stronger and wiser ones to force another action and stop the mouths of the ignorant with straw instead of bread? And was I guiltier because I accepted the risks of decision instead of surrendering myself to the flaccid fears of the scrupulous? Mel Adams had challenged me harshly, but he had not blamed me half so bitterly. But Mel Adams was not a woman and he judged me by a different set of measures.

Whether she admits it or not, every woman judges a man as a potential partner in love. Lay his face on the pillow beside her, will she wake to it with love or loathing? Join them, body to body, will there be a juncture of hearts and minds as well? If she weeps, will there be comfort for her? If she laughs, will he laugh with her?

When she commits herself into his hands, will he hold her in trust and tenderness, and strongly, too, against the terrors of night and the small death of every day? Had Anne Beldon measured me thus, and in what had she found me wanting?

As I worked through the day, the question nagged at me like a pebble in my shoe. I had been happy with Gabrielle. I knew, if I knew anything at all, that I had made her happy also. She was too free and strong a spirit to have lived for any time in an unhappy union. Then I remembered something which she had said to me a few days before her death. She knew she was going to die and she was very calm about it; but one evening as I sat in her room, reading to her, she stretched out a wasted hand and laid it on mine and said gently:

"You know, Max, everything has been so good with us; I hope you won't have to pay too much for it."

When I asked her what she meant, she answered with great tenderness:

"I was so necessary to you, Max—and that's a great and glorious thing for a woman! You gave me so much. You trusted me with so much. You never looked for anything outside me. I've often wondered if you believed in anything outside me. . . a God, a faith, even another kind of love! What will you have when I'm gone, dearest? What will you believe in? . . ."

What, indeed? And having found no object of faith, what was my life but a habit, comfortable servitude to a set of ideas that I had never examined and a physical world whose mystery I had never explored? And there, staring up at me from the mirrror pool, was the face of my true self: the unresolved man whom Cung despised, the opportunist whom Yaffa had come to admire, the halfhearted searcher whom young Groton had tried to lead into a way of enlightenment, the satrap who set his seal on warrants of life and death and, at night, dreamed of dumb birds in a bright wasteland. . . .

Then the image was blotted out by a sheet of yellow paper which Anne Beldon laid on my desk. It was the first message from Festhammer.

YOUR SITUATION SUMMARY RECEIVED AND NOW UNDER URGENT DISCUSSION. PRESIDENT DIRECTS ME SEND HIS PERSONAL THANKS FOR LUCID AND DISPASSIONATE EXPOSITION. COMPLIMENTS FROM ALL HERE. WILL ADVISE AS SOON AS DECISION REACHED. FESTHAMMER.

When I looked up from my reading, Anne Beldon was gone and I was still alone. Which was rather a pity, because now there was a question for the defense. Had I the faith of John of the Cross or the serene enlightenment of Musō Soseki, would I have done better? There was no one to tell me.

Late that evening George Groton came back from Cambodia. He was pinched and gray after a bout of food poisoning, but he had a very healthy anger against Harry Yaffa, who, he claimed, had sent him off on a wild-goose chase. Phompenh was a stamping ground for half the professional and amateur agents in Southeast Asia, and for a newcomer like himself it was a manifest impossibility to do any work of value in a few days. Wisely enough, he had decided to enjoy himself and spend a couple of days wandering around Angkor. Then he had been taken ill and, for the rest of his stay, was confined to his hotel. I could not help being amused by his youthful discomfiture and by the shrewdness of Harry Yaffa, who had sidetracked him so neatly during the new Buddhist crisis. We dined together; or rather I dined while Groton sipped tea and nibbled unhappily at dry toast. During the meal I sketched for him the events of the week, the final conferences and my recommendation to Washington. When I told him about Mel Adams and my talk with Anne Beldon, he said:

"I know how they feel, sir, because that's the way I feel myself. I don't have the experience or the information to make a seasoned judgment; but, instinctively, I'm drawn to Adams' point of view. The people have a right to determine their own future for themselves, even if the determination is made by simple inaction. I know the other point of view: that they're caught anyway in the power politics of great nations, that they're submitted every day to campaigns of subversion and political indoctrination and that the twentieth century has caught up with them, whether they like it or not. . . . But somehow this guns-on-the-table, let's-have-at--'em-now kind of action seems dangerous, if only because we can't measure the consequences."

"So you don't approve of me either, George?"

He flushed and answered me uneasily. "I said, sir, that I lack experience and knowledge. I'm expressing a personal attitude."

"Put yourself in my shoes, George. What would you do?"

"That's hardly a fair question, sir."

"Are you afraid of it?"

"No. But I'm not qualified to answer it."

"Let's say then that you have a feeling that I'm wrong. What do you feel I should have done?"

It was brutal to badger a junior like this: But I was desperate for some sign of support, or at least for some kind of absolution in return for the affection I had given him. I resented his stubborn refusal to enter the argument on my terms. There was a long pause during which Groton sat, staring into the dregs of his teacup. Then, finally, he raised his head and faced me squarely.

"You want an answer, sir. I'll give it to you. It comes in two parts. The thing we have to learn, I think, is the art of cautious inaction. I don't think we've learned it yet because we're too vulnerable to the press and public opinion. The man who saved Rome from the Carthaginians was called the Delayer. I hoped, and a lot of other people hoped, too, that you could be strong enough to be such a man. . . . You decided otherwise. Time may prove you right. And that brings me to part two. I'm a junior official. My opinions, right or wrong, carry no weight. So I'm not obliged to make the rough decision Mel Adams made. I may come to it one day. Who knows? For the present . . ."

He broke off, embarrassed, and crumbled a piece of toast between nervous fingers.

I prompted him. "For the present, George?"

"I'm committed to you. No, that's the wrong word. You've given me trust and kindness and a kind of love, I think. I want to return it. I can't do it on the basis of approval of what you do—or even of what you are. I have to say I think you're wrong—grievously wrong! I think you've done something to yourself that you can't define yet. But, for what I'm worth—and it may not be much—I'm still at your service. I don't know if I'm making any sense; but it's a family affair, like putting the old man to bed when he's drunk and curing his hangover in the morning!"

It was an odd, left-handed testament of friendship, and I was graceless enough to tell him so.

"For a budding diplomat, George, you use some damned undiplomatic language."

"Because you're pushing me out of character, sir!" I was shocked by the bitterness of his tone. "You ask too much—a total approval of everything you do, a loyalty without question. You act like a hanging judge and then expect your friends to commend you. If you want to be forgiven, that's fine! But you need a confessor for that, not a colleague or a junior assistant."

"You've said enough, George!"

"Too much or too little. I'm damned if I know, sir! I just don't have the words."

"Then I suggest you go to bed and cool off."

"I'm off duty, sir. I think I'll go to the Caravelle and have a drink."

"You do that. And in the morning you might find you owe me an apology."

He got up from the table and stood uncertainly, fumbling with the napkin. He looked so young and hurt that my heart went out to him, but I could not master my anger enough to offer him any gesture of gentleness. Finally he said:

"I'll make the apology now, sir. I've failed in respect to a superior in the Service. I'm sorry."

"I'll accept it. And we won't ever refer to this evening again."

"Thank you, sir. Good night."

I finished my dinner alone; then, desperate for company, I called General Tolliver and went across town to his house for coffee and a game of billiards. Two of his staff were with him, and we played for a dollar a hundred until midnight. It was good to be back among the professionals, and I vowed that never again would I leave them for the uncertain territory of the dreamers and the idealists.

CHAPTER TEN

At three in the morning, in the Polyclinic Hospital, on Le Loi, George Groton died in my arms.

The manner of his dying was simple, brutal and so hideously futile that even now I cannot think of it without a surge of anger and bitterness. After he left my house he walked to the Caravelle Hotel and went up to the Jerome and Juliette Bar, on the eighth floor, which was—and so far as I know, still is—the customary meeting place for the correspondents of Saigon. There he fell into talk with a photographer named Charles Kubrick, a UPI correspondent named Leonard Garbutt and Gerry Avallone, from the ABC network. They drank and talked till eleven or a little after. Kubrick suggested they move on to a night club called the Baccara, on Tran Quy Cap.

They hailed a taxi outside the Caravelle and drove across the city, past the Roman Catholic cathedral and on to the Boulevard Tran Quy Cap. There was no evidence that they were followed, nor was there anything sinister about the place to which they were going. It was a well-known bar-restaurant with a French chef, a Vietnamese band and a bevy of hostesses, no more beautiful or more virtuous than their counterparts in a dozen other resorts in the city. As Gerry Avallone put it to me, "The linen's clean, the food's eatable, the drinks are honest and where the hell do you go anyway in this lousy city!" Besides, like every other club in the city, it had its own contingent of security police—a trio of sleek, tough young men who sat always in the same places facing the door, took first choice of the hostesses and surveyed the customers with a cynical disdain.

The four men ordered drinks and sat for an hour, talking to the girls and listening to the band; then Garbutt decided to leave and put in some work at his office before going to bed. George Groton, who was still feeling seedy after his sickness, agreed to leave with him. Groton paid the check for both of them. They walked out the front door and asked the doorman to find them a taxi. The doorman left them standing on the curb and trotted twenty yards down to the corner to whistle up a cab. His story was very simple, and he stuck to it through eight hours of police questioning. Before he reached the corner he heard, behind him, a car racing at high speed along the boulevard. He turned to look back at the restaurant and saw a black Citröen almost abreast of the two men on the curb. There was a burst of fire and the two men went down. The doorman threw himself flat on the pavement and the car roared past him, along Tran Quy Cap. He picked himself up and ran back, to find Garbutt dead and George Groton bleeding from the chest and vomiting blood on the pavement. It was just another of those apparently senseless but coldly calculated acts by which the Viet Cong held the city in a state of tension and terror. Any victim would do—a bar girl, a paratrooper, a peddler of roast peanuts. Tonight it was two foreigners standing outside a popular bar.

So George Groton lay in the Polyclinic, wax-pale and coughing up a bloody foam, while an elderly nun told her beads and Anne Beldon, Mel Adams and I stood helpless, waiting for him to die. It was a long and pitiful agony, and I found myself praying desperately to a childhood deity to let it finish quickly and to give me even the smallest sign of reconciliation with this my son of adoption.

Just before three his eyes opened and I thought I saw, under the glaze of pain, a hint of recognition. I took his hand in mine and bent to talk to him, softly and tenderly, like a child. His fingers crisped hard over mine, and I took it as a sign that he had understood. Then he began to cough again, an agonizing struggle to breath through the blood that was stifling him. I put my arm around his shoulder to raise him a little, but he gave a choking cry, his head rolled away from me and he was dead.

The old nun closed his eyes, wiped the foam from his mouth and knelt to say the prayers for the departed. Instinctively we knelt with her; then something broke inside me and I sobbed like a child, with my face pressed against his lifeless hand.

They were the last tears I have ever shed. Even when we buried him, like a soldier, with bugles and gunfire, and I tossed the first clod of earth on his coffin, I could not cry. My heart had turned to flint. I hated this sodden land where he was buried; I hated the crooked, dangerous city; I hated the secret faces of its people; and most of all, I hated myself.

Diplomacy is the nearest thing to perpetual motion; and in spite of death, disaster, subornation and treason, the fidget wheels keep turning, the cogs engage, the springs wind and unwind and the illusion of purpose and direction is maintained for the comfort of the ignorant. I was hardly an hour back from the funeral when Festhammer's message was laid on my desk:

MEET ME USAF HEADQUARTERS HONOLULU 1000
HOURS WEDNESDAY 27 FOR BRIEFING CONFER-
ENCE. LOCATION AND PURPOSE OF MEETING TOP
SECRET.

The meaning of the summons was plain enough: the
hot potato had been passed from hand to hand, and
now they were tossing it back to me. No one was going
to give me a written authorization to back a coup that
might misfire or turn overnight into a bloody revolution. So Festhammer had been deputed to give me a
verbal authorization, which could then be recanted,
reinterpreted or quietly dropped from the canon of history. I could not object. This was the name of the game.
What Festhammer did not know was that I had no care
now how they played it. My heart was hardened into a
cool contempt for myself and my sorry trade, but my
mind was crystal-clear, and I was beyond the seduction of success or the fear of failure. This very detachment made me an almost perfect political instrument, for I would play the ground rules as ruthlessly as
those who had killed George Groton and those whose
intrigues and ineptitude had permitted his death.

Thirty-six hours later I was in Honolulu with Raoul
Festhammer. He was, I think, a little shocked at my
appearance. His first words were:

"My God, Max, you have taken a beating! I hope
you're looking after yourself. That was a terrible
business about young Groton."

"It was."

"I know you were fond of him."

"Yes."

He gave me a quick, shrewd glance, dropped the
subject and then went on cheerfully, "We're staying out
at Maggie Benton's place on Diamond Head. She has a
full staff, a private beach and a guest cottage that she's
turned over to us. We might as well be comfortable
while we work."

"I'd appreciate that."

We drove out, in a clear, bright air, through a mushroom city of new hotels and shopping centers, and throngs of tourists in muu-muus and flowered shirts. This was America, land of the free and the brave; and these were American taxpayers, noble folk, who paid their dollars and read the Sunday funnies and rode the surf at Waikiki because they had bought the right to forget George Groton and all the others who were buried in the distant soil of Asia. I was their servant. What I did was done in their name and with their authority. If I bled a little for them, I had no cause to complain, because they paid me well and sent me to live in state among the mighty of the world. I felt a bleak contempt for them and all their transitory works, as if I were a veteran nursing his wounds and despising those who had never seen a shot fired in anger. My thoughts must have been written on my face, because Raoul Festhammer chided me soberly.

"Take it easy, Max! You don't have to play the old Ivy-Leaguer with me! Turn on the safety valve. Blow off some steam! There's a long road to travel yet and we don't want you cracking up on us!"

"I won't crack up!"

"No, I don't believe you will. But you'll get enough hell in the business without building a private one of your own."

"True enough! Just give me a little time and I'll calm down. I loved that boy like a son, Raoul. And the night before he died, we had a fight. I'd like to think he forgave me—but I'll never know for sure."

"What was the fight about, Max?"

"The business of the coup."

Festhammer shrugged and said moodily, "I can understand it. We've had a few fights in Washington. But what the hell do you do? This is real riverboat poker— and you need eyes in the back of your head . . . !"

I told him about Mel Adams, and he was angry and snappish.

"Adams is an old woman! And he's always been too far left for my liking. I'll be happy to have his resignation. But not yet, Max. Hold him off any way you can until the fireworks are over. We just can't afford the embarrassment right now."

I told him I would do my best, and he brightened again.

"Come on. Max! We're old pros, the pair of us. To hell with all the bloody theoreticians . . . ! Let's have a swim and a drink. Maybe Maggie will take you to bed tonight! She's still a beauty, and she always did have a big yen for you!"

It was good advice and I tried to take it. I surrendered myself to Maggie's effusive welcome. I changed into swimming trunks and drank planter's punch on the lawn overlooking the beach. I swam in the warm, clear water, so different from the gray river and the stinking paddy swamps of Vietnam. And after lunch Festhammer and I retired to the guest cottage, to begin our talk. I have no complaints about what he told me.

". . . You've done a good job, Max. The report was plain and honest. The President was very pleased with it. . . . Now, before we start to talk, is there anything you want to add or subtract?"

"Nothing."

"Any doubts?"

"Plenty. But they're still the same ones that I expressed in the cable."

"Fine! Now let me show you the way it looks in Washington. There is a chance that Cung could survive this coup and even the threat of mutiny in the Army. He's done it before. He might just do it again."

"He might. It's a long chance."

"But we have to be prepared for it. If he emerges again as the man in the saddle, we have to go on living with him."

"True."

"If the generals take over, we have to live with them."

"True again. But the generals won't move without a sign from us. And that sign has to say that we will continue to back their Government in South Vietnam with aid and money and military support."

"So here's how we place the bets: money on the nose for the generals and a dollar on Cung to show. Agreed?"

"Agreed. But I don't see where you're driving, Raoul."

He gave me a lopsided smile and a sardonic answer:

"You will Max, my boy! You will! This is Washington, remember. This is democracy in action—government of the people, by the people, for the people. And the people always want to eat their cake and put a piece in the freezer for tomorrow! The word is 'Go,' Max. That's official. It comes from the man at the top. But there's nothing in writing. There's no formal directive. You act under your discretionary powers. If the generals win, we had no part in it. If they lose, we pull you out and send a new man to make a new start with the Cung regime. It's rough, Max. I know it's rough. But that's the way it goes. Any objections?"

"No."

He gave me a long, thoughtful stare, as if he were about to say something else and then thought better of it. Finally he went on briskly:

"Well, that's the theory of it. Now, as to practice, Washington regards it as very important that we should preserve, as far as possible, an attitude of total disinvolvement from the power struggle between Cung and the dissidents. We continue our current negotiations with the regime. We keep up a steady exchange of views with the Ministry of Foreign Affairs. You begin a normal round of courtesies with other diplomats—which, I notice from your reports, you have not been able to do so far."

"There are only twenty-four hours in the day, Raoul!"

He chuckled and waved away my protest. "I know! I know! But this is tactics now, Max. If you could open a hospital, announce a scholarship, start handing out prizes at speech nights—whatever the hell you can do to create an air of normalcy, even in a difficult situation . . . That's what we need."

"Nobody will believe it, of course."

"They don't have to believe it. Just so no one can print a story that connects you directly with the generals. Which brings me to the next point: How are you going to give the word?"

I told him of the Presidential dinner and he reacted with the same ironic amusement as Harry Yaffa.

"Fine, Max! Fine! . . . And how long after that will the generals be ready to move?"

"I don't know, and I doubt if they'll tell us anyway. That's up to Yaffa's boys to find out."

"Just as well. It makes us look more innocent still."

"A question for you, Raoul: How long before Washington will recognize a new government—provided we get one!"

"As soon as they are unmistakably in power. But you will, of course, be able to work with them before that. If they need working funds, we'll unfreeze enough to keep them in business."

"Another question: What does Washington say about Cung's safety?"

"If he asks for sanctuary, we give it to him. If not . . ." He encompassed the whole span of possibilities with a wave of his hand. "If not . . .*C'est la guerre!* But that's as unofficial as all the rest of this, Max."

"Of course."

It was the measure of my indifference that I could accept their proposition without conscience or complaint. Festhammer himself was surprised, because this was the whole reason for his mission: to cajole me into a commitment that would leave everyone's hands clean except mine. But having got what he wanted, he was too shrewd to ask why I was prepared to grant it. Or perhaps he knew—as Cung and Harry Yaffa knew, each in his own fashion—that there are no more terrors for a man who has come to terms with death and with his own damnation.

Our business was all over and done with in less than an hour. We swam again and drank cocktails on the lawn and watched the big catamarans homing in the sunset across a sea the color of blood. Festhammer, who was never without a woman, called a girl friend, and the four of us went to dinner at the Royal Hawaiian.

That night I went to bed with Maggie Benton. Because she was eager and I was seized with an enormous need to affirm my virility, it was a very satisfying mating for both of us. When it came time to leave, she clung to me and wept a little and we both made beautiful promises. But before the the last islands were out of sight, before we were swallowed by the empty air of the Pacific, I had already forgotten her.

This time my arrival in Saigon was a furtive affair. There were no guards and no ceremonies. As soon as the transport touched down, Bill Slavich drove my car onto the tarmac, Harry Yaffa welcomed me briskly and we set off immediately for my house. I told him of my talk with Festhammer and he grinned with cynical approval.

". . . Even for us here, Mr. Ambassador, it's the best way to handle the situation. Secrecy is as essential to the generals as it is to us. But there's something much more important. You've been told to work under your discretionary powers. Therefore I'm in a position to go to the generals and tell them that your final approval depends upon your being fully informed of their plans. We won't get all the information, but at least we'll get enough to watch their military movements and to see that our own units are not left exposed or unprepared. . . . I'll start work right away, and you'll have at least a basic briefing before the Presidential dinner. On the other matter, the innocent activity, the public appearances, and so on, I'll start co-ordinating that with our press and public relations people. You could start with a cocktail party and some dinner invitations. Then we'll arrange visits to various USOM projects: agricultural centers, training schools, medical and Army institutions, and so on. But you do have one problem—Mel Adams! He's threatened to resign, remember?"

"Leave Mel to me. I'll talk to him."

But what to say was another matter. I had great respect for Mel Adams; and besides, it was he who had
stood beside me at Groton's deathbed; it was his hand
that had lifted me and led me home. It was he who sat
with me during the hours of near madness afterward. I
was base enough, God help me, but I could not stoop
to treachery against this man. I called his home and
asked him to come and see me. I told him the whole
truth, and then I pleaded with him.

"I know exactly how you feel, Mel. I know you don't
and can't approve what I'm doing. If you want to resign
immediately, I'll sign your travel orders. But I'm asking
you to stay—not to participate, not to approve, but
simply to protect the Administration from the consequences of a decision which you believe to be wrong.
That's as honest as I can make it, Mel, believe me!"

He thought about it a long time, pacing the floor of
my study, debating aloud with me and with himself.
Finally he said flatly:

"Very well. I'll stay—on three conditions. The first is
that I handle routine business only and that I am not
required to take part in any discussions or decisions on
the coup. The second is that if the coup takes place I
am authorized to take independent action to persuade
Cung to seek sanctuary with us. The third is that when
the affair is over—whichever way it goes—you sign my
travel papers and then sight and initial my personal account of all these proceedings. I shall then forward that
document with my resignation to the Secretary of State.
Is it a deal?"

"It's a rough deal, Mel, especially the second condition. It brings you into direct conflict with the CIA and
with State Department policy."

"It's the only deal I'll make. My resignation's already
written."

"It can't be official. Because it's a contradiction of
my orders."

"Assassination's not official either. But we may still
be involved in it."

"Then between you and me, unofficially, it's a deal."

"I wish to God that we could both be a little prouder of it."

Now we had to wait and, while we waited, play out the empty little comedy of seeming to wait for nothing at all. I walked through my role expertly enough, but with little conviction. I gave a long-delayed cocktail party and began to work through a list of dinner guests. I gave a talk on American business methods to the Junior Chamber of Commerce. I visited the Pasteur Institute and presented a gift of serums from the American Red Cross. I made a solemn inspection of a stud farm where a lone Australian was raising milch cows for tropical conditions. Nobody was deceived because everybody was watching the chess game that Cung was playing in the city and in the provinces. Commands were being changed. Units were being transferred from one division to another. Three provincial governors were dismissed and, in Government departments, minor officials were made monitors over their superiors in rank. The United Nations Commission had left, angry and frustrated by the unaccountable absence of informants in the pagodas. The Archbishop of Hué left the country to take part in the Ecumenical Council, and the Minister for Education was taken suddenly ill and retired to his villa on Cap Saint-Jacques. By executive order the bank accounts of suspect officials were frozen and their houses were placed under police surveillance. Cung was playing the classic game: divide and rule. And some among my diplomatic colleagues were offering even money that he would get away with it.

Harry Yaffa, however, presented a different picture. The transfer of General Khiet was an advantage to the conspiracy since it set him at the center of events in Saigon, where he was much respected. For the rest, the generals had taken advantage of the troop movements to make their own transfers among junior commanders and N.C.O.'s in the crack paratroop, artillery and armored units. They were confident that when the time came to strike they would be ready. How long would they need after the Presidential dinner? Ten days. What warning would we have? Twelve hours at most, four at least. It was a nervous and troubled time, and the Viet Cong took full advantage of it. There were heavy attacks in the delta. A supply vessel was blown up at the docks in Saigon. And, just for a reminder that no man is an island, in Laos the Pathet Lao began moving in strength across the Plain of Jars.

Against this background of intrigue and violence, the Presidential dinner had the air of an anachronism. To get to it, the guests, Viets and foreigners alike, had to pass through cordon after cordon of armed men. Their engraved invitations were inspected with as much care as if they were passes to an arsenal—which in fact they were. When they left their cars, they left their drivers and their keys as well; and both men and vehicles were politely but efficiently searched. Yet, inside the Palace, the lights were blazing and the feast was celebrated with formality, if not with festivity. The women were beautifully gowned in silks from Thailand and brocades from Hong Kong; the men were as dapper and polished as old ivory, and the officers were resplendent in the orders and decorations of the Republic of South Vietnam; the shoulder ribbon of the Grand Cross of the National Order, the chaplet of the Commander, the breast ribbons of the Medal of Military Merit and the Distinguished Service Cross. Some of them were entitled to French decorations as well, but they were no longer in evidence except as discreet rosettes on the lapels of the French themselves.

The meal was austere, because Cung was an austere man and he would not budge from his claim that those who enjoyed the dubious peace of the capital should share, at least in symbol, the privations of the fighting man. The talk was guarded and therefore boring. Over the whole gathering there lay a shadow of mistrust and ill will; but Cung sat at the head of it, more like a mandarin than ever, and smiled a little and bent to pay his small clerical compliments to those who sat near him.

Then the toasts began, and Cung made the first one:

"To this Republic, founded in tears and blood, and sustained against enemies within and without by the courage of her people." We drank to it and the mistrust faded for a moment into a transitory pride. There was even pride for the man who gave the toast, because for that moment, if never again, they had to remember what he had done for them. I remembered it, too; and for an instant my resolution faltered. But it was already too late. My name was called, and in the silence after it I made my little speech.

"This Republic, like ours in America, grew out of a revolt against colonialism [mild applause]. The hopes of the people of this Republic are the same as ours: freedom from want, freedom from fear, freedom of speech and the right to determine their own future, without threat of armed invasion or foreign subversion [more applause]. I stand here as the representative of a great nation which shares your struggle and which spends its money, its skill and the blood of its young men in defense of what you have won and what you have yet to maintain and increase. On this your National Independence Day, I give you a double toast: Your President, Phung Van Cung . . . and the gallant people of South Vietnam."

There was no applause now. The words hung for a moment in dead air, then the whole gathering rose and drank the toast in silence. It was done. And they all knew it was done—and how and why. . . .

The following morning I received a gift from President Phung Van Cung. It was a leatherbound copy of the New Testament in the old-fashioned English version of Douai. There was an inscription on the flyleaf:

To the Ambassador of the United States
From the President of the Republic of South Vietnam.
Saint Luke XXII: 47-48.

Obligingly he had marked the text for me with a scarlet ribbon:

222

As he was yet speaking, behold a multitude; and he that was called Judas, one of the twelve, went before them and drew near to Jesus for to kiss him. And Jesus said to him: Judas, dost thou betray the Son of Man with a kiss?

I locked the book in a private drawer of my desk so that Anne Beldon would not read it. Later, as a matter of security, I showed it to Harry Yaffa, who shrugged it off with grim distaste.

"That's been Cung's trouble all along, Mr. Ambassador. He's a good man gone wrong, because he's always believed he's Christ Almighty."

I wondered what George Groton would have thought of it; but he, of course, was dead and past caring. For the first time I was glad that he was gone from me.

For the next few days I kept myself sedulously busy. I demanded a daily accounting from every department of the Embassy. I attended the briefing sessions at Tolliver's headquarters and conferred regularly with Harry Yaffa and his staff. I made myself freely available to the press and kept Anne Beldon and her girls chained to their desks with reams and reams of paperwork. I needed all this redundant activity to keep my mind occupied. I needed the company of practical men to confirm my shaky faith in the course I had taken.

I refused to eat alone now. I kept my guests talking late, and when I dined out I was always the last to leave. Before I went to bed, I drank a double whiskey and took sleeping pills, so that I would not have to face a nightly interrogation of myself. But, in spite of it all, the days were laggard for me and I fretted in expectation of a decisive move by the generals. I had little to do with Mel Adams. I wanted him to feel at least that I respected our bargain; and I hoped, though with little confidence, that he might keep some vestige of respect for me.

Anne Beldon's attitude to me was strange. She had made neither recantation nor apology for her attack on me after the conference, and I, for my part, was determined never again to be drawn into discussion with her of my own actions or of Embassy policies. On the night of George Groton's death she had wept with me, but in the end she had withdrawn and left me in the care of Mel Adams. Now, in the office, I was working her brutally; and in the evening, because of my social engagements, we were private for scarcely a moment. Yet from time to time, during a pause in dictation, or while I was signing correspondence, I would catch her looking at me with a kind of puzzled concern, as if in some fashion she feared for me yet could not express the fear in words.

Then, one evening, while I was having a solitary drink before going out to dinner at the Air Force mess, she came to talk to me. I mixed her a drink and we skirmished lightly for a few moments before she came to the point. Her girls were being overworked. There was overtime every day and very little diversion for them afterward. I was compounding the problem by brusqueness and an apparent indifference to their efforts. In the context of war and death it was a petty enough complaint, but my own guilt made me sensitive to the justice of it. I apologized for my remissness.

". . . It's a very real problem, Anne, and I'm afraid I haven't given it enough attention. What would you like me to do?"

"Just talk to them occasionally. Give them a smile or two and inquire sometimes about their health or their families. It wouldn't hurt sometimes to have a meal sent up to them when they're working late, or to make them a present of a scarf or a piece of lacquer. They're only human, you know. Some of them are lonely, and they're all living under stress in this city. They admire you very much; but when you just brush through the office, looking like the wrath of God, they're troubled. Besides, they don't really understand what you're going through . . ."

"Do you understand, Anne?"

"I didn't at first. But I began to understand the night

George died. I'd never understood how solitary you really were, nor how deep your affections were hidden. I've been feeling guilty ever since."

"You mustn't feel guilty, Anne. I'm not an easy character to know or to like. Besides, we're in a critical situation here, and I've had very little time for personal adjustment to it."

"I know that now. That's what made it seem so unfair when I attacked you and Mel Adams and even George. I still can't say I agree with what you're doing. But at least I should have given you credit for an honest purpose."

"I'm afraid it goes a lot deeper than that, Anne. The problem is that I'm not sure myself whether I'm honest or not."

"Is anybody?"

"Most people, I think."

"Only because they never challenge or examine themselves. Most of us are cowards."

"Are you a coward, Anne?"

"Yes."

"I've never noticed it."

"It isn't something that shows, like a dangling slip or a run in a stocking. It's a thing you keep hidden, like an ugly birthmark or a scar. And the hiding is part of the cowardice, too."

"What are you afraid of, Anne?"

"Do you really want to know?"

"Only if you want to tell me."

"May I have another drink, please?"

While I was mixing it for her, she got up and stood by the windows, looking out at the shadowy garden. I carried the drink across to her, and, side by side, we watched the lights of the guardhouse, the tangled outlines of the tropic trees and the misty pricking of the stars between the cloud breaks. I smelled her perfume and saw her face, half lit, like a cameo carved in profile against a dark shell. Her voice was almost a whisper.

". . . It was the night of George's death. I was terribly broken up by it because it reminded me so vividly of my own husband's death. But, more than anything, I was shocked by what it did to you. You were so naked, so desolate. You were a man with all the horror of the world on his shoulders. I wanted so much to comfort you, but I couldn't. I left you to Mel. Later, when he had gone, I heard you pacing the floor in your room. I came and stood outside your door, and I wanted with all my heart to come in and be with you, put my arms around you and be a woman to you. . . . But I was afraid. . . ."

"Of me, Anne?"

"Not of you. But that I might surrender something, give something that I couldn't take back. Oh, not virtue, not reputation or even love! It was me—the little cowardly me that I hedged and protected and refused to spend or expose in case it got hurt again. So I told myself you didn't need me. You were a big and important man and you were strong enough to survive anything that happened to you. I went back to bed and cried myself to sleep. Then, in the morning, I saw what had happened to you. You were like a stone man. Your heart was locked up and you'd thrown away the key. . . . I knew I'd failed you. I'd failed myself, too. I wonder now if I won't fail any man who is rash enough to love me. . . ."

I put my arm around her shoulder to draw her to me and comfort her, but she would not respond. She said very gently:

"No, please don't! I want to be kissed and warmed like any other woman. But I haven't any right to it, and it would make me feel like a tramp." Then she turned to me with a sad little smile and touched my cheek with her cool fingers. "We're both in the same boat, aren't we, Mr. Ambassador? We're looking around for someone to forgive us, but there's nobody. Perhaps there never will be, until we learn to forgive ourselves. . . ."

It was a haunting thought and it echoed the one I had heard from the lips of the wandering novelist: that no man can borrow another's absolution. And yet without at least the illusion of forgiveness it was not possi-

ble for man to survive as a sane creature in a mad
world. Every man, whatever his quality or his estate,
tried to create a means of exemption from his own guilt.
The Harry Yaffas of the world began with a half-truth:
that delinquency was universal and therefore unavoid-
able. They ended, however, with a whole lie: that guilt
was an illusion and impediment in the jungle battle
for survival. The egoists elevated themselves above guilt
and made the rest of the world their scapegoat. The
Buddhists, faced with a universality of imperfection,
bound man to the wheel of life and set him rolling
through an inexorable and repetitive purging, in a long
succession of existences. This, being so terrible and dis-
proportionate a penalty of existence, was in itself a
forgiveness and sometimes an inducement to misde-
meanor. The unbeliever or the unknowing, who staggered under the burden of his delinquent nature, sometimes had recourse to the curative exchanges of psychi-
atry or analysis. The true practitioners of the art aimed
at building in a man enough light and strength to accept
himself as he was and to wear his traumas with respect,
if not with joy. The others, who sought to give absolution by denying all responsibility, found themselves at
the end, inept and unworthy, because the patient himself began to cry out at the lie that destroyed his dignity
with his guilt.

Guilt and dignity . . . it was an odd juxtaposition.
But at bottom was it not a true—or at least a desirable
—one? To be guilty one had to be free, and not totally
subject to some cosmic duress. To be free was to be
able to make another choice; if not always to be potent
to change the consequences of the first. I had always
recognized a great wisdom in the Catholic practice of
sacramental confession, with its guarantee of judicial
forgiveness to the right of heart. But to accept the sac-
rament was to accept the whole faith on which it was
founded: a personal God, an incarnate Redeemer, a
continuing authority in dogma and morals. But to accept or reject was not in my power, as a wise old Do-
minican had been at pains to show me; and I must wait

in patience for an enlightenment that might never be given, by a God whom I might never acknowledge.

Whichever way I turned I was caught in mystery: the mystery of the identity, the nature and the responsibility of man. And I knew that there was no solution but to continue the blind pilgrimage and hope, without hope, for a light at the end. Anne Beldon was right when she refused to surrender herself to the fictitious pardon of a casual act of love. In a long, shared loving one might, and sometimes did, find the roots of heaven; but in the brief carnality of the little death there was no absolution—nor in the great death either, for all its illusory easement. . . . So play on, fiddler, and dance me a jig! Tomorrow I'm back to war again!

Two days later, at four in the afternoon, Harry Yaffa came to see me. He was tense and excited.

"Tonight's the night, Mr. Ambassador! Win, lose or draw, the game's on! Let's look at your maps, and I'll show you the way it goes. Take Saigon first. . . ." We spread the maps on my desk and he gave me a swift, precise lesson in the tactics of revolution. "Here's the airport. The generals have established their operational headquarters here, right next door. At two in the morning their own men take over the airfield and the communications center. Here's the radio station and there's the telephone exchange. They're the first objectives inside the city. From then on all the action converges on the Palace. Now look at the four main arteries into the city: three from the north, one from the south. One comes in from Bienhoa, one from Bencat, one from Tayninh, and there's the Southern Highway from Tânan. Already their armor and infantry are ready to move and the field guns are hooked up to the transports. By midnight they'll be on the outskirts of the city. By two in the morning they'll have the radio station and central exchange, and their tanks and artillery will be in position. Then they'll telephone Cung in the Palace and demand surrender. If he refuses, there'll be an air bombardment, an artillery barrage and then a full-scale

attack by tanks and infantry. . . . Now let's look at the
rest of the country. The Military Academy at Dalat is
ready to defect, and the local troops are organized. Hué
is considered safe for the rebels. Danang is ready, so are
Longxuyen, in the South, and Cantho. . . . It's a good
plan, sir, and General Khiet is certain it will work, without any undue exposure to the Viet Cong in vulnerable
areas."

"What does Tolliver think of it?"

"He approves, sir. His own intelligence people have
been evaluating every move as it came to their attention; and he's reasonably satisfied for the safety of our
own troops. All passes have been canceled for tonight
and all personnel already on pass have been recalled to
duty. The M.P.'s are rounding them up now, so nobody
should get caught in the cross fire tonight."

"What about our own communications?"

"All our radio links will be open and working full
schedules, and General Khiet has ordered all the lines
to the Embassy, to military installations and to your
house kept open. I think we've covered just about everything, except the question of Embassy staff. What do
you want to do about that, sir?"

"I'll stay here, of course. Miss Beldon will stay with
me. Keep the communications center at full strength,
but send the married men home to look after their families. Heads of section can remain on duty or appoint
deputies if they wish. Warn everyone to stay off the
streets and dine at home. I'll leave early and have a talk
with Tolliver. I'll probably eat with him and then be
here by nine. If you need me, call Tolliver's office."

"I doubt we'll need you, sir." He grinned and
shrugged in resignation. "It's out of our hands now.
Even Mel Adams shouldn't be too dissatisfied. After
all, it is self-determination—of the Viets, by the Viets,
for the Viets! And God help the generals if their plan
misfires!"

I could not tell him my own perverse and secret
hope: that even at this thirteenth hour Phung Van
Cung might produce a miracle and, giving the lie to us

all, emerge once more as the deliverer and the victor. For all his faults, he commanded respect, and his stubborn gallantry merited a better end than this rattrap siege that his erstwhile comrades were preparing for him.

Armed with my private knowledge, I found it strange that the city should be so unperturbed by the violence that hung over it. The clerks were ambling home from their offices with briefcases under their arms. The news vendors sat languid in their corner booths. The shopkeepers stood at the doors, gossiping with one another and with the passersby. Through the open doors of a barber's shop I saw men lying back like pashas under a cloud of lather, while pretty girls trimmed their nails and massaged their fingers. Students rode by on noisy motor scooters, sometimes with a girl, sidesaddle on the pillion, her silk blouse flattened against her body, her tiny feet trailing an inch above the ground. The amahs in funereal black scuffed along with a shiny child clutching either hand. The peddlers of soy cakes and sweetmeats trundled their little carts and the street sweepers padded patiently in the gutters, whisking their brooms at the garbage. A few sparse worshippers went up and down the steps of the cathedral, and through the open gates of a pagoda I saw the flash of a yellow robe and the slow passage of a shaven nun. Even the policemen looked languid, and the militiamen seemed more interested in studying the girls than in the defense of a beleaguered Republic.

I could not believe that so massive a movement of rebellion could pass unnoticed or unrumored, but perhaps this was the most notable symptom of the long and wasting war sickness. The people had seen so many captains come and go, they had heard so often the rumble of tanks and troop carriers that they had become indifferent. In a city full of rumors what was one piece of gossip more or less? In a life of so much uncertainty one lived from day to day, not caring to question beyond the next meal and the next night's sleep. This was Asia, where they still remembered Kublai Khan and the Ming emperors and the fabulous Trung sisters, who rode on elephants to affront the invader—but where the last princeling was nameless and a new warlord was a day's wonder.

At Tolliver's headquarters, I was back once again in the twentieth century. There was an air of bustle and excited efficiency. There was a constant buzzing of telephones and much coming and going of clerks and junior staff officers. Tolliver himself was brisk and good-humored. He insisted on showing me his situation maps and giving me his own version of the coming battle.

". . . It's a good operation, Ambassador. Good tactics, good logistics. I think they'll bring it off."

"How long will it take?"

"Anything from four hours to twenty-four, depending on the behavior of the Palace Guard. According to our information, Cung's got about four hundred troops quartered in and around the Palace. They've got machine guns, mortars and, of course, the anti-aircraft batteries. But they can't hold out indefinitely against air bombing and artillery. If the generals can move their troops into town without having to fight anywhere along the road, I'd say it's a cakewalk."

What I could not understand was how Cung, in spite of all his vaunted control of the situation, had let the generals complete their preparations so thoroughly. Tolliver, however, had an answer:

"They simply fouled up his communications, inside and outside the Palace. They fed him false information about movements and postings. The General Staff and the whole Administration is riddled with traitors."

"You'd better mind your language, General! Tomorrow they'll all be heroes."

"I know." He gave me a crooked grin. "I guess names don't matter very much when loyalties are divided. I pointed out to my staff this afternoon just how easy it would be to scramble up our headquarters once the channels of intelligence became tainted. . . . In a way, I feel sorry for Cung. He deserved better. I wonder what's going to happen to him."

"God knows. I'm authorized to offer him sanctuary if he asks for it. But that's all."

"But we don't intervene?"

"No.

"Well, thats the way the cookie crumbles. Cardinal rule for a dictator, Ambassador: get the Army on your side and keep it there! If you don't, you're dead. And by this time tomorrow Cung's going to be dead, too."

"In spite of the gurarantees? In spite of General Thuyen?"

"In spite of everything, Ambassador! Even if the Palace Guard fights to the last bullet, they'll have to surrender in the end. Then they'll start bargaining for their own safety. With what? The big bad dictator—President Cung! The generals don't have to take any responsibility, you see. He's knocked off by his own men when they realize how they've been duped and misguided."

"I didn't think of that."

"You can't think of everything, Ambassador," said Tolliver good-humoredly. "If you don't mind my saying it, I think you've done a damn good job. You moved cautiously, you kept your head and you didn't shirk a decision when you had to make it. We're all on your side. You can believe that."

Which from Tolliver was noble praise. I was grateful for the compliment and glad that he was too simple a man to understand the irony of it. . . . I wondered what Cung was doing in the Palace while the mortars were being moved into position and the armorer handed out grenades and ammunition clips and the gunners checked their field of fire. Was he afraid? Was he in despair at the treachery? Was he making the rounds of his small garrison, or smoking an after-dinner cigar with the remnants of his staff? I had a faint, uneasy suspicion that he might be praying in front of the Rouault Christus.

It was a long vigil and I was too important a personage to be welcome at the crap game in the office of the Second Secretary or the Kaffeeklatsch in the communications center. There was the usual mountain of routine work, but on the eve of an armed uprising it seemed quaintly unimportant and I had no heart for it. I sent Anne Beldon to join the other girls on standby and then took out my diary and began to write, mechanically at first, and then with a real urgency, my intimate thoughts on this last night before the roof fell in. They are strange, jumbled pages, but as I reread them now, I can afford a pang of pity for the man who wrote them.

". . . Three hours from now the shooting will begin and men will die. In the chronicles of our time it will be a minor skirmish, soon forgotten. But every battle is an Armageddon for some poor devils. . . . All the words I have spoken and written will soon be turned into bullets and bayonets and artillery shells. Strange, but true. In the end men are killed by words. Perhaps that was what the novelist meant when he said he knew the meaning of words and therefore respected them. We, who are deluged with words from the press, from television screens and transistor sets, have come to disprize and to distort them. But truly they are dragon's teeth. . . . Who reads *Das Kapital* now? Yet from Vladivostok to the Berlin Wall, from Hankow to Havana, there are bombs and bayonets transmuted from that unreadable tome. . . . We, too, are wordsmiths, and we make base coinage and wonder why simple folk toss it back in our teeth. Last week I uttered seven words in a toast, and tomorrow morning they may be a noose for a man's neck or a bullet in his head. . . . Speech is the one faculty that names us men. Why do we so misuse it that sometimes we had as lief be dumb and deaf? . . .

"The tanks must be moving in now, and the trucks and the field guns. Our tanks, our guns. We bought them with our people's money and gave them to our friends to keep them safe and free. But those who were our friends yesterday will be dead tomorrow, killed with the guns we gave them. So who is safe and who is

free under the threat of mutual malice, in the bondage
of perennial mistrust? . . .

"And I, who write this so clearly, why do I compound confusion? Or is it that I speak two languages:
one for a private truth-telling and the other for intercourse in a society whose nature and complexity I do
not understand? And if I do not understand it, why do I
accept appointment as an arbiter of its destiny? . . .

"Who am I who write? Even this I do not know
with certainty. Show me another man, though, of whom
I am equally ignorant, and I will, with great certainty,
read his attainder and sign his death warrant. In this the
man who is about to die is more fortunate than I; his
vigil, I truly believe, is calmer than mine. He knows
who he is, or at least he believes that he knows. He
knows what death is and will accept it as a consumma-
tion and a continuity. He knows what the words mean,
too: 'In the beginning was the Word and the Word was
with God and the Word was God. . . .' Nevertheless, he
has failed miserably in the affairs of the commonweal and
therein the Shining Word has availed him nothing. . . .

"At the airfield they will be filling the fuel tanks and
clipping the rockets on the racks and fusing the bomb
loads. Young men like George Groton will ride the
wind like avenging furies, raining destruction on other
young men whom they cannot see. . . . A banal
thought. A commonplace of our enlightened times. The
spirit of the tree can be placated with incense. The
spirit of the water is pleased with spread blossoms. The
spirit of the house is hungry, and one can quiet him
with a rice cake. But the avengers of the upper air, the
riders in fiery chariots, who can placate them—and
how—except with blood and the smoke of human sacrifice? . . .

"What will I do tomorrow, when it is all over? Return into a wilderness and powder my hair with ashes?
I am the oracle who must proclaim a fortunate outcome: '. . . a speedy restoration of normal relations, a
renewed effort in the military sector, stable and enlight-

ened government, liberty, equality and let's have dancing in the clubs again, a little honest whoring and to hell
with neuters and French neutralists alike!' *Dixi!*—I
have spoken! And then I'll fly home whistling Dixie
with a victory for democracy in my pocket. . . . Why
the hell don't they start? Let's get the killing over, and
then maybe we can all get some sleep! . . .

"And Pharoah said to Joseph, I have dreamed
dreams and there is no one that can expound them.
. . . Who will expound me to myself? Who will untan-
gle me the dreamer from my own dream: the dream of
the dumb bird and the flat land, and the dreamer surrounded by light, yet seeing nothing but a songless
cuckoo . . . ? I cannot endure this solitude. I must
marry and live a little and breed me a son to carry my
name. Even a little love would be enough, and I would
be grateful for it as for a new gift of life. The gift of life
is a gift of tears and laughter. I am empty of tears and
I have not laughed in a long, long time. . . .

"Gabrielle, why aren't you here? Where are you
now? Have you met George? Does he talk of me kind-
ly? I cannot think of you both bound to the wheel of
life, turning endlessly through a chain of futilities, toward the enormous calm of nothing. There is a horror
in that, an unendurable madness! . . . That I, in some
future existence, may violate her whom I have loved in
this—tread her, a worm under my elephant's foot, or, a
microbe in her blood, strike her down in a second death
—this is a primitive nonsense that affronts all reason!
But we crave so much a promise of immortality that we
are prepared to take it on almost any terms. . . .

"Mel Adams and Harry Yaffa . . . a study in contrasts. Yet whom do I respect the more? The man who
discharges with efficiency, and sometimes sexual enthu-
siasm, the most sordid tasks of Government or the man
who reserves always the right to question or refuse
them? Because I am the Government—in this place and
time—I find myself veering between the two. Without
Yaffa, I cannot function and I put the lives of many
men in jeopardy. Without Adams . . . But I am with-

out him now. He stood pat upon our bargain and refused to keep the vigil with me. Which proves—or does it?—that conscience is a dispensable item of social equipment. . . .

"Outside in the street I hear the rumble of tanks and heavy trucks. From my window I can see nothing. I look at my watch. Half an hour before two o'clock. . . . A long vigil. . . . For Cung, perhaps, an agony in his own Palace garden. For his Judas—if indeed I am a Judas—a longer one is preparing. How long did jesting Pilate rule in Jerusulem after the Crucifixion? How long will I stay here to prove that my country is blameless and filled with noble and beneficent thoughts for her gallant Asian allies? . . . A telephone call from Harry Yaffa. Everything is going according to plan. He will try to stay in contact. . . .

"Anne Beldon has just brought me a cup of coffee. I am drawn to her strongly. My night with Maggie Benton has sharpened my sexual appetite. I know I could stifle Anne's misgivings and urge her into marriage. But afterward? A mating between the hangman and the woman who has seen behind his mask. Unthinkable, unpredictable in its intimate terrors. . . . The rumble of vehicles has stopped. There is the sound of running feet: the regular, drilled jog trot of foot soldiers. Above it, the high drone of approaching aircraft. . . . Come on, for Christ's sake! Let's hear those goddamn guns!"

CHAPTER ELEVEN

It was four minutes after two when I heard the first shots: the dull duplex thudding of the anti-aircraft batteries. Immediately afterward the bombs began to fall, and the shock waves hammered at the windowpanes. As the first wave of aircraft flew away the artillery barrage opened, mixed with the sound of mortar fire and the occasional crackle of machine guns. I felt like a man locked in a prison cell while the world outside exploded into chaos. After ten minutes I could stand it no longer. I called Anne Beldon and Bill Slavich, and we drove a dozen blocks around the river front to the Caravelle Hotel. We climbed to the roof garden and looked down over the spread of the town.

It was a weird and sinister spectacle. The whole city was lit up. People were standing on rooftops, on balconies and at open windows, like spectators at a football game. The Palace area was shrouded in a thick column of smoke and ringed with gunfire. We could see the tanks, crawling like squat monsters along the roadway, while the infantry sheltered behind them or clung to the shelter of the walls. Fires were blazing in shops and tenements, mortar shells exploded on the sidewalks. The planes came over again and again, pounding at the Palace compound, and when they left, the tanks moved closer, firing point-blank down the open boulevards.

When the last wave of planes came over, there was no anti-aircraft fire and the ring of men and armor drew tighter around the citadel. The defenders fought back stubbornly, with machine guns, bazookas, mortars and small arms. Sometimes, during a lull in the firing, we heard the shouts of men, and occasionally a long-drawn scream, thin and distant like a bird cry. Around us there was a crush of people: correspondents, hotel staff, camera crews, French businessmen or simple drinkers who had stayed to watch the fun. There was a babble of tongues, and occasionally a shout as a new barrage broke out or another building went up in flames.

We stayed for perhaps an hour and a half, and then suddenly I was disgusted with the spectacle of destruction. We drove back to the Embassy, and I went straight to the communications center to catch up on the news. Fighting had started in Danang, but Hué and

Dalat were quiet and the delta towns had switched allegiance without a shot fired. Harry Yaffa had called in to report that all strategic points in the city were in the hands of the rebels, and Radio Saigon was already on the air with the news that the Palace defenses were expected to fall at any moment. I called Tolliver's headquarters. All his area commanders had reported and the countryside was quiet. Even the Viet Cong seemed to have gone to ground for the first time in months. At twenty minutes to four the firing ceased. Half an hour later Harry Yaffa came in with the news that the Palace Guard had surrendered but that Cung himself had escaped. How, when or where he had gone, no one seemed to know. Many of his staff had stayed, manning the machine guns and fighting with rifles and grenades from behind the last barricades. According to Yaffa, the Palace troops were bitter at Cung's desertion and at the costly folly of their hopeless fight.

Strangely enough, I was bitter about it, too. I had hoped for something better from this man—a last heroism, a wild charge, perhaps, against impossible odds. But no! An intriguer to the last, he had slipped away and left his garrison to die, covering an ignoble retreat. Then, after the bitterness, came a wave of relief. My decision had been right after all. I had done well by my Government, and by this country as well. I had risked much but the outcome had absolved me at last. I sent off a message to Festhammer and then sat down with Harry Yaffa to a breakfast of coffee and sandwiches.

Yaffa was jubilant. "It went like clockwork, Mr. Ambassador! A real master stroke! If Khiet can run the country the way he ran this operation, we're really in business again. Even the casualties weren't too bad, fifty or so dead in the Palace and about a hundred wounded. It's a small cost when you think we might have had the whole country in revolt. You should feel very proud of yourself. When you've finished your coffee, let's drive around the city and take a look at what's happening. From what I've seen already, it's going to be like Paris on Bastille Day. . . ."

It was an apt description. Even though it was still only an hour after sunrise, the thoroughfares were jammed with people, laughing, shouting, embracing one another, passing bottles of liquor out of the bars and offering them to any soldier who happened to be near. They closed in on my car and clapped their hands, shouting, "Long live the Americans! Long live the friends of the Republic!" Someone held up a little girl with a wreath of flowers in her hands, and when she could not reach me they sat her on the hood like a mascot and we carried her a hundred yards along the boulevard. Crowds of students were marching along the sidewalks arm in arm, with cardboard banners tied to their breasts or held high above their heads. In front of the National Assembly a man was playing an accordion and boys and girls were dancing around him to the tune of a once forbidden love song. Along the Catinat another crowd was pelting a shop front with stones and throwing lighted papers through the smashed windows. This was the bookshop owned by a member of the Cung family. Soon the place was ablaze, and the crowd and the soldiers stood cheering while it burned.

The Palace area was cordoned off with troops, but when they saw the pennon they let us drive close enough to see the rubble and the bomb craters and the fires that were still burning. The looters were still busy in the ruins, carting out furniture and ornaments and bottles of wine. In another street we had to pull into the curb for a procession of Buddhist monks carrying the heart of their first martyr in a gilt casket under a canopy of red silk. The crowd cheered them, and some fell on their knees in veneration. Flags were flying from all the pagodas, and whenever a yellow robe appeared in the crowd people pressed about him and filled his begging bowl with gifts. Whenever anyone caught sight of my pennon, there was a tumult of acclamations and we were mobbed again. Once my car was lifted off the ground and carried fifty yards by a cheering mob.

Although we made only a short circuit, it took us better than two hours to get back to the Embassy, and there I found Arnold Manson, the Australian, waiting for me with the Italian Ambassador.

Manson's manner was strained and formal. "We've been waiting for you for nearly an hour, Mr. Amberley, and the matter is very urgent. We understand that President Cung is still in hiding. Do you have any further information?"

"None at all, I'm afraid."

"Then we do have some time to act. I've telephoned our diplomatic colleagues and they are all agreed that, in simple humanity and in view of world opinion, President Cung's safety must be guaranteed. My colleague and I want to go immediately to General Khiet's headquarters and place this matter before him in the strongest possible terms."

"You are quite free to go, Mr. Manson. I personally would welcome your action."

"We'd like you to come with us, Mr. Amberley."

"I hardly think that's necessary. We have already expressed our wishes to General Khiet and his colleagues, and we have received assurances that every effort will be made to preserve the safety of President Cung's person. My visit therefore would be a redundancy. Besides, I have much to do here."

He gave me a long, hard look and then said quietly, "Would you then give us a note over your own signature, expressing your agreement with our request?"

"I repeat, Mr. Manson, we have already made our request. I see no good reason at all to repeat it."

"We should go, Manson," said the Italian abruptly. "There is no good to be done here. And we have already lost valuable time. Good, day, sir."

"Good day, gentlemen."

When the door closed behind them, Anne Beldon exploded into a passionate reproach. "Why? Why in God's name didn't you do what they asked?"

"Because I am the Ambassador, Miss Beldon, and I alone decide what is best to be done! Any more questions?"

"None, sir!" Her face was a cold, contemptuous mask. "None ever again!"

Half an hour later Mel Adams came back to the Embassy. He brought me his report, his resignation and the news that Phung Van Cung was dead.

Adams was very calm, and he told his story with the detachment of a man who had measured and accepted all the consequences that might follow from it. His calm imposed itself on me, and I heard him out without question or interruption.

". . . It was I, sir, who got Cung out of the Palace, and I was with him until a few moments before his death. The how of it was easy enough. The why is a little harder to explain, but I'll try. My duty to the Service and to this Embassy was already discharged. I had registered my disagreement on a matter of high policy. I had announced my resignation. You asked me to stay to avoid embarrassment to the Administration. I agreed, but laid down certain terms which you accepted. But I had other duties: to myself as a man, to my country as a citizen. I could not make myself or my country party to a possible assassination. So I decided to act. When I left the Embassy last night, I went to my house and telephoned the Palace from there. It took me a long time to get through to Cung, and longer still to persuade him to see me. Finally he agreed. I drove to the Palace in my own car. Already they were making preparations for the siege. They knew what was going to happen, so there was no breach of secrecy on my part.

"Cung received me in the presence of six of his senior aides. I told him that I was acting independently and why I was doing it. I offered to drive him in my own car to sanctuary in our Embassy. I pointed out that if the Palace were surrendered a needless bloodshed would be averted. He answered that he would not demean himself to the Americans who had betrayed him, and his aides approved. I offered to take him to my own house. That, too, he refused, saying that he would not expose me or my family to danger. As a last resort, I suggested the house of Number One Chinese, because, no matter what regime comes or goes, he is untouchable. All Cholon would be in revolt if their patriarch were harmed in any way.

"At that point some of the aides began to enter the argument. They had obviously been discussing the possibility of continuing the fight even if the Palace did fall to the generals. There was talk of sympathy in the countryside and support among the lesser generals. . . . Then Cung cut off the discussion sharply and asked me to wait outside. I waited more than an hour, then Cung came out with his people. He told me that he had decided to bow to the advice of his counselors and go into hiding. He had telephoned Number One Chinese, who had offered him temporary shelter in his own house. I drove him there, quite openly, at eleven o'clock. By this time the Palace and all its approaches were blacked out, and we passed through the pickets without question. . . .

"He was very quiet as we drove, but suddenly he turned to me and said, 'I hope you understand, Mr. Adams, that I could as easily have been driven here by one of my staff. The battle is hours away yet. I am still free to come and go.'

"I told him I understood that; then he asked, 'Do you know why I came with you? Because when a simple man does a good thing out of his simplicity, one should never despise him. You are a very simple man, Mr. Adams, and what you are doing is good, even if it has no importance but a moral one. Your Ambassador now is not a simple man and therefore he is a better politician than you. But what he does is not good either for himself or his country.'

"When I told him I did not want to discuss you or Embassy policy, he simply shrugged and said that the good never went far enough and the evil always went too far, so that both failed of their ends.

"When we came to the house of Number One Chinese, we were met by a servant who took us immediately to the old man's room. There the whole family was assembled, men, women and children, all dressed in their best clothes. Cung was deeply touched. Number One Chinese made a small speech of welcome. In part he said:

" 'This man is an honored guest in my house. He comes as the President of his country, and how he goes makes no matter. You will remember, all of you, that a guest is a sacred trust and that the honor paid to him is like the honor paid to ancestors. . . .'

"I understand Mandarin, and I, too, was touched by the careful courtesy extended to a man who was in fact a fugitive. When all the family had paid their respects, they were dismissed and we sat down with Number One Chinese to a meal. While we ate, a young man came in with a book and stood waiting for a signal from the master of the house. Number One Chinese explained his presence with a smile and an aphorism:

" 'When expecting a visit from the Imperial tax collector, it is advisable to drink a quantity of rice wine. It is also recommended to hear music or to listen to diverting verses. So, tonight, which may be a night of great trouble, we shall listen for a while to the verses of Li Po, the God in Exile, who was also called Tai Peng, the Great Phoenix. . . . Read, boy.'

"In a high actor's voice the youth read poem after poem . . . 'Grief for the Jade Stairs,' 'A Girl of Yüeh,' 'Song of Blue Water,' 'The Monk of Szechwan Playing on his Lute' . . . and finally he read the 'Dream of the Wanderer on Tienmu Mountain':

" 'I leave you and go. When shall I return?
Let the white roe pasture among the green rocks.
Let me go and visit the delectable mountain.
How can I humble myself to serve the mighty
    ones?
To do so would make my heart small.'

"When the reading was done, the youth bowed to the old man and to Cung and then to me. Cung thanked him and then turned to Number One Chinese with a grave compliment:

" 'No one else would have thought of such a thing on such a night. You still give me lessons, and I am grateful. You have given me light, too, and I know now what I must do.'

"Then he asked me to drive to the Catholic orphanage on the edge of Cholon and bring back Father Wilhelmson. This is a strange man, and you should meet him if you stay here, Mr. Ambassador. In the days of the Long March he did a kindness to Mao Tse-tung —cared for him when he was sick or gave him food and medicine—I'm not sure. After the Revolution he was imprisoned with other European missionaries and suffered much hardship. Then Mao Tse-tung heard of his imprisonment and had him deported. Ever since, he has been in Saigon, running an orphanage, printing a Chinese newspaper, keeping up clandestine contacts in China, through Hanoi and Hainan. He's an oddball, but apparently Cung used to use him as a father confessor. That was what he wanted now: to go to confession.

"I drove across town and brought back the Reverend, and Cung was actually at his confession in another room when the shooting started. I was left with Number One Chinese, who begged me to ignore the violence outside and then gave me a lesson for myself.

" 'Never despise this man, Mr. Adams. He has many faults. He has made costly mistakes. Nevertheless, there is in him an element of greatness. Do you know why he came with you tonight? . . . I know what he told you, but that is not the true reason. To understand it, perhaps you must be an Oriental, I do not know. Often I do not understand how an American thinks. But Cung's reason is this: he does not want to die secretly, crushed by a falling pillar or killed by a stray piece of shrapnel. He wants his enemies to take him publicly, to force them into a clear choice: either to murder him or try him openly, even if they kill him at the end. But they must do it and be known to do it. And your Ambassa-

dor will then be shamed by the bargain he has made
with Khiet and his colleagues. This is how he thinks. It
may, of course, turn out quite otherwise.'

"Then I asked him why Cung had not simply ordered
the Palace Guard to surrender outright and save needless bloodshed. Number One Chinese shook his head
and finished the explanation:

" 'That, too, is very Oriental. If there were no fight, it
would mean that there was nobody in the country who
believed in the regime—and no one willing to fight for
the belief. This way, no matter how history reads it, the
affirmation is made.'

"I asked him if he thought Cung was right in what he
did. He simply shrugged and said that the important
thing was that Cung believed it. Whatever was done
would always be half wrong because men had never
learned to read the set of the currents of history. But a
man could always act rightly with respect to himself
and his family, and this was as much as one could expect. Cung came out then, from his confession, and
Number One Chinese had the confessor driven back to
his orphanage by one of his sons. Then the old man,
who was very tired, excused himself and Cung and I sat
together, drinking tea and listening to the sound of the
guns. He was very subdued; sad, I think, but very calm.
Much of the arrogance had dropped away from him,
and that irritating didactic manner which made him
sound like a schoolmaster at the Lycée. He talked
quietly, breaking off sometimes to listen to the sounds
of the battle, but returning always to the same theme.

" ' . . . There is always a terrible dilemma for a man
like me, Mr. Adams: the choice between a moral right
and a political mistake. . . . It is the defect of my personality and my education that I made too clear a
definition of both. It is a curiously Western defect, Mr.
Adams—and for this reason I fell into it the more easily. It is also one of the pitfalls of that type of Catholicism to which I became heir by reason of a French education. It produces an arid theology and a moral attitude so rigid as to be wrong in itself because it lacks

tolerance and understanding and simple charity. . . . It is only lately that I have begun to understand how much my judgments have been colored by my own temperament. I am, I know, defective in certain capacities. I think too much and feel too little. I am stirred greatly by great ideas, but I am too little touched by their effect on people. . . . You hear the guns? I believed, and I still believe, this battle, hopeless as it now seems, had to be fought. Now, when it is too late, I see what it means in blood and useless dying. . . . It was the same with the Buddhists. Your Ambassador would never believe that I was not, at bottom, a fanatic about these people, a Catholic inquisitor. But the real truth is that I tried to force a whole Asian people into a single mold and I could not do it. Mao Tse-tung could do it, Ho Chi Minh could do it, because they have a very simple gospel which every man can understand and because they are ruthless enough to ram it down every man's neck, so that he either chokes on it or digests it. . . . I was committed to the idea of a plural society, but I was too rigid to accept all its consequences and not wise enough to turn them to an ultimate profit. . . . Strange that I should see it so clearly now, when I am powerless to change it. But there was good in what I did, Mr. Adams. There was good in me, too, and even in these last hours of my life, under the shadow of eternity, I can affirm it. . . . Now, if you would excuse me, I should like to pray awhile.'

"I must have dozed off shortly afterward, and when I woke it was already light. Cung was standing over me. He told me that he had telephoned General Khiet's headquarters and told him that he would surrender himself at seven o'clock outside the Catholic church, half a mile or so from the house of Number One Chinese. I drove him to the church and sat in a pew at the back while the six-thirty Mass was said. Cung heard the Mass, took Communion, prayed awhile and then came back to where I was sitting. He said:

"Thank you for what you have done, Mr. Adams. I accepted it because I wanted you to know that I recognize your goodwill. Now you will do exactly as I say. We will walk out of the church together. The soldiers will be waiting for me. You will stand at the top of the steps and wait till I am taken away. No matter what happens, you will do nothing—absolutely nothing. Do you understand?'

"I made one last effort to persuade him to accept sanctuary with us. He refused. We walked out of the church together. A military truck was parked beside the curb and there was a detachment of men armed with automatic rifles. Cung walked toward them. They took hold of him roughly and pushed him into the back of the truck and climbed in after him. Then they drove off. Before they had gone a hundred yards, I heard two shots. That, I think, was when they killed him. . . . And that's all, Mr. Ambassador."

His story puzzled me and worried me at the same time. Because I was tired and puzzled, and because I was challenged again in my newly found rectitude, I was angry. For a while, deliberately, I was silent. Then I asked him:

"What do you want me to say, Mel?"

"Nothing, sir. It's finished, done! Cung is dead."

"Just like that! And you're the noble friend who walked the last steps with him, the one good American in a naughty world. Is that it?"

"No."

"Let me tell you the way I read your story, Mel. I think it shows you up as a sentimental fool who makes a big spiel about action and then plunges into it himself. It makes you a party to an assassination that might never have occurred if Cung had remained in the Palace. Through you our country is joined in the act, as it would not have been otherwise. You lent yourself to a political martyrdom like the Buddhist burnings. If we are discredited by it, you will be the author of the discredit."

"That's your reading, sir," said Adams quietly. "It isn't mine."

"And what is yours, Mel?"

"That somewhere, sometime, in all this bloody tangle of politics and diplomacy, a simple human decency has to enter. Someone has to affirm that a Chinese has as much right to eat as a Californian, that a Marxist is not necessarily a monster any more than an old-fashioned capitalist and that the world can't be run by policemen and intelligence agents—or Ambassadors, either, for that matter! Maybe I have made a diplomatic mistake, but at least I kept a deathwatch with another mistaken man and perhaps helped him to die with dignity."

"And you think that's enough?"

"Nothing is ever enough, Mr. Ambassador. A man can only dig his own garden patch and share the apples with the man next door. Now, if you'll excuse me, sir."

"You're excused, Mel. Your travel papers will be ready this afternoon. But there's one more question. Have you included all this in your report?"

"No, sir. I will if you like, but I thought you might prefer it to remain private between you and me. It's over now. Let the dead bury their dead."

"I think that might be wise."

But wise for whom? For Mel Adams, who, if he were a shrewder man, might make great capital out of his last quixotic act? Or for me, who could only be shamed by it in the eyes of a sentimental public? This way I could make a personal report to the State Department and interpret the story in my own fashion.

In point of fact, I had to interpret it sooner than I expected. Just before midday Arnold Manson and his Italian colleague came back from General Khiet's headquarters. They were cold and reproachful. They told me that at the very moment when they were talking to Khiet and receiving his assurances of protection for Cung, the news of his death was received by telephone. General Thuyen had made a violent protest, claiming betrayal. He had then left immediately for his own house. So, before it was truly installed, the junta was split and Thuyen, bound by a family code to vengeance, might well prove a potent enemy.

It was clear that my colleagues held me responsible,

in part at least, for Cung's death, and through me the Government of the United States. It was a dangerous conclusion, which might have far-reaching results. So I told them my own version of Mel Adams' story, which, being true as far as it went, did not commit me to a diplomatic lie.

"I'm afraid I must have seemed brutal and indifferent when you came to me this morning, gentlemen. But I could not tell you then that one of my staff was personally involved in an attempt to save the life of President Cung. Before the fighting started last night, he drove the President out of the Palace in his own car and spent the night in hiding with him. He tried repeatedly to persuade Cung to come to this Embassy, where I was prepared to give him sanctuary, while we negotiated his safe-conduct out of Saigon. Cung refused our offer and insisted on surrendering himself. He was taken prisoner in Cholon at seven this morning, and was probably shot within a hundred yards of the place of surrender. . . . So you see, gentlemen, I am not quite the ogre I look."

They were full of apologies, of course, and they consented to have a friendly drink with me before they left. Whether they believed me or not was another matter; but diplomacy, like other kinds of theater, depends upon a suspension of disbelief and an involvement in an illusion of reality. And if that definition makes us all mountebanks and mummers, then what would you, lords and ladies all? You pay us for our bright illusions; and we are left backstage, among the dusty props with no illusions at all!

It was a long, exacting day, full of rumors and conflicting reports, all of which had to be sifted and analyzed and finally framed into an intelligible summary for Washington. I had neither time nor inclination for self-inquisition, and after a sleepless night, it was as much as I could do to stay on my feet.

Harry Yaffa was a rock of strength. He had a spoon in every pot and he seemed to be able to keep them all stirring at once. He was in and out of the Embassy all day and he had a check on every rumor and every source of news. When I asked for information he had it; when I wanted an opinion he gave it and backed it with an impressive array of facts. He seemed to revel in the excitement, yet he never dramatized and was always prepared to dawdle when the question called for reflection and discussion. After my final passage at arms with Mel Adams, I found refreshment in his amiable amorality. At the fag end of the day, when everyone else looked and felt as though they had been put through a wringer, he was still dapper in a fresh shirt and a newly pressed suit. I had him up to my office for a drink, and he summed up the situation with cynical accuracy.

"We're home and dry, Mr. Ambassador! Small casualties. A new government. A welcoming public. The provinces are quiet and there's been no major disruption of the military effort. I think we owe ourselves this drink!"

We drank, and poured another to keep the warmth going and loosen the tight fibers of nerves and muscles. Yaffa talked on:

"Of course, we've got another problem brewing, but we'll handle that when it comes."

"What's the problem, Harry?"

"General Thuyen, the fellow who walked out this morning after Cung's death. One of my agents talked with him this afternoon. He's hopping-mad. He claims Khiet broke his promise and deliberately engineered Cung's death. Which may be true, or it may not. But Thuyen has sworn not to shave his beard until Khiet is ousted. I don't put too much stock in that. Thuyen is small beer and his influence is limited. Still, we'll keep an eye on him. . . ."

He said it so casually, and I was so tired, that I almost missed the point. Cung was dead. The generals were in power. But nothing was settled, nothing secure. Already a new usurper was ploting in the shadows, and one day, soon or late, the same race would be run again. And I, the practiced gambler, would go through the same sorry play: back one on the nose and another to show . . . And then kill off the loser. I could not face it. I would not. I swallowed my drink at a gulp and set down the glass.

"Enough's enough! To hell with them all, Harry! Let's go home!"

But what was home? A haunted house with a sinister garden and guards who paced all night to keep me safe from everything except myself.

The haunting did not begin at once. Rather it crept upon me slowly, like a swamp mist, in wisps and tatters, hardly glimpsed before they were gone. When I reached my house, I felt as though I had been beaten. Every bone and muscle was aching, and I walked as if there were a great weight on my shoulders. I had Bill Slavich telephone for my masseur, and while I waited for him I soaked in a steaming bath with a glass of whiskey within reach. Slowly my body began to relax, but then a great lassitude invaded me, and it seemed too great an effort even to reach for the liquor. At the same time my mind began to spin, gaily and gaudily, like a singing top. If I had a pencil, and if I had energy to lift it, I could set down in a moment the whole history of my enterprise in Saigon. I could make it clear to the dullest and to the wisest, because the pattern was like the pattern of the spinning top: bands of bright color distinct, yet harmonious. I felt a great need to explain myself to someone; but as there was no one to talk to, I told the story to myself. Then I grew tired of it and closed my eyes and dozed a little. When I woke, the bath was cooling and I dragged myself out of it languidly, dried myself and lay down on the bed to wait for my masseur.

Normally he was a silent fellow, whose silence worked with the sedation of his fingers. But today he was full of the drama of the coup and he talked incessantly as he kneaded my flesh, I found myself talking back to him, imitating his nasal Annamite French and making him great promises and wise counsels about the future of the Republic under its new government. My eloquence reduced him to silence very quickly. The words came tumbling out, but always they were a phrase behind my thoughts, so that I became restless and tense again, and he had to beg me, "No more talk, please, monsieur. The muscles get hard, and I cannot make you tranquil . . ."

His caution made me uneasy. I forced myself to be silent, and after a little while I fell asleep under the soothing rhythm of the massage. When I woke, he was gone and I was lying naked under a blanket. For a brief instant, and for no reason at all, I was afraid. The room seemed out of focus, unfamiliar. There was a faint but nameless threat, like the aura that clings after a nightmare. Then, abruptly, everything was back in focus again. My head was clear, my body relaxed. I felt hungry. I dressed quickly and went downstairs to have a cocktail before dinner. Just at the entrance to the drawing room was a large gilt mirror, and when I looked at myself in it I found I had forgotten to knot my tie, which was hanging loose around my neck. Again that queer moment of unease, that drift of swamp mist. I must be more tired than I thought. I knotted the tie hurriedly and went into the drawing room. It was empty, and I did not care to be alone. I rang for Humphrey and asked him to fix me a martini, big and dry.

He looked at me anxiously. "You've had a long day, sir. And you didn't sleep at all last night. You should try to get to bed early tonight."

I told him I intended to do just that, and then, without warning, I was launched again on another eloquent account of the week's events. Good servant that he was, he listened attentively for a while, but finally, because I had lost the thread of the story, or had been talking too long, he excused himself and left me to my drink. It was large and potent, and I felt it warm the cold place where my heart used to be. That was strange: how long a man could live without a heart. The Russians kept a dog alive with a mechanical heart; or was it a mechanical dog with a human heart? No matter! The Russians were very clever people because they could convince themselves that everything they did was right. That was a very difficult thing to do. I had tried it and failed, and I, according to my record and to Raoul Festhammer and General Tolliver, was a very clever Ambassador indeed. . . .

But not clever enough to keep George Groton alive. Not clever enough by half! I'm sorry, George, truly sorry. I only wish I could have made you understand my problem. If you had lived to my age, you might have had the same one yourself. It's like this, George . . . I am not me. I am the symbol of a country. A symbol has no responsibility. You use it at will for a variety of purposes; on the coin you pay to the whores, on the general's cap, over the portico of the courthouse, as a seal on a warrant of execution. It is just there. It doesn't act. You don't praise or blame it. But you have to respect it. . . . And I want you to respect me, George. I need respect because I find it hard to respect myself. You see that, don't you?

I waited for his answer; but he was no longer there, and perhaps I had not spoken at all. Nerves, you know. A hard day at the office. A drink together at the end of the day is good for married couples. They share their interests; they give solace one to the other. Then they sleep together and make beautiful children, and the spirits of the air come and drop beautiful bombs on them and frizzle them up with napalm. Your health, George! And yours, Gabrielle, my love! You always did take a long time dressing for dinner.

Dinner! Now there's a diplomat's meal. You know that, don't you, Humphrey? There is a variety of dishes —variety is very important: the plural society, the plural view, each man to his taste. The meal establishes that. There is leisure—very important. It is impossible to rush a good meal, unthinkable to gulp a good wine. So one abandons oneself to a timeless dimension. Very necessary, Humphrey! A good diplomat should never look at a clock. People like to sleep on a new idea; they like to try it out on wife or mistress; they want to wear it, like a pair of new shoes, to see that it fits comfortably. That's the whole purpose of a diplomatic dinner, Humphrey; it's what the Greeks used to call *agape*—a feast of love. You've seen a lot of love feasts in your time, haven't you, Humphrey, and a lot of wandering hands and talky-talky toes under the tables! I wonder if General Khiet will give better dinner parties than Cung. That last one was very dull. He ran it like the Last Supper . . . and cast me for Judas. Sent me a gift to commemorate the opening of the show. But we put on a much better show ourselves, eh, Humphrey? Real Elizabethan drama! . . . And ride in triumph through Persepolis! . . . See, I said it! Persepolis . . . Persepolis! I am tired, very tired! I am perhaps a little drunk, but I can still ride in triumph through Persepolis. I did, too. . . . Crowds of people! Hosanna and all that! That was a popular revolution—Cung couldn't see that, but I saw it. So he's dead and I am sitting here alone, but alive. No, thank you, Humphrey. Just coffee and a brandy. Don't pester me, man! I'll go to bed when I'm ready.

I knew I was sober because I was thinking with extraordinary clarity. I was talking too much, perhaps, but the Greeks had a word for that, too: *catharsis*. The least one might expect of a good servant was a little patience. The coffee he brought me was bitter, and after tasting it, I put it aside and drank an extra balloon of brandy instead. Once again, and for longer this time, I had that sense of strangeness and menace in a once familiar scene. I walked to the window and looked out. The guards were still there, but the garden was different. It seemed to be more luxuriant, to have drawn closer to the house, like—what did the Frenchman say?—like the trees that ate the city. I felt a sudden flutter of fear. I closed the drapes quickly and sat down again in the circle of comforting light. Then my hands began to tremble, so that I could not hold the brandy glass. When I tried to set it down, it tumbled off the lip of the table and shattered on the polished floor. For no reason at all I found myself mourning tearlessly for the spilt liquor and the spilt blood and the shattered vessels of glass and flesh, and all the poor spirits bound to the wheel of life, which was now the wheel of a Juggernaut car, crushing them into the dust. . . .

Where are you, Anne? You should be here with me tonight. Not to work—I am not so harsh a master—but just to sit with me and talk a little. Is it so much to ask? Something is happening to me that I do not understand. The walls are closing in. The trees are coming to eat me. And Judas is hanging in my cupboard with silver crammed in his mouth. Anne . . . Please come!

She did not come, and after a while I composed myself, because an Ambassador is an important personage who must never show that he is afraid. I took the brandy bottle in one hand, a clean glass in the other and climbed the stairs to my bedroom. Halfway up, I remembered the strange fairy story of the man who lost his shadow. Then I knew what was troubling me. I had lost mine, too; but I did not dare to look behind in case it was there, dancing a mocking jig at the bottom of the stairs.

When I reached the bedroom I knew I was safe. I put the bottle and the glass down on the dressing table; then, furtively, I undressed and put on my pajamas. Then I took down the bottle of red capsules and shook two of them into the palm of my hand. I was tempted to take more, just to be sure, but I knew that if I did my shadow would leave me forever, and I could not bear that. . . . Hurriedly I popped the capsules into my mouth, half filled the goblet with brandy and toasted my image in the mirror.

It was a moment of pure horror. Staring at me from the mirror was the most hateful image I had ever seen: pasty gray, with red, staring eyes, flared nostrils, a trap mouth drawn into a hateful sneer, a mop of black hair streaked with dirty gray. I stared at it for a long, fearful moment. Then I threw my brandy full in its face. The liquid ran down the glass, distorting the image more hatefully still. I could not endure it a moment longer. I picked up the brandy bottle and began, coldly and savagely, to beat it to death.

In the small hours of the morning I woke, parched and sweating, and peered fearfully about the room. Anne Beldon, in dressing gown and slippers, was sitting in the glow of a shaded desk lamp, watching me. I must have cried out, because she came to me instantly and held a glass of water to my lips and then bathed my face with a damp cloth. I noticed that my right hand was bandaged. I asked Anne what had happened and she said simply, "You were very tired, Ambassador. You had a little too much to drink, that's all,"

I knew there was more because the fear was still in the room; but being still hazy from the drug, I could not remember what the fear was. I caught at Anne's hands and held them so that she could not leave me but had to sit on the edge of the bed and face me. I begged her to tell me the truth.

"Something terrible happened, Anne! I did something, said something; I don't know what. I'm desperately afraid, but I don't know why."

"There's no need to be afraid. You broke a mirror and a brandy bottle. You cut your hand. Nothing else."

"Are you sure?"

"I'm sure."

"What did I say, Anne?"

"It didn't make very much sense. When I heard the noise I came in and found you staring at the broken mirror and shouting at it, 'Sing, damn you! Sing! Sing!' . . . When you saw me, you stopped shouting and stood staring at me as if I were a stranger. As I was getting you back to bed, you said, 'He wouldn't cry either. Even while I was killing him he wouldn't cry. If you can't sing, at least you should be able to cry.' . . . Then you mumbled for a few moments and went to sleep. So you see there's no harm done."

"No harm! Oh God, Anne, if only you knew!"

Without warning it all came tumbling out of me, in a

torrent of wild words, while I clung to her and begged her, for my sanity and salvation, to understand. Finally when I was spent of words and secrets she held me against her breast and wept quietly.

"You poor man! You poor, lost, obstinate man!"

She lay down beside me and cradled my head in the crook of her arm and coaxed me into sleep like a child. When I woke again, it was bright day. The madness was gone, and Anne Beldon was gone, too. There was no sign of the broken mirror. Fresh clothes were laid out for me. There was a tray of coffee and toast at my bedside.

An hour later Bill Slavich was driving me to the Ministry of Foreign Affairs to meet the victorious generals.

CHAPTER TWELVE

I have little to say about the last months of my service in Saigon because after that last, horrible night I knew that my personal survival depended on a compromise. What was done was done; I had to manipulate the consequences to the best political advantage. I could not leave the country precipitately without an implied condemnation of our policies and my execution of them. On the other hand, I could not risk, ever again, so ruinous an assault on the fabric of my personality. So, having renounced the luxury of a moral point of view, I set about my business with a calculated detachment. I bargained ruthlessly over the renewal of our aid payments. I refused to enter into any intimacy with members of the junta. I could not afford to respect them as I had respected Cung. I could only despise them as I despised myself. When General Thuyen, bearded now and bent on revenge, moved out of the shadows to take control of the Government, I sat on the sidelines and made no attempt to intervene.

Faced with the long-drawn, unabating agony of the country, I maintained a clinical detachment. We had failed politically, but without us the military situation would have collapsed long since. The fighting man was still the noblest figure in an ignoble picture. When the bloody affrays broke out between Buddhists and Catholics, I hammered at the generals with threats of new sanctions and a total withdrawal; but I refused to embroil myself in any public comment on the religious issue. Having rejected all faith, I could despise the excesses of those who claimed to have one. When my conscience revolted at the spectacle of mere children being murdered with meat axes, I remembered George Groton and hardened my heart again. This people demanded the right to determine its own destiny. Let them do it and mop up their own blood afterward. Mel Adams was gone, so I was spared the indignity of his comparison between the repressive controls of Phung Van Cung and the murderous *laissez-faire* of the military men.

In a sense, the discipline of detachment was necessary for me. Without it I might well have lapsed into psychotic disorder. But politically it was a damning loss of face, for me and for my Government. We had connived at an assassination to prevent public disorder. Then, when worse disorders happened under a new regime, we professed ourselves powerless to stop them. There was a personal damnation, too, although I managed to hold the sentence in suspense while I rebuilt enough physical and mental strength to endure it. Although I had abdicated any spiritual position, it was the mark of my weakness that I could not achieve the total and apparently satisfying amorality of Harry Yaffa. I knew it, and I understood how rightly Phung Van Cung had judged my character. I knew, too, that in the end I must follow Mel Adams' course and quit the Service.

But my exit would bring me neither honor nor satisfaction since I would not quit for a principle, but only for incapacity—none the less real because I was the only one who knew it.

In the Service, I was still the good and reliable servant: "Leave it to Max! He won't be buffaloed. He won't be foxed"—a mixed metaphor which was uttered as a compliment across the conference table in Washington. But Max had a metaphor of his own, much nearer to the truth of the matter. Max was a veteran steeplechaser who took all the hurdles in measured style, but his wind was broken and he would never win another race.

It was a bitter feeling to find myself thus, in mid-career, bankrupt of ambition, of honesty and self-respect. I was not only the unresolved man. I was the empty man, the barren one; had no belief in what I must do and no conviction about what I should be; I saw no possible means of restoring my vanished capital. I was isolated now from any intimate exchange with my colleagues. I could not risk that any of them should see behind the mask into the hollow mannequin who wore it. Anne Beldon had applied for compassionate leave to visit an ailing mother, and while she was in Washington had asked for a transfer to a vacancy in Rome. Neither of us had the courage to face the possible outcome of that night of revelation and wasted tenderness.

So, for want of any other friendship, I began to correspond with Musō Soseki, and came, by slow degrees, to expose my problems to him. Finally, when I was able to arrange my exit, I begged him to receive me once again, as his guest at Tenryu-ji. His reply, written in the exquisite calligraphy of which he was a master, was short and simple: "Whenever you are ready, come! I know what you need. . . ." For the expression of my need he wrote the beautiful ideograph "man-under-tree," which signifies rest.

When he welcomed me at last into his house and we talked together for the first time, he studied me with grave concern, and then wrote a different sign to describe my condition. This was the ideograph of "heart-at-window," which connotes anxiety. Next he drew the symbol of "woman-under-roof" to show the state to which I must tend: peace and tranquillity. Afterward he expounded the brushwork into a parable:

"Heart looks out from window and sees what it does not understand, desires what it cannot have. Heart is troubled and afraid. . . . Tree looks but does not see, stands and does not move, grows but does not desire. Man rests under tree and is supported by the trunk and sheltered by the leaves, and he shares the life of the tree without spending his own. House shelters woman, woman encompasses man, and life is born out of their tranquillity. . . . So you, my friend, will close the window that looks outward and begin to look inward upon your true self. You will sit in my garden and become a tree. . . ."

"And tranquillity?"

"Comes with enlightenment, which is found by him who does not seek it."

After the harsh and destructive dialectic in which I had been engaged for so long, it was extraordinarily difficult for me to accommodate myself once more to the methods of quiet. For several days I moped about, restless and dissatisfied, irritated, too, sometimes, because Musō Soseki refused to engage in any discussion of the problems that troubled me. When I insisted too strongly, he smiled and drew me the word for disorder, which is a combining of "talk" and "work"; and then he drew "water-in-a-forest," which describes the nature of solitude and contemplation. It took me a long time to digest this gentle reproof; but, slowly, the quiet began to take hold of me again, and in the subtle garden, in the time of maples-on-fire, I began to experience the beginning of liberty and enlargement. I slept better; I woke each morning to a growing wonder at the simplicity of rock and lily pond and fallen leaf.

Thus refreshed, I began to be eager for the exercises of illumination which I had begun to practice long before, but Musō Soseki had other ideas.

"I, too, have learned something from you, my friend, as the water takes to itself the face of man who looks into it. We come from different countries, we are produced by different histories, we communicate, each in a different idiom. Therefore we must not accept too readily nor reject too quickly the equipment which we have. We both look out upon the same tree yet if we describe it to a stranger he will think for a while that there are two trees. So, to begin, we will each talk in our own fashion, and see what we can teach each other. First you will tell me what has happened to you. . . ."

It was, I suppose, a kind of confession; but there were many gaps in it, some dictated by the necessary secrecy of my profession, some by shame for the weaknesses of my mature years. The old man's attitude was one of detachment and a very notable respect. He was not an analyst, digging for secrets in the sour subsoil of a disturbed mind. He was not a confessor making a judicial summation of guilt and repentance before pronouncing a pardon. He accepted the story as I told it, without question, as if he were a spectator at a play, for whom the dramatist set the terms of reference and the mode of the interpretation. I mentioned this to him, and he answered me in that symbolic fashion which characterized all his discourse:

"When a man chooses to reveal himself to a friend, the friend is made witness to a spectacle of growth, like the birth of a child or the unfolding of a flower. There is an unfolding out of darkness into light; there is the revelation of a hidden life, which, if it is to develop, needs air and sun and a careful nurture. If the flower does not unfold, it withers and dies in bud, and drops from the stem. If a man does not reveal himself, his growth is stunted and, ultimately, the secret life of his spirit dies like a worm-eaten bud. However, one must be patient and not ask to see all the growth at once. First the small shoot pushes up timidly to the sun, then another appears, and the stalk grows strongly into bud and blossom and fruit. . . . You have reserves with me.

I know that. To be timid is not to be afraid, only careful of the fragility of the inward self."

I told him, with some resentment, that others whom I had loved and respected had not been so careful. They had made summary judgments and brutal withdrawals.

He shook his head and chided me quietly. "Summary, yes. But not brutal. They, too, were timid, you see. They depended on you for what they lacked in themselves. When you could not supply the lack, they were angry, disappointed and, possibly, afraid."

"But they would not concede me the right to be afraid."

"They were younger and of lower degree," said Musō Soseki tolerantly. "I am older, and I concede your right. So now let us begin where we left off. Did you find the answer to the question of the cuckoo?"

"I found it. I killed the cuckoo."

"So now there is no song for you in winter or summer?"

"No song and no bird. Only a reproach with which I live every day."

"Did the cuckoo reproach you when you killed him?"

"In my dream, no."

"But what else was the cuckoo but a dream?"

"When the dream was over, the cuckoo turned into a man."

"Did you kill the man?"

"I spoke the word that woke the hunter who killed him."

"So the cuckoo is dead and the man is dead. Let us talk about a river."

"What river?"

"What is a river?"

"A river is water that flows from high ground to low ground to meet other water."

"The water is never the same water, yet the river is always the same. So how can the water be the river?"

"The river is the place where the water flows."

"But without water the place is an empty valley."

"So the river is the place and the water and the flow."

"Look, now! I throw into the river a stick and a stone and a man. What happens to them?"

"The stick floats. The stone sinks. The man swims or drowns."

"And the river?"

"Changes but is always the same."

"Whether the man swims or drowns?"

"Whether he swims or drowns."

"Does the river care what the man does?"

"No, only the man cares."

"Why does he care?"

"Because he knows that he is not a river. And he knows that he knows. And the knowing is wonderful and terribly lonely."

"Now let us talk about the knowing. You knew when you spoke the word that it would wake a hunter?"

"Yes."

"Why did you speak it?"

"Because if I did not speak wild beasts might come and eat us all. But the hunter, too, was a beast."

"But the hunter was a man, also."

"Yes."

"So you woke man and beast with the same word."

"Yes."

"And in yourself a beast woke, also."

"That, too."

"Could you have prevented the waking of the beasts?"

"By not speaking—yes."

"But you were sent to speak. It was a charge on you to speak."

"I should not have accepted the charge."

"Then for this you should blame yourself—but not for the death of the man."

"But the one is an extension of the other."

"How do you know?"

"It seems so to me."

"What seems is not always what is."

"I wish I knew, truly, what is."

"Look at the maple trees. It is autumn now, the time of falling leaves. Is it the wind that strips the tree or the tree that tosses the leaves to the wandering wind?"

"It does not matter to me because I am neither leaf nor wind!"

"But you are! You are leaf and tree and beast and wind. Being a man, you are involved in all, and are a compendium of all."

"No! No! No! . . ." I was surprised by the vehemence of my own protest. "Don't you see? This is the whole mistake—the personal mistake, the political one. I am not a tree, and if I try to determine how the tree must grow, then I stunt and distort it like the bonsai in your garden. We are not Viets or Japanese or Malays. How then can we say how they must live and what they must believe to be content? There is murder in this! Destruction and a sowing of hate! I know. I was the instrument of it."

The old monk was very patient with me. He did not balk at the proposition, but mused over it with me, pacing the graveled walks, pausing occasionally to contemplate some small and hidden beauty in the ancient intimacy of the garden.

". . . You must not be too harsh with yourself, my friend, nor expect too much of the imperfect processes by which mankind governs a complex planet. This is the paradox, you see, the visible contradiction beyond which we try to penetrate to the invisible harmony. This, in Western terms, is the purpose of *satori:* to illuminate the harmony and the unity and to make man himself part of it again. But even *satori* is not a permanent state, only *Nirvana* is the permanent and eternal illumination. You say you must not determine the growth of the tree but if the tree threatens your house do you not lop and prune it?"

"Kill it, too?"

"If the tree falls on your house, the tree dies and the house is destroyed and you are killed, too."

"Are three deaths worse than one?"

"All death is one dying, and yet there is no death. The beast you kill becomes a beast in you. The good you kill springs up again like moss on a grave."

Abruptly I was invaded by fatigue and a distaste for this symbolic dialogue, which now seemed like a slow groping through cobwebs. I was not the same man who had come to Tenryu-ji with George Groton. I was changed. I did not belong any more in this garden. I was weary of the subtle language of the *mondō;* now I was truly *gaijin,* the outside man. I needed another kind of illumination than that which Musō Soseki offered me. It was hard to explain all this without seeming impolite to my master, but he understood it intuitively and absolved me from any discourtesy.

"This is what I thought might happen. This is why I told you I had learned something from you, too. You are changed. You have spent a part of yourself which cannot be replaced. The language and the symbols which we have used together are now an obstacle and not a help to your enlightenment. You must not be dismayed by this. It happens to many. The way of pure illumination and contemplation is for the few, and I think that it may now have serious dangers for you."

"Can you tell me what has happened to me?"

"I think I can. You are like the old-time traveler who sets out to make the journey from Kyoto to Edo, which, everyone tells him, is full of interest and diversity. He begins very confidently; he has money in his purse, good clothes, stout limbs and companions to lighten the journey. But before the journey is over he finds he has miscalculated. The inns are expensive, the girls are grasping, he is cheated by ferrymen and clever rogues. So long before he reaches Edo he has no money, his clothes are too light for the coming winter, his companions have dropped off along the way and he is in a province whose dialect he does not understand. He is older, too. Time is shorter. When he talks to the girls in the teahouses, his heart is still at home. When he watches the merchants haggle, he knows that gold is soon spent and silk wears out. What does he do? He wants to kill himself, but he lacks the courage. He wishes he were a clever rogue like those he has met on his journey. But for this he has neither taste nor talent. He sits down by the roadside and weeps for himself. But after a while there are no more tears to shed. He hears the gongs from the monastery and he sees the maples-inflame and he says, 'Here is light and the compassion of the Compassionate One.' But he finds no light because light is a gift to each separate man. It is not held in common. And the compassion cannot touch him because he clings to his own guilt and will not be forgiven. Does my parable tell the true story, Amberley-san?"

"It is true. But is it ended there—the traveler motionless, without tears, lacking light, refusing compassion? There is a word for that in the West: *accidie;* it signifies the false and terrible *Nirvana* which is founded not on union but on separation, not on the extinction of desire but on contempt for it. And this is where I find myself now. This I think is why I cannot continue the *mondō* with you."

"There is another end to the parable, my friend. If you will be patient a little longer, I will try to show it to you. We are left, are we not, with our traveler, all alone by the roadside, bereft. He cannot go back; there is nothing to urge him forward. But, without desire, he continues walking. By the side of the road he sees an image of the Buddha, of the Goddess Kuan Yin, of Raijin the Thunder God, a *fumiejesu,* perhaps, or even the Great Bear of the Ainu people. It is a dead thing of wood or stone or baked clay, which, for our traveler, has no meaning. But, because he is a man, he knows the image has a meaning for other men: an expression of their need and their desire for enlightenment, harmony and elevation above the self. He stops by the image which has no meaning for him. He recites a prayer in whose efficacy he does not believe: 'If there be light, show me light. If there be power, extend it to me. If there be forgiveness, forgive. If there be tomorrow, grant me a hope in it; and if there be these things, but not for me, give me the patience to endure the not having.' "

"And how will I know if the prayer is answered?"

"When you have the courage to live without an answer."

"But if I have no courage?"

"Then you will walk just a little farther along the road and you will come to a habitation of men."

"How can I be sure of that?"

"Because where there are images, there are always men!"

"And then?"

"Then you will see what the Lord Buddha saw: an old man, a sick man, a dead man and a man with a shaven head who has no home. And then you will say: 'None of these is more fortunate than I so why should I complain?' And then you will either accept to live again in the habitation of men or you will join the homeless one and continue on the road. And so, either way, your prayer will be answered and there will be a beginning of light and a desire for more light."

"And forgiveness? Who forgives me for what I have done?"

"The dead man whom you bury, the sick man whom you succor, the old man whom you support, the homeless one whose loneliness you share."

"And the image?"

"Is still an image of the Unknown and the Unknowable, who may, one day, choose to enlighten you—for the All-Enlightened One has pity on mankind."

It was a bleak and Spartan philosophy, and as he expounded it to me I felt my heart quail at the harshness of it. The prayer to the unknown God is a terrible and desperate act that may launch a man into madness or into undreamed-of revelation. It is the leap through darkness that may hurtle him into eternal silence or the sublimity of a Divine embrace. And yet what else was left to me? My small inheritance of good manners, polite custom and traditional morality had been laid waste by the processional march of history. My action, any action, was a futile gesture against the trampling might of the elephants. That I had survived it and that Phung Van Cung had been destroyed by it was an unimportant accident in the long, violent evolution from the first biotic form to that chaotic creature, man, who nevertheless has managed to impose an order on the spinning planet. An accident or a design? A light or an illusion of total darkness?

If it was all accident and illusion, I wanted no part of it. Time was too long, life too lonely in the flat and empty landscape of my dream. But if, as Musō promised me, there was even a hope of light, a need of pardon, a meaning in service, a tranquillity in love, then I could agree to continue to be a man. But how, ever again, would I know for certain, I who had killed the dream bird who did not exist, and killed a man without touching him, and, having destroyed his own image, now looked into a blank mirror?

As if he had divined my thoughts, Musō Soseki bent and picked up from the path a small pebble, round and polished and veined with green. He held it out to me in the palm of his hand.

"Is it not beautiful, my friend?"

"It is beautiful."

He tossed the pebble into the pool and watched while the ripples spread out and broke against the grassy bank. Then he turned to me and said in his grave fashion:

"It is still beautiful, even though you do not see it. It will still be beautiful when the fish have forgotten it and the water grass covers it and no one but you or I knows that it ever existed."

"Is the beauty enough—against all the ugliness?"

"No. But that there is someone to see the beauty and delight in it, this is much more."

"But not yet enough."

"Not yet, but to know that one has seen and enjoyed is to know that one may do so again."

"Even when one has destroyed beauty and created ugliness?"

"Sometimes because of that. . . . You have never asked me, my friend, how I came to this place."

It was true. From the first moment of our meeting I had accepted him as a permanence, like the pine trees and the rocks and the patterns of sand and moss. He was so much at one with them that it would have seemed an impertinence to question how he came there. I told him this, and he acknowledged the compliment with sober humor. Then he told me:

"I am seventy-five years of age. I have been in this place for more than thirty years. In 1931, I took part in the invasion of Manchuria. I was an officer then, proud of my long lineage as a member of a Samurai family. I killed many men and was decorated by the Emperor for valor in the field. Then I fell sick and came very near to dying. For the first time I understood the nature of the death I had inflicted on other men; how much promise was destroyed, how much dignity was violated. I too, wanted pardon, but instead I had only praise. I wanted to pay, but of what use is a coin in the mouth of a dead man? Like you, I found myself in darkness and wandered in it a long time. Then I came to this place, looking for light . . ."

"And did you find it?"

"I learned not to demand it."

"Are you changed?"

"I am the same. But I am changed because I know that I cannot change what I was or what I did."

"And the light?"

"This is the light."

"But you have paid nothing."

"I have paid everything by accepting that I can pay nothing."

"The Christians exact a penance for sin."

"The Lord Buddha taught that life itself is a penance for wayward desire."

"The Christians say one waits upon the mercy of God."

"For us there is the Compassion of the Compassionate. What is the difference?"

The sun was gone now. The garden was filling with shadow. The maples were no longer in flame, but dark against the evening sky. The fat carp hung motionless in the black water and the lilies had folded themselves into sleep. Musō Soseki laid his old hand on my sleeve and led me into his house.

Saigon—October 1963.
Sydney—October 1964.

Now in paperback!

*The #1 bestseller throughout
the nation*

THE SHOES OF
THE FISHERMAN

BY MORRIS L. WEST

author of THE DEVIL'S ADVOCATE

A towering novel of the modern Papacy, "a triumph—'The
Shoes of the Fisherman' is rich in characterization, from
the poor of Rome to the Princes of the Church, from the
worldly and corrupt nobility to the humble and the self-
critical; it is told swiftly and stirringly; it is strong
and honest in its treatment of great and challenging
questions."—NEW YORK HERALD TRIBUNE

"A novelistic drama of great power and immediate
concern . . . brilliant!"—TIME

A DELL BOOK   75c

ARMAGEDDON
Leon Uris

A magnificent novel of Berlin in the grim,
turbulent days immediately after World
War II, by the author of EXODUS and BATTLE
CRY. The struggle for power among the victors, culminating in the breathtaking drama
of the Berlin Airlift.

"A vast panorama of people and places ..."
—New York Herald Tribune

A DELL BOOK   95c

Don't miss this towering, behind-the-scenes novel of the automobile industry!

AMERICAN CHROME

BY EDWIN GILBERT

"A huge novel that ranges back and forth from executive suites and country clubs to sleazy hotels and garish used car lots. AMERICAN CHROME is devoted to the power of our machine-god, the automobile, and the society which has grown up around it . . . unusual . . . absorbing."
—Louis Untermeyer, *Life Magazine*

A DELL BOOK   85c